CLOUD NINE
NAILED IT!
BOOK 2

FEARNE HILL

Copyright © 2023 by Fearne Hill

All rights reserved.

No part of this book may be reproduced in any form or by any electronic or mechanical means, including information storage and retrieval systems, without written permission from the author, except for the use of brief quotations in a book review.

AUTHOR'S NOTE

I wish to express my thanks to M.A. Hinkle, for their editing skills, and to Sarah Coppin, my proofreader. Any errors are mine alone. Please heed the trigger warning for one episode of bullying.

CHAPTER 1

TRISTAN

Favourite things about living in the penthouse: part one: the hot tub. Although only when no one else was around, restricting my visits to late at night. Frankie, my brother, would blow a gasket if he found out about my regular solo rendezvous with the bubbles. Once he'd got over himself, he'd insist on joining me. Then, to make matters worse, his boyfriend Lysander would tag along too, which would be a dreadful bore, as he'd strip down to his skinny Speedos, and Frankie would prance around him like a dog in heat, entirely forgetting the reason we were there in the first place. They'd end up canoodling, sucking each other's faces off, and leaving me wishing I was anywhere *but* in the bloody hot tub.

Hence tonight, I conducted my usual subterfuge. Patiently, I waited until the mutual foot-stroking and petting, a love language more eloquent than any of the fancy speeches Lysander hated making, overwhelmed them and they took themselves off to bed.

Affording me opportunity to creep out.

For safekeeping, I left my hearing aids behind in their plastic case on my bedside table, rendering me deaf as a post. It didn't matter; experience had taught me the penthouse door emitted nothing more than a weary sigh and a soft *click* as it closed behind me. Its quietness colluded in my exploits, as did the thick carpet of the hallway, cushioning the pad of my bare feet almost in a caress, as my shaky legs carried me towards the lift.

The lift conspired with me too. Several scions of engineering must have put their heads together to design it—a soundless, smoothly engineered transition from our comfortable home at the very top of the building, down past the lower floors until, with a dull *thud*, which I couldn't hear but sensed, a gradual halt at the sports complex in the basement.

Under the hardly there glow of dim night lamps, the twenty-five-metre pool offered up its usual shimmering invitation, but I steered well clear of it. By this time of night, the water had settled into a brilliant rectangle of calm, and honestly? It could stay that way. My unpredictable balance and the slippery edges of swimming pools were never a good combination. A few years ago, on holiday with Frankie, he'd taken his eye off me for less than a second, plenty long enough to entertain the greasy, hot holidaymakers on the front row of loungers as, fully clothed, I tumbled headlong. Someone actually fucking cheered and clapped after Frankie jumped in to hoick me out.

Letting my eyelids droop, I inhaled the warm, chloriney scent. Long, deep steadying breaths in through my nostrils, a pause, then a protracted easing out through my mouth. With every breath in, I imagined the rich humid air trickling like warm honey down the ever-decreasing branches of my lungs, seeping into my bloodstream to wash over my tired bones, warming me from the inside out. And every exhale carried away all the built-up tension stored in the weary muscles of my back, shoulders, and calves.

As if designed especially for me, the basement hot tub had a handy low bench next to it. Sleek planks of warm, smooth pine to match the pine of the sauna. Lowering myself down, I propped my sticks in the little triangular gap between the bench and the tub, then unhurriedly undressed, laying my T-shirt and joggers in a neat pile alongside my folded square of towel.

Stripped to my boxers, I lurched from the bench to the wide steps leading up to the water, my transition more of a controlled fall than a purposeful movement. I'd become quite adept and not misjudged it for weeks. The tricky part which followed ensured I only ever visited alone and at night: an ungainly, exhausting slithery crawl up the steps, followed by a crablike shuffle over the lip, finishing with an uncoordinated *flop* into the giant bath.

Of course, my siblings—Maddie and Frankie—had seen me exposed and vulnerable like this thousands of times. My friends Mungo and Milo, not to mention Maddie's partner Darren, had caught an occasional glimpse too. But no one else. I even tried to hide the worst of it from Lysander, as his body had been carved out of the finest alabaster, underlining mine, hacked from Tesco's economy blancmange. My shyness around him was ridiculous, because he understood how uncomfortable being stared at could feel more than anyone.

Sometimes, when I performed this manoeuvre into the hot water, my feet slipped on the wet tiles, and my head disappeared below the surface for a few seconds. I always righted myself soon enough—the tub wasn't more than couple of feet deep—and then kicked myself for being so clumsy. Because who wanted to be remembered as the idiot who drowned in a puddle of water?

A seated position in the hot tub successfully negotiated, I pushed the big red knob next to my shoulder and, with a contented sigh, nestled my head back on the little foam pad. Familiar rumbling vibrations swelled under my bum, heralding the best bit. Two seconds later, like bullets from a gun, powerful jets of hot water shot across the muscles of my aching lower half, pummelling my withered buttocks. Better than any expensive masseur.

As the jets levelled out, a few softer eddies spritzed across my belly, tickling and nudging at my balls. Lapping up the tingling pain and with no one to overhear, a vibrating sensation left my throat—a groan of pleasure. Sinking lower, I dipped my chin under the water and wriggled out of my boxers, toeing them off my legs, and watched them float to the rippling surface and jiggle about. My legs, generally scissored closed, spread a fraction wider as my spasming thigh muscles relaxed, inviting soothing swirls into every hidden fold of flesh.

It goes without saying I fondled my dick.

With a grunt of satisfaction, I let my hips and legs float up to the surface to join my boxers. My dick bobbed on the surface too, half hard. Only here, alone in the semi-dark of the empty pool room, could I ever experience weightlessness. For these precious few minutes, I allowed myself to imagine that the two useless pillars of bone, masquerading as a pair of legs, with muscles as weak as tissue paper, belonged to someone else.

Hot jets blowing up the divide of my arse were an added bonus.

The throbbing in my hips faded and my achy shoulders and neck took a break from complaining they hadn't been designed to support my weight through two sticks. The humming from my weary brain receded.

Most of the time, I forgot the world pigeonholed me into a box marked deaf and disabled, in the same way a person with green eyes didn't walk around all day with a smug awareness others identified them as green-eyed.

Nevertheless, reams of trite out there were only too keen to remind me. Books and websites, and magazine articles, full of shite about how I mustn't let my disability define me or destroy me. News flash, guys: it didn't. On the inside, I was just like other people. I could be petty and anxious, for instance. I was frequently obnoxious. Sometimes witty (although Frankie would disagree), sometimes moody, and sometimes sad. I had inherited my mother's dislike of the texture of bananas. Like my dad, I could waste an entire Sunday afternoon snoozing on the sofa in front of televised snooker. I hated the current state of British politics and thought *Happy Valley* was a good series but overrated. (James Norton was hot.) If I developed a headache, like everyone else, I worried it was a brain tumour and googled the symptoms. I fretted about not recycling enough but still bought packaged sandwiches and bagged fruit. I hoped to have a dog one day, when I owned a house with a decent-sized garden.

I hadn't always been so cool about my disabilities, but trust me, all things were relative. I experienced bad days, like everyone else. When I did, my disabilities provided a useful hook on which to pin the blame for all my other inadequacies. For a period (most of my teens and into my early twenties), I used to detest being Tristan Carter, the disabled triplet, and despised anybody who tried to help. I'd read articles spouting well-meaning crap, then seethe and rail against the unfairness.

Now I was older, at worst those homilies bored me, and at best, they made me smile, reminding me why I didn't belong to online or in-person groups designed to support 'varyingly abled' folk like me. These days, seeing as most of my energies were taken up with getting from A to B without falling arse over tit, able-bodied people could get their knickers in a twist over the right language to use or rail against the lack of pubs with wheelchair-accessible toilets on my behalf.

I'd been born this way, and I was done with feeling sorry for myself, which wasn't to say I wasn't fucking depressed about it from time to time. In all honesty, I wished people did see me before they saw my disability, or whatever the hackneyed phrase able-bodied folk liked to trot out.

But it could be worse. I was lucky enough to have siblings who would walk over hot coals for me, although they would never admit it, and parents brave enough to let me go, even when it diametrically opposed their base instincts to hold me close. And at least I had working arms (mostly) and could wipe my own fucking arse. In comparison to that, my dodgy legs and ears, whose single attribute was holding my sunglasses in place, didn't sound too bad. And if people took one look at me and assumed I was half-witted? Then they were folk I wouldn't want to hang around with anyway. And, if I really loathed the company I shared, I took my hearing aids out and escaped reality for a while, like I was doing now, in the hot tub.

After the jets switched themselves off, I lay for a while longer with my eyes closed, enjoying the gentle lap of warm water against my skin. Once, I'd nodded off like this and woken God knew how long afterwards, when I'd slid sideways and choked on gallons of water rushing into my open snoring mouth. Fifteen minutes, I decided, in a drifting haze. Fifteen minutes and then I'd clamber out.

More like half an hour later, my eyes blinked open in dismay. Because, standing with his back to me near the far end of the swimming pool, was a man. I squinted in the gloom. Maybe I was mistaken, and it was a towel rack? I reached up for my boxers, which had settled next to my shoulder, and to my horror, the shape moved. Fuck. Who the hell in this posh apartment block came for a swim at one a.m. on a Tuesday night? And how did he get in? Frankie had led me to believe that, after hours, only the penthouse floor had access to the basement.

The man tilted his head up, as if reading the printed instructions on the wall. It was one of those pointless signs that basically told you not to drown because the pool wasn't lifeguarded, and if you did, Lysander's company—Cloud Ten Management Corporation—weren't to blame, because they'd put up a sign full of complex legalese reneging all responsibility. The man had a nice back, as far as I could see, tapering down to a short black towel secured around his hips. He ran a hand through shaggy brown hair, then made as if to turn, which was probably my cue to announce my presence with a cough or something, so it wouldn't be awkward when he realised he had company.

So what did I fucking do instead? I remained silent. Because who wanted to make polite conversation in the middle of the night with a deaf bloke who'd left his hearing aids upstairs? And as much as I wished my boxers were covering my wanger, they were actually still clutched in a death grip in my right hand. My deformed legs were frightening enough on their own; add in the slashes of scar tissue and my floppy dick bobbing around, and the poor guy would be traumatised for months. Whoever he was, he'd come down for a relaxing, late-night dip in the pool, not to be accosted by a deaf, naked disabled bloke. In his shoes, I'd scream the place down, then call the apartment block security team.

So I did nothing, except lie rigid as a statue, with my head poking above the water and my gaze fixed with dread on the intruder. If he dived into the pool and started some laps, I'd attempt to slip out unseen. A terribly simple plan to execute... for anyone who wasn't me.

Having satisfied himself with whatever had caught his attention on the noticeboard, he ambled to the edge of the swimming pool and stared down into it for a moment. Stretching out a leg, he prodded the glassy surface with his toe, and a tiny wave of ripples fanned out across the water. Evidently pleased with the effect, he did it again.

And then, casual as you like, he dropped the fucking towel.

Not being a regular visitor to sports changing rooms, I'd only ever seen two blokes properly naked, in real life: my dad and Frankie. Oh, and my friend Milo, once, when he staggered, drunk as a skunk, into the wrong bedroom. No offence, but none of them were much to write home about. My dad's got a dad bod, obviously, and no one stares too hard at their dad's willy if they can help it. Milo could have done with a good square meal and afterwards insisted he was really, really cold. I'd seen more meat on a dirty fork. Frankie's body and dick were just much more aesthetically pleasing versions of my own.

Whereas this geezer was living, breathing proof that God had his favourites.

He teetered on the edge of the pool, providing me a better view, although most of his face was still in shadow. He had a soccer player's build, the nicest kind, in my humble opinion, all long lean muscles, and an athletic grace. Something metallic attached to one of his nipples glinted in the greeny-yellow glow of the pool uplighters. With his left hand, he scratched at the side of his ridged belly, then moved lower to give his soft dick a friendly squeeze, letting his fingers linger as he contemplated the water below. He squeezed it again, giving it a couple of distracted, half-hearted pulls, and fondled his balls.

All the tension erased by my dip in the hot tub returned tenfold as every individual muscle fibre in my arms and legs leapt to attention. My right calf muscles ganged up on me, threatening to spasm, to jerk out; controlling the build-up of pressure sucked up every ounce of my concentration. Was it possible to sweat whilst bathed in water? As the tub temperature mysteriously soared about five million degrees, I stopped breathing.

In a single fluid movement, the man dived in, cleaving the surface of the pool in two. The swiftness caught me by surprise, and with a hiss of pain, I gave in to the spasm. My right knee shot upwards as he broke the surface, then ploughed down the pool towards me. Desperately, I rubbed at my calf, willing it to relax. The distance between us shortened, my heart leaping to my throat. If he hauled himself out now and looked up, he'd spot my folded clothes, my towel, and the tsunami my errant knee had made across the surface of the hot tub. My head poking out from the top of the water.

With barely any strokes at all, the man reached the end wall. But instead of coming to a stop, he performed an elegant tumble. As he pushed off, his legs splayed apart, and before his thighs came together again, he gifted me the quickest flash of the secret dark divide between his white arse cheeks. He ploughed down for a second length. And then a third and a fourth, building a solid rhythm.

He wasn't as proficient a swimmer as Lysander, but very few people were. Lysander purred through the water, as if powered by a hidden electric motor. This guy crashed through it, almost furiously, as if in a hurry to reach the other end. His front crawl technique was decent—certainly rapid enough, but he could have been doggy paddling, and the play of lean muscle across his shoulders, the twin white domes of his bare buttocks, the hard sinews of his rangy arms, still would have transfixed me.

Each length he swam away, I fumbled with my wet boxers

under the water, eventually finding the holes. I slid them up, over my useless legs and suddenly hard dick, never taking my eyes off the body in the pool. I'd timed his lengths. There was no hope. During the course of a twenty-five-metre dash, I couldn't possibly clamber out, slither down the steps and onto the bench, then grab my sticks and totter to the door. He'd spot me straight away and know I'd perved him naked, seen him touching his dick.

Irrational thoughts swarmed my panicky mind. Who was this guy? He could be anyone, a mad psycho! An addict. He could have broken in off the street, looking for a fix or money to steal. He could be high on something. What if he became enraged and shouted and threatened? I'd have to sit here and take it and pray he wouldn't attack me.

Shivering, despite the heat, I imagined myself cowering here two hours from now, all because some exhibitionist wanker decided to go for a nighttime, five-mile swim. My skin had already taken on the texture of an out-of-date raisin. Any longer and I'd be forced to piss in the water. Shit, could they have put that dye in? What if the water turned red, and naked swimmer guy chose that exact moment to get out, and saw that I'd pissed in it? Oh God, please no.

I craned my neck to the side, urgently eyeing the distance between the hot tub and the door. My canes taunted me from the corner, just out of reach. Fuck. I was going to have to make a run for it. This guy was powerful and fit; he could go on for several more hours, or decide he wanted to end his evening workout with a soothing soak in the hot tub himself. And my bladder needed serious attention. When I needed to go, I needed to *go*.

Steeling myself, I decided to give it another minute, then haul myself up with as much dignity as possible. When he spotted me, which he undoubtedly would as soon as I flopped over the side, I'd pretend I'd just arrived and hope to God he believed me.

Of course, when I swivelled back from willing my canes to teleport their way into my hands, the guy had climbed out of the pool. He stood not three feet away, dripping wet and watching me. Water streamed from his chin and hair, coursing over the planes of his smooth chest. Coalescing into a fat river down the valley of his pecs, before fanning out across the grooves of his abs like the fucking Mississippi delta, before regrouping and dripping into the thick, wiry brown thatch at his...oh, fuck.

Chest heaving, he caught his breath. He shook his head vigorously, and a fine spray arced through the air, like a shampoo advert. Except in shampoo adverts, actors pouted in an erotic, sensual way, as if, off camera, someone was sucking their dick. This guy, in sharp contrast, looked as if someone had sunk their teeth into it.

He shouted at me, I think. He waggled a finger, lips snarled in an animated, cruel fashion. I managed to lipread the word 'fuck' and maybe another expletive too, but the rest became blurred in a mess of panic and shame and concentrating on trying not to wee.

In two quick strides, he closed the distance between himself and the hot tub, then leered over me, gripping the sides with his hands. Sharp, pissed-off, dark eyes bore into mine. His lips moved.

"I can't hear you." I cringed, cowering. My voice without my aids came out as a nasal whine, making me sound stupid, but I didn't know what else to do.

"I'm deaf," I added and signed it with shaky hands.

At that, he stepped back. Realizing their opponent couldn't hear them took the wind out of even the nastiest people's sails. If his nakedness bothered him, then he hid it remarkably well. His fat dick hung inches from my face, but no way could my eyes stray to it. He said something else—I had no idea what, but from his sneer and body language, I'd have bet the penthouse it wasn't complimentary. With one last glare, he twisted away. Swiping my towel from the bench, he deliberately knocked my clothes onto the wet floor, then sauntered out.

CHAPTER 2
DOMINIC

Things I hated about London: fucking *everything*.

Like radioactivity, clubbing in a city full of strangers had a half-life. Great the first time—a sweaty dance floor full of sexy people I hadn't met yet. Second time half as great. I'd met the hottest ones, and realised that the good time folk desperate to Instagram themselves in the VIP area didn't hold a candle to my old college buddies. Third time verged on tragedy, which was why, after two weeks kicking my heels in London, I was pining for the San Diego sunshine. And wishing my brother Lysander would hurry back from his trip. There were only so many stuffy art galleries and crummy old palaces a man could visit.

I regretted not expediting an earlier start date. A couple of guys I knew from college had started their internships already, leaving me contemplating my navel. Expecting sympathy, I'd whined to my mom on the phone about it. None was forthcoming. *Beggars can't be choosers, honey*, she'd said. *You've made your bed, and now you're gonna have to lie in it.* Gee, thanks, Mom.

Despite my temporary boredom, things could be a hell of a lot worse. Albeit this was an impromptu extended sabbatical from college, but I was in *London*! England! Which had to be a good thing, right? A city crammed full of history and culture, soccer, and rain. On an intellectual level, I'd known this world existed outside of the good 'ol US of A, but getting to see it with my own eyes? Awesome, once I got going. Unreal, once I'd found my feet and made friends. And even better once, after living out of a hotel room for the first couple of weeks, my brother handed me the keys, or rather swipe pad, to my own 'sub-penthouse', one floor below my older brother Lysander's even swankier one. I couldn't complain too much; the view was sublime, the super king bed to die for, and Uber Eats at the top of my speed dial.

Yesterday afternoon, I christened the bed with a hookup from the club. She slinked off to do her bar shift, afterwards, panty-less and a damn sight more dishevelled than when she'd arrived. Shame she wasn't still around to keep me occupied.

Seeing how I was big sister Daphne's favourite, she bestowed on me a whole four weeks to get settled prior to my hurriedly organised mini-internship at the family firm, Cloud Ten Construction. The unsexy world of shovels and stucco wasn't my ideal choice, but why put myself through the trauma of application forms, interviews, schmoozing, and trying to wheedle experience anywhere else? Instead, I could just rock up, no questions asked, and kill time at the huge Cloud Ten conglomerate until all the hoo-ha died down, *and* get to live one story below Lysander. An ace move: keep the fam happy, sneak under the radar for a few months, experience the European dream, then toddle back to SDSU to finish my business studies course and live out my days partying in the SoCal sunshine.

I may have omitted to mention to Daphne the sub-penthouse came fully furnished. Dumping my two suitcases of clothing into the vast closet took less than five minutes. After my hookup left, I found myself at a loose end, prowling around the basement sports complex and plumping for a late-night dip in the pool.

And *that* proved interesting, to say the least. Lysander never mentioned the apartment block came with its own resident fucking deviant. I'd ask my brother whether I should report him to the concierge or something.

My phone buzzed on the counter. *We're back. Come on up!*

At last! No sooner had I'd pitched up in London a fortnight earlier, Lysander and Frankie had up and left. We'd scarcely spent thirty minutes together, what with my jetlag and paperwork rubbish. Nothing personal, just bad timing—some eco-charity thing they were expanding into a place named Cornwall, and they'd combined it with a romantic holiday, AKA screwfest. Judging from the utter contentment on Big Bro's ugly mug as he buzzed me into the penthouse, the trip had been a success in every way.

St. Clouds were plentiful in the UK, but only Lysander and I shared the same two parents. And as big brothers went, they didn't come any better, even with ten years and an ocean separating us. Despite hating the media circus attendant on being the fastest man in the world across fifty or so meters of water, he'd always found time for me. He handed out awards every year at school and college, without fail, even though he detested the clamour of autograph signing and relentless gladhanding.

We were apples and oranges in that regard. Whereas his gold medals lay hidden in a dusty box in the back of a closet, I was an attention whore. After the horrors of his public break up with his ex, living the quiet life with a *guy* (jeez, that had blindsided me) and doing a job he loved in a country where he walked the street unrecognised couldn't have suited him any better.

"Cool pad, Lys." I cast my gaze around.

The penthouse footprint was bigger than mine, and yet they'd added enough homey touches to create a cosy, lived in feel. Two fat-ass blue sofas either side of a huge fireplace begged for two bodies to snuggle up together on them. The bright bolts of colour —cushions, curtains, abstracts—were Frankie's doing. He had a good eye, although I suspected Frankie could have spray-painted the whole place purple with pink spots, and Lysander would have gone all gooey-eyed. Maybe I'd invite him down to mine for some interior design advice, help me break up the acres of dull beige and chrome. And give me a chance to get to know this easygoing, laid-back guy with whom my hitherto straight big brother planned on spending the rest of his life.

"Sure is." Lysander dangled his long legs from one of the work surfaces. "We're very happy living here, aren't we, Frankie?" He shot a sweet smile at his lover. "I could stare at the fabulous views all day."

He raised an amused eyebrow in the direction of Frankie, bent over and hunting through the fridge, a pair of tight white jeans stretched beautifully across his cute little ass. Wow, I hadn't seen this side of my cautious older brother before, but I wholeheartedly approved. Although with his wavy blond locks and soft, fuck-me mouth, Frankie's pale prettiness would turn any guy's head.

"We're so happy, in fact," he continued, "we're taking things one step further. Right, my love?"

Frankie held out a bottled beer for me, then backed himself into the space between Lysander's open legs, smiling up as my brother slid two strong arms around his waist. *So this is what true love looks like.* A rumpled apartment, peaceful domesticity, and warm thighs to nestle into, just for the hell of it. As they shared a moment, a rose blush stole across Frankie's cheeks. "You tell him, Lysander."

"Are you sure? Don't you want to do it?" Lips twitching, Big Bro tore his gaze from Frankie to glance across at me.

Frankie shook his head. "No, it's your turn."

Oh my God, these two were freaking adorable together.

"Okay… sooo… our… um, business trip turned into something a little more, Dom." A bashful grin spread across Lysander's face. Trying to hide it, he pressed his lips tenderly to the nape of Frankie's neck, and I found myself grinning back. Knowing what was coming next wouldn't take a genius.

"And we… well, I asked this gorgeous, wonderful guy here if he'd give me the great pleasure of becoming my husband. And he only went and said yes."

Did I mention they were freaking adorable? Multiply that by a million. "That's crazy, man! Congratulations!"

As my big bro crushed me in a bear hug, I'd have struggled to find a prouder, more delighted guy in the whole of London. Pleased as punch, he was like a rooster locked in a henhouse, and his pretty boy wasn't much better, piling in for a cuddle too. As we were cheesily fond of saying in our family, Lysander and Frankie were riding high on a St. Cloud.

"We need to celebrate, guys! Crack open the champagne!"

"We will, we will, don't worry about that." Peeling himself away, Lysander resumed his position on the counter. "Frankie here has it all in hand. Some of our friends are coming over later—you're going to meet the whole gang."

"A gang?" My reserved brother had never been a group setting kind of guy. "Is that why you have such a huge pad? Because you have a *gang*?"

Frankie laughed. "It needs to be this big to store Lysander's medal collection."

Lysander threw him a gentle punch. "You mean your shoe collection, more like. And if you think this place is big, have you checked out the sports complex in the basement yet, Dom? I think you're going to love it."

"I had a look around last night. It's great. Haven't used the weights room yet—maybe we could hit it together sometime?"

As my brother high-fived me in agreement, Frankie chuckled.

"You have no idea how long he's waited for someone to say that to him. I'm... um... I tend to skip leg day. And... um... ooh, arm day too." He rolled up his sleeve and flexed. "But look, I did find a vein on my bicep yesterday. Let me show it to you. It's here somewhere."

Pretending to peer at Frankie's lean, lily-white arm, Lysander swooped in with a playful nibble. Someday, I looked forward to finding love like these two shared, but Christ, way off in the future.

Promising half-sister Daphne I was partied out and ready to experience working for the fam at Cloud Ten had been a big fat lie. As soon as I found me some decent buddies, London was a city waiting to be conquered, and I was the guy to conquer it.

"It must be a wet dream for you, Lys, having that big-ass pool in the basement. I went for a late swim last night. To be honest, I hadn't expected it to be unlocked. Felt great to be in the water, seeing as I'm missing the beach already." I took a sip of cloudy beer and tried not to wince. Seemed Lysander had embraced all things British, not only the men. The sooner we uncorked the champagne, the better.

"It's yours to use whenever." He drank from his own bottle, sighing with appreciation. "The management keep it open 24/7, but some hours are only for your apartment and mine. On my request. I swim early some mornings, like four-thirty sometimes." His face flushed. "Old habits die hard, I guess."

Frankie and I exchanged grimaces of horror. Who chose to get up at four-thirty to exercise? I'd often just hit the sack.

"Buddy, you can keep the early slot to yourself. I'll stick to the occasional late dip. Although you might want to double check the security arrangements down there. Last night, some creep decided he fancied a midnight soak, too. I'd assumed I was alone —found out a little late in the day I had unwanted company."

"Oh yeah?" Lysander's forehead creased into a frown. "Between about ten p.m. and six in the morning, it should be locked, except for the penthouse and your apartment to access."

"Maybe it was one of the security guys on his break." Frankie threw me a cute smile. His eyes were stunning. Me and Lysander's future husband were going to get on just fine.

I nodded at him. "Yeah, maybe. But the perv hadn't switched on the lights, so I didn't spot him straight away. Anyhow, seeing as I'd left my swim trunks up in the apartment, and no one was around, I decided to bash out fifty quick lengths in the nuddy."

Wagging his head, Lysander rolled his eyes. "This isn't the frat house, dude!"

"What's a guy to do? It was the middle of the night, I was bored and needed to check out the pool!" I shrugged. "Turns out this loser had the same idea but didn't bother announcing his presence. 'Cos when I climbed out at the end, the guy had been hiding in the fucking hot tub, watching the whole show. Getting off, probably."

"What?" They frowned in unison. "And he didn't say anything?"

"Not a word! And it's not like I arrived and jumped in straight off the bat. I was killing time since I couldn't sleep, so I wandered around the pool beforehand, checking out the sauna and the showers. I found a towel and stripped, then read the notices and stuff. He had plenty of opportunity to say hi or turn on the lights. Not gonna lie, dude, it freaked me out."

Frankie's expression was both amused and appalled. "What did you say to him?"

"I told him he was a fucking weirdo and to get a goddamned life. Didn't get much of a read on him because it was so freaking dark, but the guy looked like he was going to shit himself. He didn't even bother standing up when I confronted him! He just came out with some crap about how he was deaf, in some kind of freaky, horror movie voice. He said he couldn't hear me and couldn't communicate, or some ass-wipe shit."

Remembering what came next, I gave a clipped nod of satisfaction. "Any rate, I gave him a mouthful of good old American cuss words, swiped his towel, and accidentally on purpose tipped his clothes onto the wet floor. That'll teach him." I let out a bark of laughter. "Or not. Maybe he's still jerking off over it now."

I registered a noise behind me, hovering in the periphery of my mind: a dull tapping sound, like a casement window rattling. Or a door knocking against the frame in a draught. At the same time, Frankie's generous smile abruptly faded, replaced with a tense stare. Lysander, too, drew himself up higher, and his eyes flickered to something over my shoulder.

"What, what is it? Do you know him? Has this wacko spied on you too, Lys?"

Another long pause. Carefully, Lysander placed his beer bottle down onto the countertop next to him. Frankie stepped forwards out of the triangle of Lysander's thighs, remarkable turquoise eyes narrowing to two glittering laser beams.

"Dominic." He addressed me in a tight, cool voice I'd never heard him use before. "I think it's time I introduced you to my brother, Tristan." His gaze darted over my shoulder, before homing back onto me. "You'll have to speak clearly to him, however. You see, he's quite deaf."

I didn't need to twist around to see who stood behind me—the look of pure disgust souring Frankie's pretty features said it all. Nor did I need to digest my own brother's hardened expression, warning me too late how monumentally I'd fucked up.

Gut clenched and my throat closed, I performed a slow-mo 180 anyhow, until my eyes landed on Frankie's brother.

Oh shit. Not only deaf.

A guy hovered in the doorway of one of the bedrooms, short and blond, dressed in baggy blue sweatpants and an old Nirvana T-shirt. In reality, he wasn't that short, but his hips were flexed forwards and his legs bent at the knees, knocking a few inches off his height. His shoulders hunched in on themselves, his head lowered to the floor. A straw-blond curtain obscured his features. If he stood straighter, pulled his shoulders back, and looked up, he'd have been roughly as tall and of a similar build to... oh fuck.

Had Lysander mentioned Frankie's brother, who would be living with them? Yes, but at the time, back in San Diego, I'd been hammered, or under a pile of girls or boys. Most likely both. So I'd not paid much attention. Tedious domestic adult detail. Boring family and health stuff, about people I hadn't even met yet.

Twin canes supported the guy's weight. His knuckles gripped them so tightly I half-expected balls of shiny white bone to pop through the translucent layer of skin. His legs twisted to one side, and his skinny thighs trembled as they hugged each other, almost as if braced for another verbal onslaught from the arrogant asshole taking up floor space in the kitchen of his beautiful home. Resolutely, he stared at his feet, his thin chest heaving underneath the cotton fabric of the T-shirt. Behind a swathe of wavy hair, his face remained hidden.

"Tristan can't move very fast, Dominic," Frankie continued in his icy tone. Leaving his spot in front of Lysander, he walked—quickly, as if in contrast—over to his brother's side. "Especially from a seated position. Like, in a slippery hot tub, for example. If he tries to stand up in a hurry, then he risks losing his balance and falling over. Damaging himself. Cracking his head open, for instance, on the hard tiles."

His words dripped unconcealed fury, though the look he gave his brother as he slipped an arm around his narrow waist couldn't have been more tender. Seeing this Tristan guy now, upright but precariously balanced on two sticks and useless legs, I couldn't imagine how he managed to get *into* a hot tub unaided, let alone climb out of it. And then try and find a towel to dry himself. And dress in dry clothes. Oh… shit.

The beer from earlier revolted in my belly. I felt sick as a dog.

"Oh, and I should reiterate something else," Frankie added grimly, as if he hadn't already crucified me enough. "It sounds as if Tristan tried to explain all this to you himself. But perhaps you weren't listening, too full of righteous moral indignation that he caught you with your pants down. Is your dick really that small, Dominic, that you had to scream and hurl abuse at him? My brother is deaf and has cerebral palsy, you arrogant fucking prick. He's. Fucking. Deaf. And fucking *disabled*."

Tearing his eyes away from me, he gave another of those unbelievably tender looks to his brother, who hadn't moved from his spot. Tristan's T-shirt was rucked up at his waist, and Frankie straightened it for him.

"Tristan is wearing his hearing aids now, as he was looking forwards to meeting you. Oh, and celebrating our happy news. He struggles to communicate without them, so he wears them most of the time. Except if he thinks they might get wet and damaged. Like in a fucking *hot tub*, for example."

He spat out each syllable, even as he wheeled his brother

around and propelled him back into the bedroom. If Tristan hadn't been his primary concern, I'm fairly certain he'd have hit me.

To compensate, he yelled over his shoulder. "And he's worth two wankers like you any fucking day of the week."

With a furious slam, the bedroom door closed. Which left me and my big brother staring at each other in shock across the silence of the kitchen. All the colour leached from Lysander's face.

"I didn't know, did I? How was I to…"

"Shut the fuck up, Dom. Just… fucking shut up. And… and clear off. I don't want you here right now, and Frankie most definitely won't want to see you. And Tris… fucking hell, Dom."

"I can't go, Lys. I need to say sorry, at least. I can't…"

"Go," he ordered. "Right now." Rubbing a hand across his stubble, he blew out a long breath. "Let Frankie calm down. Let me talk to him. Let him… just go, okay? I'll come over and see you later."

Things I hated about London? That I was still fucking there.

'Go and work as an intern in the dazzling cultural capital of Europe,' they said. *'It will be fun,'* they said. Hah! I was ten seconds away from calling a cab and heading back to Heathrow Airport. Whatever shitshow I'd left behind in San Diego couldn't be any worse than this; I should have stayed there and faced the music. I paced the floor of my apartment, loathing everything about the bloody city stretched out beneath me. They could take their grey skies, their red buses, and their fucking disgusting real ale and stick it up their asses. Sorry, *arses*.

I'd really excelled myself this time. In the space of about four minutes, I'd succeeded in upsetting my favourite brother and alienating the love of his life, probably forever. And on the day they announce to the world they're getting fucking married, too. Not to mention the tiny matter of humiliating and abusing a disabled person. My insides tumbled into each other, sick with the horror of it.

Anger and mortification apparently lived side by side. Every time I hit a blank apartment wall and stomped in the other direction, I oscillated between the two. Had my behaviour down in the pool truly been that terrible? As I wore a groove in the floorboards, I tried to convince myself otherwise.

Why the fuck hadn't Tristan alerted me to his presence in the hot tub? With some splashing, or a wave or something? I'd have waved in return and said hi. And cursed because my swim shorts were back in the flat. And then I wouldn't have had a swim, I'd have postponed until another time. I wouldn't have gotten cross, I wouldn't have yelled at him, I wouldn't have pinched his towel and knocked his clothing to the floor.

So what was I saying? That *Tristan* was to blame? That going for a swim in my birthday suit was somehow his error? That stealing a towel and dropping *his* clothes into a puddle of water, clothes belonging to a guy who couldn't walk without sticks, or communicate without hearing aids, was somehow *his* fault, not mine? Christ, what kind of shithead would do such a thing like that?

A shithead like me, apparently.

I thought back to the abuse I'd slung at him, cringing, wanting to crawl into a hole and die. Nasty words had a hell of a lot in common with poison-tipped darts. Once they left your lips and penetrated human flesh, that fucking shit couldn't be sucked back out again.

The fact the guy turned out to be Frankie's brother was the freaking icing on the cake.

As a low buzz sounded from the hallway, I froze. Was Frankie coming for round two, in case the message hadn't been clear enough the first time? Or Lysander, ordering me to pack my bags and find accommodation elsewhere now Tristan didn't feel safe with his fucking abuser living one floor below? Who could blame him?

Oh, Christ, what if they told Daphne? And the rest of the Cloud Ten board? Or my mom and dad?

A firmer knock this time. With a heavy heart, I opened the door. Lysander, alone, fortunately. We weighed each other up.

"Can I come in?"

Nodding, I opened the door wider. "Sure."

He strolled across the threshold, casting his gaze around my empty apartment. "Nice."

"Could I come up and apologise to Tristan, Lys? It's the least I can do."

"Tristan doesn't want to see you again today." He gave me a humourless smile. "And it's better for your own safety if you stay away from Frankie until he's in a more reasonable frame of mind. That might take some time."

"I'm so sorry, Lys. I'm so sorry. I didn't know. I... really... I'm not that sort of person, you know that. I don't know what came over me. I must have been tired or excited or... not thinking straight anyhow."

Turning his broad back on me, Lysander gazed out across London. I'd been so thrilled to be visiting under the circumstances. Now, I wished I'd never set foot here. And I hadn't only been looking forward to the London adventure, but spending time with Lysander, and the rest of our relatives, too. Exploring the world outside of SoCal, to show everyone that the spoiled baby of the family was finally all grown up, putting his stupid mistake behind him.

Seemed I still had a hell of a lot of growing up left to do.

"It's not me you need to apologise to." With a short huff of laughter, he cast me a glance over his shoulder. "Just be glad it was Frankie and not his sister, or his sister's partner giving you the hairdryer treatment. Darren would have chucked you onto the next flight back to the US."

"I'm thinking of chucking myself on one, save him the bother." I clutched at my hair. "Christ, Lysander, I've fucked up, haven't I?"

"That's one way of putting it."

Embarrassingly close to tears, I sucked in a couple of deep breaths. Had I reduced Tristan to tears? I hoped not. Maybe he was a braver soul than me and shrugged it off. Sticks and stones and all that. Except, deep down, everyone knew that rhyme was horseshit. Cruel words cut and stung like hell. A fresh wave of mortification washed over me.

"I'm a good guy, Lys," I wailed. "I'm a nice person. I'm kind! You remember Mrs Sullivan from next door to Mom? After she broke her hip, I drove her to the grocery store every week for three months straight. And the carwash I organised at college, for the new homeless shelter? All that money I raised?"

"I'm not sure those good deeds are going to stack up too highly in Frankie's mind, against what you did to Tris, dude." Arms folded, he stared out into the night, his disappointment almost tangible. "I can't understand it, Dom. What the fuck were you thinking? What was running through your head? Didn't it occur to you to at least sound him out a little before you balled him out?"

The $10-million question, one reckless young men like me never had an answer for when they got caught. In my psych minor we'd learned the young male brain didn't fully develop until aged twenty-five or more; mine had apparently stalled altogether aged around thirteen.

"I don't know, Lys. Maybe I was embarrassed I'd been caught swimming naked. That maybe I'd get into trouble or something. And… I was frustrated and bored or some shit like that. Angry too, that you and Frankie weren't around. That I'd been sent here to London in the first place when I didn't want to come."

"You brought that on yourself," he cut in sharply. "I've spoken to Mom. Was that the work of a nice person too?"

I swallowed hard. I didn't know he'd heard about that. "It was the work of an asshole. Just like last night. Christ, Lys, what am I going to do?"

Fuck, I was trembling. Fucking trembling. A howling silence

stretched between us, and the sinking feeling in my gut worsened, like it was filling up with concrete. My chest ached; I was suffocating. I'd well and truly ballsed everything up. Again.

Coming to stand beside me, Lysander placed a comforting arm I didn't deserve around my shoulders. I blinked rapidly, swallowing down the tightness in my throat.

"Good people make mistakes, Dom." He gave my shoulder a squeeze. "And you're good people. I know that. I've watched you grow up. Unfortunately, you're also young and spoiled and forget it sometimes. When they are ready, I know you'll apologise to Tristan. Frankie too."

"Let me go up and apologise now. Let me see Tristan and say sorry."

"Not a wise idea, dude." Lysander shook his head. "Give them some space. Give Frankie time to calm down. They'll get over it eventually. But first, you're going to have to show *them* you're not that sort of guy."

"How the hell do I do that?"

He shrugged. "You'll think of something."

And what did I do in the meantime? I had two more weeks before I started work. Weeks supposed to be full of fun, spent with Lysander, letting him and Frankie show me the sights, meet their friends.

"Are we still good, Lys?" I sounded horribly desperate and in need of a reassuring hug, which wasn't forthcoming. I wouldn't want to hug someone as despicable as me either.

I had to settle for another shoulder squeeze. Better than nothing.

"Yeah, we're good." He sighed. "And you won't want to hear this, but Mom pretty much filled me in on everything that's happening back home. I'll say it again. You're not that sort of guy."

Ah. So, this was even more fucking awkward.

"I think I've just demonstrated I am."

"No, you're not. I know you. But this internship is a convenient opportunity for you to take a break from all the highjinks at college, get stuck into a quiet routine, and impress us all. To grow the fuck up."

I brushed at my eyes, hoping Lysander hadn't spotted my self-pitying tears, but another comforting shoulder squeeze said he had.

"Have you told Frankie about that stuff back home?"

"No. And if you don't want me to, I won't."

That stuff. Another hugely embarrassing situation with me in a starring role. It left my mom talking to my dad for the first time in years, so he could make calls and pull strings. Get me a plane ticket out of San Diego before I'd even sobered up.

"Have you had any more news about it?"

"No." I sniffed noisily. "Dad's lawyer is still on the case. I guess I'll be the last to hear."

As we both contemplated the shitshow I'd left behind, I swallowed down another fat lump.

"Oh well, I'd better get back." Lysander let go of me. "I'll see myself out."

I watched him go, easy athletic walk less sure than usual. With a hand on the door, he turned, rewarding me with a glimmer of a smile. "And Dom? It's for the best if you avoid the pool for the time being. Especially at night. And if you do choose to go for a swim during the daytime, make sure you wear swimming trunks, yeah?"

CHAPTER 3

TRISTAN

Favourite things about living in the penthouse: part 2: my bedroom.

I'm the youngest of triplets. Maddie's the eldest (and don't we know it), then Frankie, and then me. Three babies in one fell swoop must have been a living nightmare for my parents. But scroll on a few years, and three hormonal teenagers peaking in sync must have been a hell of a lot worse.

From my recollection, Maddie had determined to be a depressed goth for at least a two-year stretch, all the while insisting she was sunshine and roses, and everyone else was miserable. Frankie went through a delightful phase when his feet and armpits stank to high heaven, only communicating with an array of grunts, his middle finger answering every question.

Of course, I behaved, and continued to behave, perfectly.

When we reached an age deemed safe for us to be left home alone, my parents tried to claw back a semblance of half-remembered fun adult lives before surprise triplets came along and flipped them upside down. One of my abiding memories was my mum asking Frankie to keep an eye on me, and him scowling: "I'm not my brother's keeper." My dad used to say if he had a pound each time Frankie grunted those words, he'd be a rich man.

Times change. Teenagers eventually mature into responsible young adults. These days, my siblings had woven me so closely into the fabric of their lives that worries about coping alone, or in sheltered accommodation, or, heaven forbid, back home with our parents, were a distant memory. From the outset, Lysander knew Frankie and I were a package, and he welcomed me into his home as if taking on his lover's disabled brother was easy and natural as adopting his pet goldfish.

Goldfish swished around in titchy glass tanks, whereas I had a vast private space, all to myself, and I loved it almost as much as I loved the hot tub. An alarm cord in my en-suite bathroom connected me to the rest of the penthouse and to the concierge service downstairs, meaning help was never more than minutes away. Lysander had installed more handholds in the shower cubicle than a climbing wall; our friend Milo once demonstrated this by climbing up them, banged his head on the shower nozzle, and almost knocked himself out.

My bedroom in the penthouse boasted its own telly and a comfy sofa. I suspected this was the benefit of Lysander's privacy as much as mine, but I wasn't complaining. By the time evening swung around, I was more than content to disconnect from the world and wallow in my own silent company. Conversations with other people didn't passively happen to me; I had to actively listen and process through the clever microtransducers clamped on the sides of my head. By the end of some days, I was more than ready to switch off.

So, all in all, the sanctuary of my bedroom felt like a wonderful place to be. Although tonight, it struggled to work its magic.

"Tristan, it's me."

A light knock on the door preceded Frankie's soft tread. He found me curled up on my bed, fully clothed.

"You okay?"

I nodded, shaken from last night's horrible incident down in the basement, let alone overhearing Lysander's brother's callous retelling. Over the years, I'd experienced much worse than him, but the suddenness of the abuse hurt the most. The lack of preparedness in a situation where I least expected it. When I'd been merely minding my own business in the haven of my own home.

Frankie perched awkwardly on the edge of the bed. He looked after me for sure, helping me from A to B and carrying stuff, but at the end of the day, we were brothers, not soulmates. If we spent all day together, we bickered and wound each other up. We never shared deep meaningful chats, not unless something dreadful happened.

"I wasn't perving him, Frankie." Shame bruised my cheeks. "You need to make sure Lysander knows that. I was half asleep, and then I opened my eyes, and there he was, exposing himself. I didn't know what to do. And I didn't have my hearing aids."

And I didn't want him to see my horrible legs. But there was no need to spell that out, not to Frankie; he already knew.

"I know you weren't. Chill. Lysander knows, too."

"I think I just hoped he'd have a quick dip and then get out, without spotting me at all."

"Tris, I get it. You don't need to explain. He's the wanker here, not you."

Why the hell did it have to be Lysander's bloody brother? It was going to cause all sorts of ructions. "Thank you for wading in. I was too shocked to say anything. But you didn't need to do that, you know. I don't want to cause strife between you and Lysander."

Frankie huffed. "Yes I bloody well did! I'm fucking furious with him! And don't you worry, Lysander is as cross as I am. Well, disappointed mostly. He was so excited Dom was coming to the UK—he wanted us all to get along."

I'd felt the same. I'd heard a lot about this younger brother and his college antics. Frankie and Lysander hardly set out to make me feel like a third wheel upstairs, but I still did, and I'd hoped

Dominic's arrival would change everything. Instead, I'd be more confined to my bedroom than ever. Just in case he decided to pop in to visit big brother. And what if he made a regular thing of his midnight dip in the pool? Soaking in the hot tub had been the best medicine for my taut muscles for years. How dare that bloody inconsiderate twat take that simple pleasure away from me?

"Tell him to stay clear of the pool," I ordered fiercely. "At night, anyhow. I don't want to ever bump into him down there again."

Frankie's eyes lit up. Shit, I shouldn't have brought up the pool.

"Aah. I was coming to that. When were you going to mention your little midnight trips?"

He sounded amused, rather than annoyed, thank God. Probably because he still felt sorry for me. The last thing I needed was to fall out with Frankie, too.

"I wasn't. Just don't tell Maddie, okay?"

"Of course I'm going to tell her! That wanker deserves everything he's got coming to him. I want to be there when she rips his balls off."

"I'm still going to go down to the hot tub, though. As long as he's never there. Don't try and stop me."

He snorted. "I won't. But promise me you won't drown. Lysander says the paperwork would be terrible and will reduce the rental value of the apartments."

Neither of us laughed. Frankie tried to lift the mood by filling me in on his trip to Cornwall and the romantic proposal. I asked him if he had any ideas about the wedding. Wrong move. I then had to pretend to be interested in his fifteen-minute monologue on venue options, likely the first of thousands. He didn't totally succeed in taking my mind off Dominic's behaviour, but it helped. We could have dissected last night's incident at the pool to death, and the one in the kitchen earlier this evening, but what was the point? I'd still be deaf and have rubbish legs, and ignorant dim-witted fools like Dominic would still roam the earth. He'd bruised me, but I'd had worse. I'd survive.

Favourite things about living in the penthouse: part 3: Maureen.

From the day we moved in, Lysander insisted I use a driver from the company driving pool. And for once, I didn't argue. Instead, my heart danced a little jig because the unpredictable mix of public transport and calling for Uber's had been an arduous affair. Costly, too.

At the start, my private chauffeur was a huge embarrassment, but I soon became prepared to stab anyone who tried to take my driver away from me. Maureen improved my day-to-day immeasurably. Yes, I could do public transport—my nearest Tube station was only 300 metres away, and the other end spat me out almost opposite the record shop where I worked. And Tube staff were surprisingly sweet and helpful with cripples like me, although the usual woman who let me through the special wide ticket barrier had hinted I'd find it much easier in a wheelchair. But she meant well, unlike a certain young man I desperately tried to banish from my mind. For several reasons.

That night in the pool ranked as my worst in aeons. The agony of crawling on my hands and knees out of the hot tub, praying he wouldn't come back to hurl even more abuse. Another half an hour spent retrieving my wet clothes, scrabbling into them, then dragging myself back upstairs to my bedroom, where I'd tumbled under my duvet, humiliated, shocked, and shivering, my legs itchy from my own hot piss. So yes, on a scale of awfulness, it stuck out right at the top of the fucking end.

However, until the moment it all went to shit, one wonderful aspect of it played like a film reel in my head. Almost constantly. The able-bodied world desexualised folk like me, with parts they considered ugly. Even small plastic attachments like hearing aids detracted from 'normal' ideals of beauty. But though my hearing was useless, my vision was perfect. I knew my twisted, pathetic legs were hideous; I could see them myself. I didn't need the averted eyes of able-bodied folk to remind me of that.

But... drum roll... people like me still felt horny too. And since witnessing Dominic's strong fist wrapped around his dick, some of us felt very horny indeed, most of the time.

"Our Gina's only got eight weeks to go," Maureen remarked, as we stalled in the heavy traffic chugging across Vauxhall Bridge. I reckoned by now I knew more about her daughter's pregnancy than Dean-the-plumber who'd impregnated her. And indeed, about a whole host of other colourful characters who made up Maureen's world. I didn't only adore her because she drove me places. She was my surrogate mother, protector, sounding board, *and* chauffeur, all rolled into one.

"How's the Gaviscon helping with her heartburn?" I shifted in my seat. Maureen could always be relied upon to kill an incipient erection, too.

"She's swigging it straight from the bottle." Maureen chuckled. "If heartburn is a sign the baby will have a full head of hair, then our Gina's giving birth to Chewbacca!"

Another reason to love our car journeys: Maureen ploughed the tricky furrow of acknowledging my disabilities but still treated me like her mate. It was a rare skill, made even more special as I don't think she realised how brilliantly she accomplished it.

Some folks pretended to ignore my mobility issues altogether, which I daresay helped the person feel like they were paying me a compliment—*hey, you're one of us!* This cunning plan, though, painted disability in a negative light, something shameful, something to pretend not to see. And made for very awkward conversations at the bottom of a staircase.

Maureen never overlooked my disabilities. She always helped me out of the car, and, on wet pavement days, all the way into the record shop, her brawny arm tight around my waist. Deathly embarrassing. Nevertheless, she still treated me as someone she considered a friend, just like her neighbour Brenda and Janice from bingo at the Red Lion.

'Differently normal' was the fashionable expression promoted by organisations a hell of a lot more on message than me. Sincere attempts to view disabled people in a positive light were noble endeavours, even though cynical me argued they were a mask to cover up ableists' own uncomfortable feelings about disability.

Anyhow, to Maureen, I was simply her disabled mate, Tristan, and I was very cool with that.

After we pulled up outside the record shop, Maureen honoured me with a whiskery kiss on the cheek, then fiddled around me on the pavement. She didn't kiss me every time she dropped me off, thank God, but after today she'd be gone for a fortnight, chauffeuring Lysander's Uncle Paul around on an extended trip to Ireland, 'between the pub and the golf courses', according to her.

"Don't know who's taking over from me." She adjusted my collar as if we were outside the school gates and she was my blooming mother. Though I gave her the eye roll, I let her fuss. Maureen's name sat at the top of a very short list of people allowed to rearrange and touch my person without seeking permission first.

"If it's Pete, don't let him drop you off at the end of the road, the lazy bugger. And if it's Doorman Dave, then don't grow too fond of him. 'Cos I'll be back."

She said 'I'll be back' in a rubbish growl, and I groaned. The worst Schwarzenegger impersonation ever.

"And don't let your Neil talk you into going to any underground drug dens," she added darkly, with a finger waggle. Did I mention that Maureen had a vivid imagination?

"He's not my Neil."

"Good! Keep it that way! And keep away from that wacky baccy he smokes, too."

I groaned again, loudly. "Do I strike you as a man whose existence would be improved by hunger and paranoia?"

"Don't get fresh with me, young man. That Neil's not special enough for you. I can't be having you wandering the streets on your own or with him, and me in a foreign country fretting about you."

"I don't know what you've got against Neil, Maureen. He's just a friend."

"His lips are too thin. My grandmother told me never to trust a man with thin lips."

This was the same grandmother who told her never to pick blackberries in September because witches pissed on them. And eating bread crusts made your hair grow curly.

"Ireland is hardly foreign."

"I'll be getting on a boat and sailing across the sea. Spending euros, not pounds. That's foreign enough in my book, young man."

Whoever turned up to collect me this evening would have big shoes to fill.

An assistant position in a vintage record shop just off Ladbroke Grove didn't sound like much of a career game, set, and match, but I'd been employed there for over a year with no plans to move on. When Maureen began dropping me off in the swish Lexus every morning, none of the other members of staff uttered a word. The record shop was a judgement-free zone, even if a mug with Little Lord Fauntleroy imprinted on the outside appeared on my desk two days later. My boss, Emily, her employees, and friends formed a broad church, as did our regular clientele.

"Your groupies are in the front, over by the trad jazz rack," she mouthed, close to my hearing aid. "Go on, make their day."

Blimey; Arnie and Dirty Harry in the same morning. I threw Emily my best withering look, and she stuck out her tongue.

"Where's Irene? Why can't she go?"

"She's nipped to the bank, before it gets busy."

Yep, smug satisfaction. With a despairing sigh, I clambered to my feet.

My particular skillset—i.e., sitting on my arse for long periods of time—lent itself well to working in the back room, sorting the internet orders. Emily's long-time partner, Irene, blessed with boundless enthusiasm and a ready smile, manned the shop, along with a couple of part-timers. These days, our core business was online and international; Emily had branched into vintage band T-shirts and gig memorabilia, as well as maintaining a reputation for sourcing rare vinyl. She strategized, marketed, and also consumed a staggering number of chocolate digestives in her office out the back, and completed all three rather well, too, if our increasing revenues and her expanding waistline were anything to go by. Even more cuddly, Irene said. I wholeheartedly agreed.

I didn't actually mind the groupies, smiling to myself as they whispered, sneaked a peek at me, and whispered again, pretending to be fascinated by Acker Bilk's *Golden Treasury*. Three of them skulked around today, two boys and a girl. Sometimes, they materialised in a shuffling group of four or five. Non-conformist emo kids, who dressed and made up their faces in an identical fashion as all the other thousands of non-conformist emo kids.

"Anything I can help you with?" I queried.

They shook their heads in a chorus of no's. One of the boys caught my eye, and his cheeks pinked. I swear he was only about sixteen.

Every now and again, I got hit on. Flattering, sometimes, and sometimes not. People attracted to me fell into three categories. First, the weirdo disability fetishists, of whom way too many roamed the streets, easily spotted from a mile off. They wandered into the shop and wandered out again just as quickly, after getting short shrift from myself or Emily. Mostly male, but a few women fell into this loose category too. Often older and with mummy complexes, wanting to take me home and pet me like a doll. Nice enough but confused and seeking love in the wrong places.

Then there were the romantic, idealistic youngsters, like the lad peeking shy glances in my direction. I knew my face was okay. I was a washed-out, pale, and less radiant version of Frankie, who got hit on all the time. *Same guy, less popular font*, was how our friend Milo charmingly put it. (Fortunately, I was very fond of him.) Boys like the one in the shop, making eyes at me from under his long fringe, saw me as a poor man's Kurt Cobain, a tragic hero with a tormented soul, and all that bollocks.

In reality, of course, I was just a deaf guy with cerebral palsy working in a record shop. On the inside, I was ordinary, and if any of those kids ever spent twenty-four hours in my company, the daily grind would soon strip them of any sexy fantasies.

And then there was the third, much smaller category containing folk like Neil, a musician and one of the record-shop regulars, who simply fancied me. Presumably because of my razor-sharp wit, fathomless, penetrative sapphire stare, and hot body—yeah, right.

Fuck, I don't know *why* they fancied me—why did anyone fancy anyone? Sadly, most people who landed in this unfortunate category tended to be women. I'd made a few friends this way, even snogged a couple of them, but… nah.

Unfortunately, any blokes pigeonholed in this group so far had found their feelings unreciprocated. Neil was okay, pretty enough to look at, but laboured under the misapprehension I wanted to hear about Cuban hip-hop from dawn till dusk. Or the dire state of the Amazon rainforest, and how I should tie myself to a lamp-post outside the Houses of Parliament in protest. On a couple of occasions, we'd been out for beers after work; once he invited me back to his flat, but I declined as it was on the fourth floor of a building without a lift. I had to feel way more comfortable with someone to let them assist me up several flights of stairs, let alone lead me into a situation where I might have to undress.

In my experience, attractive young gay men were a fickle bunch. Guys lacking classical ideals of beauty like me were mostly invisible. Which posed a problem, because I wasn't lowering my standards, as though my disabilities made me a second-class citizen and I should be grateful for what I could get. So although I hadn't found him yet, my Mr Right was still out there somewhere. In the meantime, I contented myself with remembering the night of the *thing*, and what he-who-shall-not-be-named looked like in his birthday suit with his hand on his...

"Do you have any Wythenshawe Waltz T-shirts?"

Emo boy, a black flop of hair covering most of his face, sidled up to the counter and nibbled nervously on chipped black fingernails. I shook my head and reached for a notepad. One day, the British disaffected youth's love affair with Morrissey's music would wane. Until that time came, it made a healthy contribution to my wage packet.

"Still on order. Maybe try again from next Tuesday onwards?"

I took his contact details, promised to let him know, and watched as he reported back to his huddle of friends. A few minutes later, they left the shop, and Irene returned.

My day settled into its comfortable routine, revolving around internet enquiries and hatching plans with Irene for Emily's fortieth birthday party in a few weeks' time. Frankie pinged me a couple of texts asking me to give him a call, reassuring it was nothing concerning. Being a dick, I let him hang, to remind him he wasn't the only family member with a demanding, very busy day job.

Towards late afternoon, the steady trickle of customers thinned out, and Irene left early to sort the birthday cake order, leaving me to handle any last-minute sales. Settling behind the counter, I flicked through a pile of gig flyers, letting the minutes wind down. I'd not had much time to dwell on the bad part of the *thing*, but as I waited to discover which driver Cloud Ten had freed up to collect me, my anxiety mounted.

What if Dominic had made himself comfortable in the penthouse when I got home? What if Lysander had taken sides, and him and Frankie had fallen out over me? Maybe they would ask me to move out? Fuck, what if the row had been so bad, they'd called off the wedding? Was that why Frankie had phoned?

Spoken aloud, these thoughts sounded irrational, which didn't stop them churning around in my head. First and foremost, Lysander was kind and generous; he'd never kick me out. If I went, then Frankie would leave too, and Lysander worshipped my annoying, bossy brother. And yes, in all likelihood, Dominic would come up to the penthouse tonight and attempt some sort of half-arsed apology, if only because Lysander insisted on it. To keep house and future family dynamics running smoothly, I'd be expected to accept, and we would all pretend to draw a line under it so we could move on in a mature, adult fashion.

But Dominic, my future *brother-in-law,* would still label me as a pervert. In private, anyhow. The damage was done. No one liked admitting they were in the wrong, especially cocky, good-looking wankers like him.

All in all, I didn't feel ready to be an adult about the situation. Not yet anyhow. Maybe I'd ask the driver to take me over to my sister Maddie's, and I could spend the evening cooing over the baby. That would take my mind off things. I could even stay the night. She had a spare room, and I had an extra set of hearing aid batteries in my bag.

At two minutes to five, the shop door jangled, setting off a flare of irritation. My Cloud Ten drivers were an enormous luxury, of which I was hugely appreciative. The least I could do was be on the pavement, ready and waiting. Faking a smile, I looked up. And did a double take.

Framed by criminally long lashes and boasting all the fabulous shades of autumn, a pair of wary eyes locked onto mine.

Oh my God, this had to be some sort of elaborate joke. No way would Frankie do this. I was going to fucking kill him if he had.

Clutching a familiar set of Lexus car keys, my new driver appeared to be following the same untenable train of thought, looking ready to puke. We eyed each other in mutual horror until I found my voice, thick and sluggish, as if I had a mouth full of marbles.

"Sorry. We're closed."

CHAPTER 4
DOMINIC

EIGHT HOURS EARLIER

Things I hated about London: It was cold, wet, and over five thousand miles away from California. And that wasn't the worst of it.

"What the fuck?"

The most stupid idea *ever* was what it was.

I wrapped my robe more securely around my waist; I didn't need to expose myself to *both* Carter brothers. Lysander and Frankie had hauled me from my bed, where I'd been enjoying less than five seconds of wakefulness before the ghastly state of affairs hit me all over again and left me wallowing in the miserable chasm accompanying the dawning of a new day.

I assumed Lysander and Frankie had exited for work for the day, but no, here they were, suited and booted and shoulder to shoulder in my living room. Two against one.

"We think it's an excellent idea," Lysander continued. "Not only will you be helping Tristan, but it's a step to improving overall relations between the four of us. Before the wedding."

And receiving a twice-a-day visual reminder of how badly I've behaved.

"Why can't I be the one to drive Uncle Paul around his golf courses, and that Maureen woman can carry on here? I'm his nephew, whom he hasn't seen for umpteen years. I love golf!"

"Because *that Maureen woman*, a highly valued employee and of whom Tristan is very fond, has family in Ireland, and she's staying on afterwards for a few days." Frankie's clipped tone was frosty but preferable to the bitter hatred of last night. "And before you say it, no, none of the other drivers are free. Daphne's in town, and she likes to keep Dave at her beck and call. The other driver, Pete, treats the streets of London like his own personal racetrack. Tristan is not a suitable co-driver."

"Why can't he get an Uber for two weeks? I'll pay for it myself."

Frankie's fists clenched. Without Lysander, he might have launched both barrels. Was I coming across as selfish and whiny? Yes. Probably. Definitely. But Christ. What the hell were they thinking?

"Because I said so, that's why," Lysander answered with an unfamiliar sharpness. God, he sounded just like our mother. "Have a little bloody empathy for someone else, Dom, for once in your life! Has your little escapade back home taught you nothing?"

Frankie eyed him curiously, and a flush of heat swept across my face. If he brought that up, then Frankie and his brother would despise me even more.

"Whatever your opinion is on the matter, Dom, you're doing it. You never know. Having to think about someone other than yourself for a change might do you good."

"Okay, but I don't know how to look after a disabled guy."

Frankie treated me to that slitty-eyed, glittery gaze again. He was awfully good at it. "He isn't a *disabled guy*—he's Tristan. And Tristan doesn't need looking after. He just needs a fucking lift."

Lysander sighed. "Jesus, Dom, let me make this perfectly clear. You have fucked up. This is a chance to remedy that. And we're not asking you. We're telling you."

"Oh, and by the way," Frankie added, with more than a hint of satisfaction, "seeing as you'll have some time on your hands in between dropping Tristan off and picking him up again, I've arranged for you to gain valuable work experience on one of the building sites. You know, an opportunity to get your hands dirty down on the shop floor. Daphne thought it was an excellent idea when I suggested it."

Asshole. Me, working on a bloody construction site? Didn't the fucker realise my trust fund could buy a fucking construction site ten times over?

"And I know you think that's beneath you," he added, as if he could read my mind. "See it as a lesson in humility instead."

"Starting tomorrow," Lysander butted in. "Straightforward manual labouring. It will afford you plenty of thinking time, which sounds exactly what you need right now. Time to reflect on how you would like the rest of the world to view you. Consider it payback for what happened at home, as well as treating Tristan so badly."

When had my genial older brother stopped being such a pushover?

"I can't believe Tristan wants this." I pulled a sulky face. "Does he know?"

"I'm phoning him later," answered Frankie calmly. "Given the choice between you and the scrum on the Tube, a warm Lexus—even with you next to him—might just about win out. You have a fortnight before you begin your internship, and Tristan needs someone we can trust to see him safely to and from the record shop. It makes perfect sense."

Not to me it didn't. "Hey! But I've never driven in the UK before! I've never driven a stick-shift car. Or… or one with the steering wheel on the wrong side. Or on the wrong side of the road, for that matter."

Lysander sighed. "They call stick-shift a 'manual' over here. And you're in luck because the Lexus is an automatic. Doorman Dave is coming to give you a quick practice lesson on how to drive on the *correct* side of the road in…" he glanced at his watch, "ten minutes. So, little brother of mine, hop in the shower, throw some clothes on, and be out on the pavement waiting for him."

Fuck me, they really had thought of everything.

Dave treated me like a spoilt pampered brat, and to be fair, for the first half hour of the lesson I behaved like one. I was one, dammit! And spoilt pampered brats weren't used to being told what to do. By Dave *or* Lysander. I had to admit, though, the Lexus was a smooth ride, very pokey accelerating away from the lights, and Dave made the whole drive-on-the-wrong-side thing seem pretty straightforward.

He'd placed a handy sticker on the steering wheel with the reminder 'keep to the left!' in block capitals, which I ripped off as soon as I dropped him back at the offices. And then wished I hadn't, because as I drove out of a gas station (sorry, *petrol* station) after filling the Lexus with gas (sorry, *diesel*), I almost careered into a white truck hurtling towards me in the wrong freaking lane. Yanking down his window, the driver eloquently informed me, in words of one syllable, all about my error.

His look of disgust, however, was nothing compared to Tristan's expression of downright horror. From his muttered swearing, he'd attended the same charm school as White Truck Guy. Nevertheless, I was not to be deterred. As I'd driven across town, I'd practised how our first confrontation since my fucked-up swim would play out. So I was one hundred percent prepared. Facing him square on, I dipped my head to his level and enunciated clearly.

"I'm. Here. Because. Lysander. Has. Made. Me. Your. Replacement. Driver. For. A. Fortnight."

I flashed up all ten fingers, then added another four before doing some pointing. "Fourteen. Days. Driver. Me. You."

From the look of consternation crossing his face, this must be news. "Frankie. Said. He. Would. Phone. You. And. Let. You. Know."

I mimed the last part, pointing again and forming the universal hand signal for speaking into the phone. He stared at me blankly. Oh God, the guy had learning difficulties too. This was going to be even harder than I'd imagined. Taking a deep breath in, I began again.

"Driver. Me? You?"

"Er...Dominic?" Tristan voiced my name very clearly; I guessed he must have been practising too. "Why are you shouting like an arsehole and speaking like this?"

He waved his thin arm around as if conducting an orchestra, accompanied by a series of bizarre facial contortions, which yes, I possibly had been making. I felt myself flush.

"Because you... you... Frankie and Lysander said you were..."

"Go on, you can say it," he interrupted. "The D word. Deaf. It won't upset me. I worked through the stages of shock and denial ages ago, and for the last twenty-five years, I've found acceptance. Oh, and a set of cochlear implants."

Sarcastic jackass. His voice with hearing aids sounded nothing like the nasal monotone speech of the pool.

"I was only trying to be nice to you."

He shrugged. "Lucky me." He indicated to a stool on my side of the counter. "Wait there. I'm just going to phone my brother to tell him he's an utter prick and to make the most of his last hour left on the planet. And then I'll grab my coat."

So, that went well.

People like me didn't hang out in murky record stores hidden down anonymous side streets, so I took the chance to look around. First up, what seemed like a pokey shop from the outside opened into a surprisingly airy industrial space. Watery evening sunlight, pouring through two enormous skylights, made it seem larger still. Neat racks of vinyl records were screwed into bare red brick walls. Framed vintage T-shirts hung like pieces of modern art between the racks, and sepia photos of sixties kids with daisy chains in their hair and strumming guitars ran around the back of the counter. Very cool. In one corner of the store nestled a low coffee table, piled high with back copies of music magazines. Battered leather armchairs tempted music lovers to take the weight off and while away a few hours.

"Ready."

Not one to sit still for long, I'd migrated to the nearest racks and flicked through the vinyl. At his curt announcement, I pulled back my hand as if burned. The artistes didn't even register; I was too busy absorbing my chill, urban surroundings and realising Tristan must be a part of them. In my preppy navy chinos and button-down, I felt oddly out of place, a whole new experience.

"I see you're a Coldplay fan." He smirked, looking over at the rack I'd been perusing. "That figures. Never mind."

"I was just…"

"Yeah, yeah, that's what they all say."

A slow shuffle to the door began, sticks first then legs dragging behind. Frankie advised not to offer Tristan any help unless he requested it. Having spent all of five minutes in the guy's company, I thought I knew better.

"Hey, I'll grab that bag for you, so it doesn't interfere with your balance."

I held my arm out for the old-style leather messenger bag slung diagonally across Tristan's small frame. Ignoring me, he continued with his bent, knock-kneed dragging walk. I hovered around him, overly large and useless.

"Let me open the door for you."

He graciously inclined his head, only for the shop door to swing outwards on its own as my dart towards it activated the motion sensor. Jackass.

"The car's parked just here." Christ, I'd been less anxious on freaking first dates. I wittered on, feeling more out of my depth with every step. "The silver Lexus next to the kerb, in front of the blue Honda with the…"

"My eyesight is fine, thanks. I can see the car perfectly. I'm more bothered by tripping over the huge bloody elephant clod-hopping around in front of me."

He should have been more bothered about the driving skills of said elephant, because... bus lanes. Hundreds of the damn things, snaking out across the road at all angles. Rush hour and pedestrians with a death wish stepping off the sidewalks (sorry, *pavements*). Zigzag lines around crosswalks, orange flashing globes. I mean, what the fuck? Cab drivers, hooting everywhere, like we were crossing frigging uptown Manhattan. Cretins driving Audis like they were screaming off the grid at the Daytona 500. Mini rotaries—what in God's name was the point of those? And the yellow box things at traffic lights?

Navigating central London at five o'clock, with a furious ball of precious cargo in the seat next to me instead of placid Doorman Dave, was madness. I didn't need a purple post-it note on the steering wheel reminding me to drive on the left—I needed the whole freaking highway code. And the verbal dexterity of a hostage negotiator.

"I hadn't realised it was possible to stall an automatic," Tristan observed blandly. Cursing, I restarted the engine.

"Nor had I, but did you see those massive orange bollards swerve out as if they were going to hit me? Jesus, that cyclist in the red helmet is a psycho! Look at her! And are all your black cab drivers on cocaine or something?"

I glanced over to see him staring out of the side window, his mouth covered with his hand. His hair was even lusher than Frankie's, soft waves of golden spun silk reaching down to his shoulders. A shield to hide behind. Sensing me looking, he glared.

"Eyes on the road! Any more of this and the satnav woman will beg you to drop her off at the next bus stop. I'm very close to asking if I can join her."

We made it home alive, bumping down the ramp into the apartment block underground carpark with choreographed sighs of relief. Parking without mishap, I then spent several embarrassing minutes working out how to switch off the damned engine and remove the key, a feature Doorman Dave had omitted during his whistle-stop tour of the Lexus.

At least it left me too occupied to offer to help Tristan manoeuvre himself, his bag, and his sticks out of the car, which he accomplished with a minimum of fuss. Already, in the short time I'd spent with him, I appreciated how significant inconsequential acts like traversing a busy sidewalk or opening a car door became if your legs didn't work properly. And how long travelling the minimal distance between the car and the elevator took. I dallied, unsure whether the etiquette was to walk at his pace alongside or go ahead and wait for him to catch up, as if deliberately contrasting his slowness with my agility. Shit, how did people work all this stuff out?

"For God's sake, go on in front of me. You make me nervous standing there—I swear you're going to trip me up. If I need you hovering next to me, I'll tell you."

Huh.

Feeling bold, I pressed the buttons for my floor and the penthouse. Surely that was normal, wasn't it? I rested my hand on the open door to prevent it closing on us while Tristan was half in, half out. Apparently, that was okay too. As the doors glided closed, he sagged against the back wall and rolled his shoulders, wincing. Having to think out every step of every trip, no matter how short and familiar, must be exhausting.

"Tristan, I need to say sorry."

"Yeah, you do," he replied dully, staring up at the ceiling.

Last night, I'd lain in bed planning a whole apology speech. About how I should have checked I wasn't alone, how I shouldn't have been so judgemental or so fucking vile, how next time I went for a dip I'd take my goddamn swim shorts. But watching him here in the lift, witnessing his reliance on drivers and elevators and brothers and sticks and hearing aids, merely to accomplish simple daily activities the rest of us took for granted... none of it felt appropriate.

"So here it is. I'm sorry. Truly, I am. I was a horrendous

asshole. My parents brought me up to behave better than that. I won't let them or myself down again. I can't change what I did, but I can show you the real me is better than that. So I'm here at your disposal for the next couple of weeks to help you any way I can. Which won't make up for it, not by a long shot, but hopefully will show you there is a decent side of me."

An understated *ping* signalled my floor. As the doors swished open, I hesitated, wondering what else I could add. Nothing, I concluded. The words to make the situation better hadn't yet been invented.

Dropping his eyes from the ceiling, Tristan pinned me with his gaze. In the bright artificial light, he was more delicate than Frankie, his skin thin and fragile. The eyes sizing me up matched the turquoise of the swimming pool, strangely luminous against his pale cheeks, as though lit from behind.

"Will you be okay travelling up to the next floor on your own?"

A stupid question. As soon as the words had left my lips, I braced for the sarcastic putdown.

It never came. "I'll be fine. Thank you. And thank you for apologising."

CHAPTER 5
TRISTAN

Favourite things about living in the penthouse: part 4: the posh surroundings drew our friends like a magnet, saving me the hassle of hauling my wrecked body out. Mungo wrestled me to the sofa when I'd barely set foot through the door. The list of people allowed to do that had only his name on it.

"Princess! How's it hanging?"

Surprise, surprise, no one else got away with calling me Princess either.

"Bloody hell, get off! I'm being bearded to death!"

Mungo's much-loved younger sister suffered from significant spina bifida, which featured a different set of obstacles but meant Mungo had never handled me with kid gloves nor assumed what I could or couldn't do. In other words, he greeted me with the same big-hearted hugs he showered on all our friends, and I found myself suffocating under fifteen stones of hairy tattooed lawyer.

When he allowed me to right myself, he beamed, a naughty grin splitting his luxurious facial hair. Years ago, I'd hoped… yeah, whatever. Not long afterwards, I'd accepted Mungo was in love, and would forever remain in love, with somebody else. Until that lucky individual, currently occupying the far end of our sofa cottoned on, he'd only ever be in the market for casual, and our friendship was way more important.

"Are you okay, flower?" Milo, said lucky individual, shot me a concerned look. "Frankie told us about Lysander's horrid brother. Do I need to go downstairs and beat him up for you?"

Mungo and I both snorted. Milo weighed even less than I did.

"Nah." I shook my head. "I'm over it. I think Frankie was more riled than me."

Not entirely true, and neither of them were fooled, but I'd developed a tough shell. I loathed anyone's pity, and no way would I portray myself as that awkward, chippy disabled guy.

"Anyhow, he's apologised."

"I should bloody think so. Gone on his knees and grovelled, too. And then performed any other service you might have requested while he was down there."

The picture he painted was far too close to the Dominic fantasy bouncing around my brain since—the *thing*. Before Milo sniffed it out, I shoved it to one side. I hadn't had a moment to process his apology but, suffice to say, I'd been impressed. Saying *sorry* out loud, followed by a full stop, and without a 'but' or justifying his behaviour with mitigating factors was hard. I knew because I rarely managed it myself. Even harder was to delve into your soul and admit a need to do better.

"Seriously, though," continued Milo, "How could you stand being in the car with him? And having him living one floor below? In your shoes I'd insist on a restraining order."

"If he wasn't going to become my brother-in-law in a few weeks' time, I probably would." My voice sounded glum. "But he is, and for the sake of Frankie and Lysander, I need to get over it. And, as I said, he's apologised and managed to sound like he meant it."

"Well, seeing as he's not about to become one of my nearest and dearest, forgive me if I'm not so generous." Milo had a tongue as sharp as a knife; I almost pitied Dominic.

"Now that's out of the way," Mungo said, with a nudge-

nudge, wink-wink look, "is this Dominic hot? Tell me he's hot. Lysander's hot, so he must be."

"And don't tell me you were so horrified you didn't gawp at his dick when he went for his impromptu skinny dip, flower, because we won't believe you."

I pretended to weigh up Dominic's assets, as if the scent of his aftershave filling the car interior and the map of veins crisscrossing his tanned hands hugging the steering wheel hadn't given me a semi all the way home. Vein porn. Was that a thing? A small shaving cut had blemished his otherwise smooth-shaven jaw, and I'd had to quash a reckless impulse to touch it.

"Meh, he's not bad, if you go for the trust fund, preppy look."

Milo smirked. "Any look preceded by *trust fund* gets my vote."

"What about the trust fund-but-I-haven't-shaved-for-six-months look?" Mungo waggled his eyebrows at him, and I rolled my eyes. Someone needed to point out to these two what was at the end of their noses.

"More of a trust-fund-but-I-blew-it-all-on-wine-women-and-song look, to be honest, Mungs." Milo smiled fondly. As they carried on teasing each other, I cast my mind back to Dominic and his clumsy attempts to help me. Confidence walked a fine line next to arrogance. At the pool, he'd crossed it, whereas this evening when he picked me up, he'd been all enthusiastic clumsy Labrador puppy. Drove the car like one, too, oh my God.

Lysander strolled through the door, all sweaty in his gym kit, and the three of us sat straighter, endeavouring to make coherent conversation. Out of nowhere, Milo developed a stutter, while Mungo regressed to the language capability of a toddler, leaving me to keep up our end of the conversation.

"Did Dominic pick you up okay?" Lysander turned towards the kitchen, where Frankie was throwing a dinner together. I'd deal with my brother's heavy-handed management of Dominic and me later. "He was a little anxious about the driving." Casually, he pulled off his damp T-shirt, to reveal acres of Olympic torso.

Next to me, Milo whimpered and crossed his legs.

"So was half of London," I quipped. "But he got through it. He'll be better tomorrow."

Goodness, tomorrow we would be thrown together again. And the day after that. For two whole weeks. Why didn't that thought fill me with dread?

The next morning, Dominic dressed more scruffily, in a faded pair of blue jeans and a long-sleeved T-shirt. Scruffy for him, anyhow. The jeans were Armani, and the silver Breitling flashing at his wrist hadn't been picked up cheap on Camden Market. Under the bright lights of the lift, his damp, messy hair gleamed. We exchanged awkward greetings, and I hoped he wouldn't attempt another apology. Time would mend my wounds; more words would only remind me of them.

"I'm going to one of the building sites later, after I've dropped you off." He sounded almost sheepish. "To work. Your brother very helpfully thought I would need occupying between dropping you off and picking you up. I think the atrocious weather forecast might have played a part. In his decision making."

Sounded like Frankie. Revenge a dish best served cold and all that. Maybe I'd forgive him for forcing us together after all. Biting back a smile, I concentrated on clambering into the car without looking like an incompetent fool. In the shower this morning, my legs had spasmed like buggery, and my left one still hadn't made its mind up whether to cooperate. If Maureen were here, she'd have eased them into the footwell for me. Another trip to the hot tub beckoned, perhaps tonight if I had the energy.

One of my sticks clattered to the ground and rolled under the car, and I cursed.

"I'll get it." He hopped out and dropped to his knees to retrieve it, then appeared at the open door.

"Thanks." I gave him a stiff nod. My leg chose that moment to play dead.

He threw me a wary look. "Would you like me to help you?"

Not really. I'd like to be able to leap out of the car like you did, balanced on toned, muscular calves like yours, instead of ones that insist on squeezing themselves into an excruciating, tense ball of anger.

"Thanks." I inclined my head again. His warm, capable fingers encircled my calf as if holding a newborn lamb, leaving behind a scorching band on my skin, even after he'd taken his hands away and tucked himself back into the driver's seat.

"Just… yes, like that, thank you."

I needed Maureen home as soon as possible, manhandling me with the same impersonal firmness as peeling potatoes, all the while chattering on about Gina's indigestion and Janice's husband's coronary bypass. Not this, not this oh-so-careful lifting, from a man with eyes that changed colour with his mood.

The journey passed in silence, with me staring out of the window and surreptitiously massaging my calf, and Dominic concentrating on not killing us both.

"How about that, we're still alive," he observed drily, as we pulled up to the kerb outside the record shop. "And I'm certain the alloys were already scuffed anyhow."

He side-eyed me through thickly fringed lashes, a hint of humour playing at his lips. Bloody hell, he was going to be a difficult person to stay annoyed with. And I don't know who had warned him, or whether he'd worked it out for himself, but he'd never once fiddled with the radio or asked if I minded him switching it on. People assumed cochlear implants were a cure, but they weren't. They merely allowed my brain to process electrical signals as sound. Since I'd had them from a very young age, I handled them well, but hearing still required full concentration. Music blaring through the car stereo confused my processing powers. No irony at all that I worked in a record shop.

"Would you like me to see you inside?" he queried politely.

"Just onto the pavement will be fine, thank you," I replied, equally polite.

This time, my muscles relaxed enough to propel me out of the car on my own. In some ways a disappointment, as I didn't get to experience his hands again, but I decided it was no bad thing judging from the effect they had on my dick. Once I balanced upright, he gave me a nod.

"Same time tonight, yeah?"

Oh yes.

CHAPTER 6
DOMINIC

Things I hated about London: every north-south route slowed traffic to the speed of a thirteen-year-old teenage dirtbag forced to help wash up.

Nonetheless, as I drove off, I felt an absurd satisfaction. I hadn't injured any cyclists, and I hadn't pissed off my tricksy passenger. I hadn't coaxed a smile from him yet, but neither had he snarled, so I chalked the journey up as a win. Manoeuvring Tristan's legs into the car had been a strangely intimate experience. His calf muscles had jumped under my fingers. If he'd been one of my football buddies cramping up, I'd have eased it with a brisk rub, no question.

Turning up at a construction site in a fancy Lexus, aged twenty-one, was akin to wearing a sticker on my forehead advertising 'over-privileged asshole', but the guys knew who I was anyhow. If nothing else the surname tended to give me away. I held my hand out, and my temporary overlords gave it three gnarly shakes in return.

"Mick. Yer helmet and coat's over there."

"Dick. Yer on 'odancuppa duty."

"Jason. Don't fucking crack any of the bricks."

Charming. And what the hell was 'odancuppa duty'? I

deduced it was something to do with cinder blocks, although the only blocks lying around were less than half the size of the ones back home and a darkish orangey red in colour.

"Mine's white with two."

"Black with one."

"White with three. And three chocolate Hobnobs."

Or maybe not. Talk about two nations divided by a common language.

"Yer related to the bosses?" asked Mick, or possibly Dick, sometime later. For the third time that morning, I'd been instructed to lay down my hod of blocks—sorry, *bricks*, and focus on my principal reason for existing, making the tea and delivering cookies (sorry, *biscuits*) to their exacting specifications.

"Yes, sir, I am." I felt a tinge of familial pride. "Daphne, the CEO is my half-sister."

"She's all right, that woman," grunted Mick with satisfaction.

"That she is," I agreed.

"Why are yer 'ere then?"

I'd been asking myself the same question all morning. One of my palms was scraped raw and the other smarted from a cement burn the size of a dime. The construction site appeared to have its own microclimate too; despite the sun shining high in the clear blue sky, an Arctic gale whistled down the top of my hi-vis. My three companions seemed immune. Mick (or maybe Dick?) had stripped down to shorts under his fluorescent jacket.

"I reckon he's got 'imself in a spot of bother." Jason sized me up like I wasn't fucking standing next to him.

"Yeah, that'll be right," agreed Mick/Dick, slurping an entire scalding mugful of tea in one gulp.

"Our Emma works in the head offices up on Canary Wharf. I'll get her to put her feelers out."

"He's not even putting in a full shift," remarked Dick/Mick, whom I'd gleaned to be vaguely in charge. "Foreman says I've got to let 'im off at four."

"What for?" Three sets of eyes studied me as I sipped at the mud-brown fluid, even more revolting that Lysander's cloudy beer.

"Mebbe he's checking in with 'is parole officer."

"Can't see a tag on him."

"Nosy buggers, aren't you?" I observed mildy, quashing my annoyance; for all I knew they were reporting straight back to Lysander and Frankie.

"I'll give our Emma a call now." Jason pulled the world's oldest cell phone from his pocket. Checking they weren't watching, I tipped my tea onto the ground; I'd be bringing soda from tomorrow.

"Guys, no need. I'm leaving at four because my brother Lysander, one of the bosses, has asked me to pick someone up for him. And I'm here because I have a couple of weeks to kill before I start an internship in the offices."

"And you've got yourself into a spot of bother." Mick eyed me shrewdly. "You 'ave, 'aven't ya?"

Christ, these three should be employed by the CIA. And they weren't going to drop it.

"Okay…yes. As a matter of fact, I have."

"That's a tenner you owe me, Micky," crowed Dick. "And you as well, Jason, you tight bastard. Cough up. I told you he was shifty."

"I'm not freaking shifty, okay?"

"He's shifty," Mick agreed. "But he makes a good cuppa, so I'll let 'im off."

"Tell us what yer did, then. Drug dealing would be my bet."

"Nah, he's buggered over here from America 'cos he's got some bird up the duff."

"He don't look druggie."

"He don't look capable of being a dad neither."

Oh, for fuck's sake.

"Hey, guys." I picked up my empty hod. "No one's pregnant, and no one's dealing drugs, okay? I did something monumentally stupid back in the US, which is why I'm in London, and then I did something even more monumentally stupid here, a few days ago, which is why I've been sent to sweat it out with you guys. All right? Questions over?"

Surprisingly, when four o'clock rolled around, I'd almost enjoyed myself. Dubbing me Pablo, they ribbed me all afternoon, coming up with the most outlandish crimes possible. Apparently, I now led the SoCal branch of a Columbian drugs cartel.

Even if the bulk of their humour was directed at me, the guys were funny and smart. Mick was a walking encyclopaedia of films starring Jason Statham, and Dick was the captain of an unbeaten pub quiz team, feared throughout the East End of London. Jason had spent the weekend visiting a coastal town called Portsmouth, touring a maritime museum. From the knowledge he'd accrued, I reckoned he could get a job there as a tour guide.

And, despite my hands being ripped to shreds, manual labour suited me, even if mowing my mom's yard was the closest I'd come to experiencing it. Since arriving in the UK, I'd missed my regular college sports. Building up a healthy sweat and humping house *bricks* with a load of guys didn't feel too far removed from football training.

Over the course of the day, as general dogsbody, I learned I'd pronounced *vitamin* wrong my entire life, the West Ham soccer team was being managed by a muppet (but they didn't elaborate which one), and that it had been far too long since Mick had enjoyed some decent how's-your-father. By the time I was showered and back in the Lexus, I was cream-crackered and, bizarrely, looking forward to tomorrow.

I made it across London in record time. Driving the wrong way down a one-way street proved a bowel-clenching, but time-saving, shortcut, resulting in half an hour spent relaxing in one of the cosy armchairs at the record store waiting for Tristan to finish his shift. I was alone, apart from a group of super-cool Londoners rummaging through a rack labelled '90's German techno'. Peaceful, lowkey Latin rhythms thrummed through the store's sound system.

"You must be Dominic! Hi and welcome!" A plump, friendly-looking woman descended on me; a rainbow-coloured stripe through the centre of her greying hair giving her the air of a cheery gay badger. A treasure trove of silver danced on each arm as she spoke.

"I'm Emily. Tristan's told us all about you."

Great. And she was still smiling?

A coffee, not more freaking tea, thank God, appeared at my elbow, which I accepted gratefully. "Make yourself comfortable. He won't be too long. He's just finishing up going through some orders with Irene."

Sounded like he was having a party, judging from the bawdy laughter floating through from the back room. One of the voices definitely belonged to him. Tristan's hearing voice was much clearer than his deaf voice, but still discernible. And when he found something funny, like now, he laughed like a hyena—who knew?

"Nice to hear them having fun." Emily jerked her head in the direction of the noise. "Irene's had a rotten week. She's had to put her mum in a home. Dementia. But you know our Tristan—he can cheer anyone up."

Seemed I didn't know Tristan at all.

"Has he worked here long?" I took a sip of coffee. The nicest cup of anything since I'd arrived in London.

She cocked her head onto one side. "Just over a year. I don't know what we did without him. Half the customers only come in here because of Tristan, I reckon. He's got a real fan club."

The dull tap-tap of Tristan's canes on the wooden flooring announced his approach and also alerted the group crowded around the racks. Two of the guys hurried over, placing their hands over Tristan's right one clasped around the cane, in lieu of a handshake. I stored the gesture as one to use for the future and acted like I wasn't listening by fiddling with my phone. Names of bands I'd never heard of, gig venues and such, sallied back and forth. Tristan held all the wisdom, and the guys lapped it up. More laughing, even gentle backslapping.

One of the customers, laidback with dreadlocked hair, rested his hand on top of Tristan's way longer than a normal handshake, which was… interesting. He found every word that came out of Tristan's mouth super fascinating too.

After five minutes or so, Tristan wound the conversation up. "Sorry about holding you up," he said, as we began our slow shuffle towards the door. I left his big-ass leather satchel exactly where it was, slung across his body, and made sure my giant feet stayed well clear of his.

"No worries. You're a popular guy."

He flushed, his eyes glued to the floor. "Not really. They're just musos. One of them, Neil, is in a band signed to a minor indie label."

"Is that the cool dude with the dreads?"

"Yeah." Tristan's amused eyes swung my way. "Between you and me, if he spent more time practicing guitar and less on his hair, or his mission to find the cheapest organic nut roast, the band would be doing even better. But Neil's okay. He's always hanging around—they all like to chew the cud. I don't mind."

"Can I ask you a question?"

He let out a cautious huff of laughter. "That depends. Is it a general one, that anybody gets asked, such as who's your favourite football team? Spurs, by the way. Or is it about being deaf, or having cerebral palsy? Those tend to crop up more."

We traded a glance. "What, from total strangers?"

"God, yes. Especially from total strangers. Yesterday, a customer asked me to put something on order for her, then checked whether 'deaf people could read and write'. Once, a random woman on the Tube saw my hearing aids and asked me if deaf people had sex!"

"Jeez, I can't believe you get asked shit like that."

He shot me warning look. "Trust me, they do. So I'll answer

most things in the general category. If it's a question in the second category, it had better be a good one."

I felt annoyed on his behalf, and I hardly knew the guy. Today, humping bricks around the construction site, he'd crossed my mind a lot. To be honest, I had tonnes of questions. Some said more about my total ignorance about living with his disabilities than I was ready to acknowledge, but I wasn't so dumb as to come out with those. That's what Google was invented for.

"Real tossers also ask me if cerebral palsy is catching, or whether I'm friends with so-and-so's daughter, as she's in a wheelchair."

As if I was an idiot, I slapped my head. "Damn, then it looks like I've been beaten to it. I know this amazing blind lady back in San Diego. I was sure you'd know her too."

He laughed again, a proper laugh this time, like he'd shared with Irene. On reaching the car, I opened the passenger-side door, holding my hand out for his canes. His eyes briefly left the ground and flicked up to mine, his nod of thanks leaving a few strands of blond hair trailing on his cheek. The trace of a smile brushed his lips, a taste of the ones he gave to other people, like those guys in the store, and a warm fuzz spread across my chest at my tiny triumph.

"I just wondered if the music playing in the store made it harder to hear customers, that's all."

Seemed this was a fine question. As we joined the queues of vehicles snaking through the middle of the city, he explained how Irene played the heavy stuff, then in lulls in trade, or whenever Tristan took a turn out front, they switched it to mellow jazz or Latin, pushing the bass down low. They'd discovered customers browsed longer with the chill-out vibe, especially in the afternoons, and were more inclined to buy coffees and hang out with their friends. Different days of the week brought different people into the store, Emily's regulars had become friends, and he sometimes went to gigs, but not too often. As he put it, 'his head was flinging itself around the mosh pit while his body was plonked in a wheelchair next to a massive speaker'. Which was cute and funny and sad all at the same time. I wanted to ask him about wheelchairs, but I reckoned I'd filled my quota for the day.

"Can you drop me at my sister's?"

We approached a complicated junction where you had to veer left to turn right. And why were the lanes so narrow? Back in San Diego, performing this manoeuvre in my Dodge would have taken out the entire front row of pedestrians queuing at the bus stop. A comment that made Tristan laugh, even as he held onto the edges of his seat, white-knuckled.

"She's not far from here. I'll get a cab back later."

"Yeah, sure."

On his instruction, we zigzagged through a maze of even narrower side streets in South Kensington, with way too many cars parked either side for my liking, before pulling up into a disabled parking spot outside a row of old redbrick houses converted into apartments. The variety within districts of London was an endless source of fascination. One second, you were in a bustling downmarket high street crammed with laundrettes and chip shops, the next in a genteel leafy avenue, like this one.

"That's hers. On the first floor." He pointed upwards through the dash at an elegant, cream-stuccoed apartment with views over a small park. Terracotta tubs bursting with geraniums underlined each of the tall sash windows. Very pretty. A set of narrow steps, tiled in a chequerboard of black and white, led up to a side entrance.

"Hate to break it to you, but I'm pretty sure that's the second floor, buddy."

"Sixty million Brits would disagree."

"Does she have an elevator?"

"No." He snorted. "She doesn't have a lift either. These conversions are tiny, although the amount she paid would have bought a four-bedroom detached house fifty miles out of town. Prices around here are crazy." He gathered his sticks. "I usually phone her when I'm out on the pavement, and Darren, her boyfriend, comes and gets me."

"I'm not in a hurry. I'm happy to see you to their door, save him coming down."

He gave me a doubtful side-eye, gauging whether a man who drove as incompetently as me could be trusted with this new task. "I can do stairs; Darren added an extra handrail, so there is one on both sides. He just stands behind me, so I don't lose balance and fall backwards."

I flicked my gaze over his slight frame, then pretended to puff out my chest. Another half-smile: I was on winning form. "Hey, I might not be a brawny scaffolder, but I reckon I'm up to the job. I work in construction too, you know."

A boyish giggle escaped him. "You've done one day! And already sucked and blown on your blisters twice!"

So he *had* been shooting me covert glances when he didn't think I'd notice. Tristan's sexuality hadn't crossed my mind, which I liked to think was because I was a devastatingly mature individual who didn't obsess about sex twenty-four seven... and not that I'd dismissed it altogether due to his CP. With confidence, I concluded the former and gave myself a metaphorical pat on the back.

"Did the regulars on the building site know who you are? Did they ask you why you were there?"

Did they ever. "Yeah, and I told them the truth—that it was because I'd fucked up. Not how, though," I added hastily. "They told me I'd pulled a blinder today, whatever that means."

"Did they try and prank you? Darren always asks the apprentices to fetch six feet of fallopian tubing, or a lefthanded screwdriver from the van, or something."

I chuckled. "No, but thanks for the head's up. I'll look out for it tomorrow. I think they were just feeling me out today."

Half the expressions Mick, Dick, and Jason had used flew straight over my head. I'd felt useful, though, for the first time since arriving in the UK. Did this mean I was on the path to redeeming my hideous transgression back in the US? Or against Tristan? Or was the hard graft simply putting some space and thinking time between the immature acts I'd committed, and the better person Lysander and my parents wanted me to become? That I wanted me to become? Whatever. The work and chauffeuring Tristan gave me structure, and the physical exercise would help me sleep better.

Gathering his sticks, Tristan pulled the car door handle. "Come on then, Bob the Builder. See me up the stairs."

Once he'd gotten some momentum, the stairs proved no trouble, although Tristan was out of puff at the top. A willowy female version of the Carter brothers flung wide the door to the apartment, and she flew at him, burying him in a bear hug. Tristan was a seriously popular guy. Someone took her place in the doorway —Darren the scaffolder, who could easily have doubled as a windbreak. Nope, I wouldn't like to get on his wrong side.

"Maddie, Darren, this is Dominic, Lysander's brother. I told you about him."

Judging by the pleasant welcome, he'd not yet divulged my appalling behaviour. We shook hands, and, introductions made, I stepped away.

"Thanks, Dominic. I'll see you tomorrow."

I hesitated. Tristan struggling on his own later with a random cab driver didn't sit well with me, though I was sure he'd navigated his way home solo hundreds of times, especially before Lysander put a company car at his disposal. A fellow intern had digs somewhere around here. If he wasn't around, I could always find a bar and grab some food. All that waited at home was an empty apartment and the gym; my aching builders' muscles wouldn't atrophy if I missed a workout.

"I'll come and pick you up later. It's no bother."

In the end, I sat on my own in a pub, very much an outsider amongst a crowd of locals. This alien city and its inhabitants, with their mangled English spoken in busy clipped tones and brisk, no-nonsense approach, wearied me. I missed the heat, my friends, and Milwaukee's Best Ice straight from the cooler.

So I did what any maudlin homesick boy would do: called my mom. Of course, my mom's lazy elongated Californian vowels, imagining her pottering around our cosy yellow kitchen, preparing brunch five thousand miles away, only made it worse.

"What's wrong? You sound a little flat. Are those St. Clouds giving you a hard time? Don't let them push you about, honey."

I sighed, blowing away the stresses of the day, and touched by her concern. This time, however, she was way off. My mom put up with the St. Cloud clan for ten years before realising my dad was a dick and dicking an even younger model. Although a decent enough father, my old man viewed wives as commodities to buy and sell at will. My mom walked away with pots of money, her beautiful home in Carmel Valley, and a fierce instinct to protect her naïve Californian boys.

"No, they're good. Lysander and Frankie are good. And I've gotten my hands dirty with some construction work today, and that was… good, too."

She tutted down the line. "Honey, with so much good around, you're sounding awfully down. Is it a girl? A guy?"

I groaned. How did mothers intuit this stuff?

"It's a guy," I confessed. "But not how you think. Not a *guy* guy."

"You mean a guy *friend*, not a guy *not-friend*?"

"Uh, yeah, I guess so?"

"Or is he a guy *friend* that could become a *guy not-friend*?"

Okay, so now she'd confused me. I'd not ever considered Tristan in a *guy* guy way. Was I as guilty of seeing the disability and not the person as the random jerks throwing insensitive questions at him? Would I be sexually attracted to him if his legs worked properly? Was he even my type? Or was it because we'd gotten off to such a bad start, meaning my thoughts on the matter were irrelevant, because he'd never consider *me* that way?

His face sure was pretty, though.

"Uh, I don't know how I feel about him, yet." Wasn't that the bare truth. "Anyhow, I behaved badly towards him and upset him—a nice man. I've apologised, but I still feel bad, you know?"

"Were you drunk? Tell me you weren't drunk again, honey. Your dad and I don't need another..."

"No, Mom, Christ. No. I wasn't drunk. Just… just…"

I cringed for the millionth time, recalling the raw fear on Tristan's face as he cowered in the hot tub. I could chauffeur him around for another fifty years and it wouldn't be apology enough.

"I don't know what I was. Tired, maybe? And homesick? Angry Lysander wasn't around, angry I'd been sent here in the first place?"

"You brought that upon yourself, honey," my mom butted in sharply. "And about that—your dad's managing to grease the right palms. I'll forward you his latest email. So I think you will soon be able to put all that behind you."

I squirmed. Painful events taught us lessons we didn't think we needed to learn. On the one hand, my dad and his money came running whenever shit went down, and I was full of gratitude, especially on this occasion. Otherwise, I'd be facing a short spell behind bars. On the other, a little voice wondered whether my punishment should have been, like, an actual punishment? Instead of days of heated wrangling with my parents, followed by a flight to London? In business class? And the sub-penthouse was hardly a jail cell.

"So what did you do to this guy? Did you hurt him? Did you get into a fight with him? You're not a fighter, Dominic."

Tristan's weak, pale body popped into my head. He couldn't fight his way out of a paper bag. I had hurt him, though, and in some ways, the harm was worse than physical.

"I… no. I… I bullied him, I guess."

"Oh, Dominic, no."

A fresh flood of shame coursed through me. Glad to be hidden amongst uncaring strangers. For once, I thanked God my mom was on the other side of the world. What I'd done to Tristan would horrify her. Rolling my achy shoulders, I picked at the last of the cooling fries—sorry, *chips*—on my plate.

"I fucked up, Mom." I sighed again into the silence, as my mom digested the thrilling news: once more, her pampered youngest son had behaved like a douchebag. "Again. But I've apologised and he's accepted my apology. Things are still a little awkward between us, and he's someone I'll be seeing a lot. I behaved in a way that… wasn't the true me. I could have done much better. I *am* better."

"Damn right you are, honey."

She hummed down the phone line. I hadn't given her much to go on, to be fair, but I didn't need Lysander *and* my mom lecturing me with the whole disappointed spiel. If I'd told her, then she'd realise I was talking about Frankie's brother. She'd be on the phone to Lys before I'd finished my very gassy half pint of something German and expensive.

"Can you do anything to make it up to him? To this person?" she offered at last.

"I am already. I'm helping him however I can."

"Well then, honey, that sounds good enough. An apology on its own isn't always adequate. But following it up with action will help you sleep."

The remainder of the phone call switched to mundane matters, like her new pool guy, less thorough than the last, and the neighbour's cat shitting in our yard. They only served to deepen my homesickness. Before embarrassing myself with public tears, I signed off, paid up, and walked back to the Lexus. At least the London traffic would have died down a smidge.

CHAPTER 7
TRISTAN

Favourite things about living in the penthouse: part 5: my sister Maddie, her partner Darren, and baby Rosie lived somewhere else.

Don't get me wrong, my sister was great, but when we lived together, if I asked her to rustle up some dinner, I'd receive a thirty-minute rant about how women weren't handmaidens born to serve the patriarchy. If I wanted lasagne, I knew in which cupboard to find the bloody pasta sheets, blah blah blah. Cerebral palsy be damned as a pitiful excuse.

These days, she'd transformed into some kind of motherly domestic goddess. If I invited myself over requesting lasagne, then a plate of steaming lasagne is what I'd get.

(Favourite things about living in the penthouse: addendum 5.1: Frankie's lasagne. Bland, a bit gloopy, but reliably delivered without a lecture and loads of garlic bread.)

"Bloody hell, Tris! You could have warned me Lysander's brother would be dropping you off. I'd have put some lippy on!"

"Darren, you are so weird. Anyone ever tell you that?" I gave the bundle of flubber wrapped in his arms an uncly kiss on the top of her blonde curls. She smelled an appealing malty mixture of rusks and baby shampoo.

Darren grinned like a Cheshire Cat. "Yes, you and Frankie, all the time."

"But seriously," said Maddie, as she led me into the kitchen. "You should have said. I feel bad I didn't invite him to join us. He's going to be family."

Thanks for the reminder. "He had plans," I lied.

"He's rather easy on the eye, isn't he?" She gave me a knowing, sisterly look.

"Is he?" I aimed for nonchalance. "I hadn't noticed. He's… he's, well, we got off to a bad start."

Once settled around the table with delicious grub in front of me, I talked them through the *thing*. They'd hear it from Frankie anyhow, sooner or later. For the hundredth time, I regretted not drawing attention to myself the second I spotted Dominic, even if he would have seen my legs, and maybe my dick, too, as I fumbled around with my boxers. Honestly, neither scenario would have ended well. Although the guy chauffeuring me around, who let me haul myself up the stairs to my sister's without chivvying or offering unwanted assistance, didn't seem like the kind of man who would've been repulsed by my legs.

"Don't you dare blame yourself," said Maddie when I'd finished. "Don't make any excuses for him. If I'd known all that, I'd have kicked him back down the staircase when he brought you to the door."

"We just need to move on." I swallowed a mouthful of cheesy perfection. "I'm over it. And you're right. Dominic is going to be family; he's going to be our brother-in-law. So we need to find a way through this. He's apologised and is trying to make things up to me by driving me around. So, please, don't say anything when he collects me later."

Baby Rosie picked that moment to join the conversation with a gruesome squelch from her rear end and an appreciative gurgle from the top. Darren gave her an adoring look, as if she'd outlined Fermat's last theorem.

"Who's a good girl?" With a practised move, he plucked her

out of her bouncy chair. The guy was barely twenty-one, but his commitment to my sister and their baby was pretty awesome. Dominic was a similar age, but the thought of that overgrown college kid being trusted with a precious scrap of a child? Oh my God. Maddie pulled me out of my reverie.

"How's Neil?"

For goodness's sake, why were people so obsessed with my non-existent sex life?

"I have no idea, Maddie. He's probably propping up some cool bar in Clapham droning on about The Velvet Underground's unique use of chord changes and boring the tits off a poor guy regretting his decision to go out for a drink, instead of parking himself in front of the telly."

An unpleasant odour wafted towards me. "Your baby smells."

Dominic rapped on the door at ten o'clock precisely. For the last quarter hour, I may have been watching the minutes tick by. Maddie and Darren vowed to be polite to him. As I picked my laborious path to the door, Maddie by my side, I heard him and Darren exchanging pleasantries about scaffolding poles. A surefire technique to get Darren on side. The sight of Dominic fired up all sorts of inappropriate tinglings in my lower belly. Almost as if he'd come to pick me up as his date.

"Hey!"

"Hi!"

Yep, I behaved as if I was on a date too. I didn't need to see Maddie's raised eyebrows; I could sense them.

"All set?" He threw me a smile of such unabashed sincerity I found myself grinning back at him. Christ, I needed to pull myself together.

Maddie thrust out her hand, and Dominic gave it a firm shake. "It's been nice meeting you, Dominic. Future brother-in-law."

Huh. Maddie sounded positively sweet. Something was off.

"You bet," answered Dominic enthusiastically. "The wedding is great news. Lysander is buzzed about the whole thing."

"As are we; Darren and I are looking forward to getting to know you."

"Likewise. I'm around for a while, so maybe we can get together sometime when I've found my feet here in London?"

"Great," agreed Maddie.

Having relaxed him with good manners, she then skewered him with a look undoubtedly familiar to her class of ten-year-olds. "Tris has filled us in on your plans for the next few months, and what you've been up to so far. I gather you're a keen swimmer?"

No subtlety, my sister. Worse than Frankie in some ways. But, as I'd accepted years ago, being a triplet was my superpower. Like a three-headed monster, cut one of us down and another one reared up, ready to fight your corner.

"Yes, I am." Dominic shuffled his feet.

"Good," responded Maddie happily. "In that case, you should invite Tristan to join you for your late-night dips, so someone can keep an eye on him. It would set my mind at rest. I hate to imagine you struggling in and out of the hot tub, Tris, on your own. What do you think?"

A terrible idea. And being a triplet was the worst ever. I should have anticipated she'd say something about my solo expeditions.

"I'd like that," Dominic answered. "It's the least I can do."

"Tristan?" Darren nudged me. "Didn't you mention your legs were spasming today? You should go for a swim tonight, with Dominic, when you get in."

I gave Darren a filthy look. He threw me a wink in return.

"And then Frankie and I won't have to worry about you falling when no one is around." My bastard sister beamed at me. God, this was mortifying.

Face prickling into a blush, I concentrated on arranging my canes. "I'm sure Dominic has plenty of other things to do tonight."

"I'm cool," breezed Dominic. "I'm aching all over from the

building work today. A dip in the hot tub would do me the power of good, too."

Two very interested individuals followed our slow descent down the steps. Ensuring my feet landed in the centre of each tread took enough of my energy, without having those busybodies making the back of my neck hot. Descending a staircase was trickier than climbing one. My taut calf muscles tended to force my weight forwards, onto the balls of my feet and toes, which could very easily have me tumbling from the top to the bottom. With my canes clasped in one hand, Dominic took backwards steps in front of me while I gripped the stair rails. Disappointingly, I didn't trip and tumble into his waiting arms.

"I don't expect you to take me down to the pool complex, by the way." We reached the bottom. "That was Maddie having a dig."

"It's okay. Lysander's already warned me off. And she's only looking out for you. I behaved like a piece of shit, so I deserved it. Frankly, I deserve much worse." He handed me back my canes. "You're a popular guy, Tristan, you know that, right?"

"It's my devastating good looks and charm. You should have picked up on them by now."

He laughed, a soft, smoky huff of air into the chilly night. "Maybe now you've forgiven me, I might just do that."

"Er… I'm sorry. Who said anything about forgiving you?"

I might not have tripped on the stairs, but I almost fell on my backside as we crossed the flat, dry stretch of pavement to the car. If I wasn't mistaken, this felt very much like flirting. Reaching the car, Dominic opened the passenger door with a flourish.

"Your chariot awaits."

"So does my dodgy charioteer." I failed to prevent a grin. "Maureen's job's safe, anyhow."

"I'm much improved!"

"You couldn't have become any worse!"

I flopped down into the passenger seat, and his eyes flicked wordlessly to my knackered legs, still dangling outside of the car.

Nodding my consent, for the second time today, he lifted them into the footwell for me. Weary, tense calves were a much-underrated erogenous zone.

"Does it tire you going up and down stairs?" He settled next to me.

"Yeah, but I'll sleep better. Tired muscles don't spasm as much."

A text vibrated in my pocket. "Talking of charioteers, it's Maureen, checking up on me." I read out from the text. "She says, *'how's my temporary replacement?'*" Laughing, I thumbed a reply. "This could take a while. Is there a character limit for text messages?"

The car jolted as Dominic swerved around seemingly nothing. Again. I smirked.

"Texting and grabbing the dash with both hands is proving a challenge. I might have to work out how to do the voice recognition thing. Does the software recognise screaming?"

Dominic chuckled and threw his hands off the steering wheel. I braced. "Don't be so dramatic, Tristan! You didn't die, did you? And I swear that guy in the blue Mazda wasn't honking at me! I was in the right lane!"

"Dear Maureen," I pretended to text. *"Message from my new driver: I didn't die, did I? Quote unquote."*

CHAPTER 8
DOMINIC

Things I hated about London: Brits have no idea they pronounce oregano and yoghurt wrongly. If they think it's cute, they're mistaken.

"You got a bird warming your bed then, Pablo?" We were drinking tea, served by Mick for a change, with a slice of gluey brown stuff called malt loaf. Slathered in butter, it stuck to the roof of my mouth and coated my teeth like a plastic dental plate, forcing me to empty my first mug of tea ever, to wash the freaking thing down.

"No." Idly, I wondered if I'd puke the whole lot up again later. Although it sat in my belly as if I'd swallowed one of the tiddly red house blocks, so probably not.

"Good-lookin' young fella like you?"

"No."

I'd been out with Luke the night before, an investment company intern I knew from back home. We'd hit a couple of bars, more than we should have done on a school night, and boy, was I feeling the pain now. I stretched out my back, wincing. Sure,

I was young, but my body felt about eighty-five after last night's beers and a week of unaccustomed construction labour.

If I ever joined the St. Cloud conglomerate for real—not that I was planning on it anytime soon—I'd insist all the suits spent some hours on a site getting their hands dirty. And perhaps they should also spend that time trying to budget food and household bills in an expensive city like London, when they only took home the equivalent of $400 a week after taxes. Like Mick managed, who had four kids. His wife worked nights at the hospital to make ends meet. In the mornings, it sounded like they crossed the threshold of their apartment (sorry, *flat*) like ships in the night.

Last night, Luke and I had blown the best part of his paycheck on dinner, drinks, and a taxi ride home without breaking a sweat.

"Maybe he's got a really small todger."

"Or maybe he likes the fellas."

"Maybe he likes the fellas *and* he's got a really small todger."

"The fellas won't like 'im much, then."

The truth—I liked the fellas *and* the birds—might blow their minds. The size of my dick was none of their business. Time to change the subject.

Vowing never to go near the stuff again, I dislodged a lump of malt loaf with my tongue from one of my back molars. "Tell me, if you could run this company for a day, what would you change to make lives for guys on the shop floor, like you, better?"

"Eh?"

"I'm serious. If you could change one thing, what would it be?"

"Get 'im to buy the first round on a Friday night," grunted Mick. "Tight bastard."

"Any round would be a start," quipped Dick.

Good idea, but I wasn't going to get anywhere. These guys happily talked soccer, the state of London traffic, and the price of beer from dawn 'til dusk, but the second I tried to delve deeper into opinions or real matters, or, heaven forbid, *emotions*, they clammed up like kids in a classroom refusing to grass up the guy who threw the eraser.

"Have someone listen to us, for a change," said Jason. "A bloke came down here the other day, eyes glued to his fancy iPad, to tell us that this lot here," he gestured behind him at the footings of a monstrously sized area mapped out for a storage warehouse, "needed to be done by the end of the month. He thinks this is Cloud Cuckooland, not Cloud Ten."

"Why?" I asked, curious. I picked up my newly acquired sturdy gloves.

"Because he hasn't got a fucking clue, that's why! It'll take two weeks just to finish those trenches over there so they're twelve inches below the frost line. And at this time of year, you can add another week on. It's going to piss it down tomorrow. And that's before we even start on the shuttering."

"Did you tell him?"

"Yeah, course I did! Not interested, though. He's got his targets to report back to the brass, and that's that." Jason shrugged, resigned.

Nothing more was forthcoming. The other two had risen to their feet already. Standing up too, my bones creaking, I collected the empty mugs. Lysander described the management layer between the top corridor and the construction workers as a wet sponge, and from what Jason was telling me, Clipboard Guy was sunk right into it. Lysander and Frankie worked hard to bridge the gap between the reality of the shop floor and the idealism of the brass. Sounded like there was still a long way to go.

Despite all the ragging, I'd miss these guys when I started my internship. I'd been the butt of their jokes for two weeks straight. It was time for some payback. "You really want to know my sexual preferences?"

Three sets of eyes gleamed. Finally, they were going to get the gossip. Taking my time, I treated them to a lascivious look.

"Often."

· · ·

My presence was expected at a board meeting, which meant I escaped an afternoon of hod duty. Attendance was a three-line whip for all family members who happened to be in London on the dates the board meetings fell, whether old and retired, or young and disinterested, like me.

Lysander's descriptions of these board meetings had become the stuff of legend, so even though the main source of provocation, Uncle Paul, was gallivanting around the golf clubs of Galway, observing the key players in action was still an improvement on shivering outside in a hi-vis jacket. And I looked damned fine in a designer suit, even though I did say so myself.

The Scottish cousins were plain weird. I mean, threesomes were cool—I'd tumbled into one or two myself, but I couldn't help wondering what the hell was going on under the table. Our chairs were huge, fat-ass leather things, but the cousins were all squashed together like a single six-armed, three-headed beast. And what was with the non-stop touching each other? A hand on an elbow, a pat of a leg, finishing each other's sentences, whispering in each other's ear... whew.

In comparison, Aunt Pauline was positively approachable. I hadn't seen her for a number of years, but her blunt manner and habitual expression of a bulldog chewing a wasp hadn't improved with time or divorce. And soured even further when her ex's PA, Natalie, wafted in.

Making up for Uncle Paul's absence, the world's noisiest silent partner, Cousin John, leered at Natalie and another blonde PA as if he was two willing ladies short of a threesome himself. Or maybe a foursome, from the way he kept trying to semaphore to me when he thought no one else was looking.

Thank God for my dowdy half-sister Daphne and her dull husband Gerald. And Lysander, of course.

Once the meeting was underway, I switched off. Disappointingly, the Scottish cousins stopped pawing each other. For the first ten minutes of Daphne rabbiting on, I tried to figure out how someone had gotten the enormous mahogany meeting table through the door. The next ten was taken up wondering if John voiced terrible ideas for the sole purpose of making the meeting drag out longer and to piss the rest of us off. By that point, I'd already taken my pen apart, put it back together and taken it apart again, so if anyone had said anything worthy of writing down then, I wouldn't have been able to anyhow.

A few times, Frankie tripped in and out, to hand over some papers or pass a message on to Lys. He was no slouch in the suit department either; his tastes ran a little skinnier than mine, which suited his frame, and he could get away with a light grey too. He'd tied his hair back in a cute little topknot, accentuating his razor-sharp cheekbones and smoking-hot eyes.

Yep, those Carter boys were fine-looking specimens. The sister hadn't been bad either. With my thoughts drifting in a very pleasant direction, I missed the next item on the agenda—until my name was mentioned.

"All our interns do it, so Dominic won't be the exception. Of course, his stay with us is that much shorter, but he's a St. Cloud, so our expectations of him are greater. I'm confident he'll make a decent stab at it."

Lys had warned me they pulled stunts like this. At Cloud Ten, you were either seated at the table or on the menu. I kicked myself for letting my mind wander. Politely, I asked Daphne to clarify.

"A presentation to the board on the topic of your choice. Within reason and relevant," she added, putting paid to my discourse on Ten Things I Hated About London. "However, we encourage most interns to focus and reflect on their experiences here and come up with suggestions for improvement. Examine our corporate behaviour with young, fresh eyes."

Freaking hell. That was brave of them.

"We don't always agree with their recommendations, of course, but it's vital we invite feedback, both positive and negative."

"I'm sure Dominic can find something suitable within the timeframe," Lysander interjected. "Can't you, Dom?"

"Sure, I'm game."

He leaned into me, dropping his voice. From the paper shuffling and keyboard tapping, everyone else had moved onto the next agenda item, so my scolding went unnoticed. "Maybe something around respect and interpersonal skills? And the importance of recognising you're a damned lucky guy who is walking a very thin line right now? So the least you can do is put that pen down and look like you're bloody paying some attention? You never know, you might learn something relevant to that business major you're supposed to be studying for."

Folding his arms, Lysander sat back and resumed flicking through the notes Frankie had prepared for him. Colour me told off.

The annoying thing was the bugger was right. And not just the lucky part, although while I was sitting here on a comfy leather chair with a pot of decent coffee, Dick, Mick, and Jason were out in a muddy corner of London freezing their balls off.

The next agenda item summarised the acquisition of an old warehouse site in a part of northern England I'd never heard of. Cloud Ten had put in a change-of-use bid for a sustainable housing development including green spaces and cycle lanes. Pauline gave a run-through of the financials without checking her notes once, and the Scottish cousins gave a savage précis of our competitors bids, identifying areas we knocked them out of the park. John had finagled his way into the pocket of the town council, and Lysander had already reached out to local subcontractors to thresh out some finer details and begun dropping positive spin to the media. All in all, the well-oiled machine did its thing.

I sat up straighter, started jotting a few things down. It was kind of...cool.

"Frankie told me to tell you you're invited up for dinner tonight," announced Tristan as we pulled away from the kerb. If he'd noticed I'd swapped my flannel shirt for a damned fine Armani suit, he pretended he hadn't. Although how anyone could avoid comment on how freaking fabulously I rocked the whole Harvey Specter vibe was beyond me.

"Is he still too pissed to ask me himself?"

"Frankie doesn't hold grudges." Face half-hidden behind a curtain of hair, Tristan threw me an amused sidelong glance. His eyes momentarily skirted down to my tie and back up again. "He cuddles them, nurtures them, and then sets them free when you're least expecting. He'll get there. He's just…he just worries about me. Him and Maddie both do."

Everyone did. Since sharing the car journeys with him every day, I was headed that way myself.

"And anyhow," he continued, so entranced by the bland row of fast-food outlets on his left that he couldn't possibly look at me, "we need to get on with each other. We're soon going to be family."

"We do get on, don't we? Now?" Him agreeing suddenly felt terribly important.

"Sure," he said slowly, as if weighing up the pros and cons. "But we need to show that, so Lys and Frankie can enjoy their wedding. Frankie's already got his knickers in a twist about the flower arrangements. Seems the wedding planner hadn't quite understood she'd be dealing with Bridezilla."

Having been at the wrong end of the full force of Frankie's ire, I had some sympathy. Wrapped up in that sweet, smoking-hot bundle of twink was a fire-breathing dragon.

"So I guess you're cool if I hang out with you guys tonight?"

Thanks to royally fucking everything up with Tristan down in the basement, anticipated cosy evenings chilling with my brother hadn't materialised. Once or twice, Lysander popped downstairs for a drink, or we'd hung out in the weights room. The one time I bumped into Frankie, he'd been decidedly frosty. So I skulked around my own apartment, used up a few hours in the gym, or caught up with guys I knew from home, like Luke. If this dinner was an olive branch from Frankie, then I'd grab it with both hands.

"Sure." Tristan shrugged, with a little less enthusiasm than I'd have liked. "It's their apartment."

"Is that how you feel?" I kept my eyes on the road. Judging from how I'd had to assist him into the car, he seemed pretty whacked tonight. He'd even passed me his messenger bag, which was a first.

"Sometimes?" He inhaled deeply. "Not that they do anything to make me feel that way. And I pay Lysander token rent, not that he wants me to. But I don't have a lot of choice, do I?"

"Have you always lived with Frankie?"

"No." He shook his head soberly, voice flat. "I tried living on my own for a while, but it didn't work out. I fell a couple of times. I broke my ankle on one occasion. I used to have this big thing about independence and not having to rely on anyone. Lasted about six weeks."

"I heard the UK healthcare system is pretty good. Don't you have stuff like… um… caregiver options you can access?"

I hoped the fact I had absolutely no fucking clue what I was talking about wasn't too obvious.

He sighed. "Yeah. There are care packages. I qualify for things. But basically, it boils down to a choice between a bunch of strangers coming to check up on me a couple of times a day or staying with Frankie for as long as he'll have me. Frankie wins, every time, even if I do feel like a third wheel when they start batting their eyes at each other."

I felt his pain. My old roommate in my first year at college had been sickeningly in love with his girlfriend. Or in lust, at least. They'd pawed each other every chance they got. After I caught them fucking on my bed, for the second time, I'd moved out.

"You're always welcome to come downstairs if you want to get away from the lovebirds for a while. I'm not exactly great shakes in the kitchen, but I do a mean takeout."

"Thank you. And…" Continuing to stare out of the window,

he twiddled with the ends of his hair. "All joking aside, Frankie will take a while to get over what happened. Longer than me. Maddie too; it's just how they are."

I hesitated, but he seemed pretty open to conversation on this journey. Truth was I'd never known someone with disabilities like his. Over the years, in class at school and then college, people who used wheelchairs had come and gone. A girl with a withered arm had been in my biology class throughout, and a blind girl in the last year of college with a cute dog. I'd not even spoken to either of them, and I wondered why. Ignorance maybe? Not knowing what to say or how to behave, like how I'd felt around Tristan at the beginning of our two-week stretch and less so now?

Or maybe I just couldn't be damn bothered?

As I drove, I frowned. More reasons not to like myself very much.

"Tell me to shut up if you like, but can I ask you why you don't ever use a wheelchair?"

His striking blue eyes narrowed on me, sizing me up.

"I'm not suggesting you should," I added quickly. "And I… just…" I blew out a breath. "Look, I'm an insensitive asshole. I think we've already established that. But I'm trying to do the right thing now. So I have no idea how to say the right things to you, how not to upset you, how not to present myself as an overprivileged, thoughtless dick."

A silence stretched out between us. "There's more to me than my CP, you know. I mean, it probably is the most interesting thing about me, but a lot of the time, I forget I even have it."

I could have told him that he was plenty interesting without his CP—he seemed to be a very cool guy. But our conversation was awkward enough without me acting like I was hitting on him. Christ, a bully and a creepy stalker. God knew how Frankie would react to that news.

"For your information, I'm not anti-wheelchair. I don't see using one as a failing or something to be ashamed of or anything. And I'm fully aware a wheelchair would make my life easier. In many ways. I'd be less tired, for one. And get around quicker. But then I'd stop using my leg muscles and if you don't use them, you lose them. I'd risk losing the ability to walk altogether."

"And with it, the choice of using a chair, right? I hadn't thought of that."

Tristan's blue gaze slanted over me. Not irritated, nor in appreciation of the suit either. Just assessing. Sizing me up.

They really were the prettiest eyes.

"Why would you, Mr All-American College Boy?" If I didn't know better, his voice sounded almost flirtatious.

With a ludicrous flutter of my eyelashes, I gave him my best deep south drawl. "Aw, shucks, is that what you think of me, honey?"

CHAPTER 9

TRISTAN

Best things about living in the penthouse: part 6: Lysander St. Cloud.

Not in a sexual way, although if Cloud Ten Construction ever took a nosedive, an alternative career as a male model begged. Anyhow, he was besotted with Frankie; he found my brother's foibles endearing instead of fucking irritating. Even if Lysander was a smelly green goblin, he'd still rank as one of my favourite people to walk the planet, because of the immense consideration he'd shown me from the day we'd met, as if nothing gave him more pleasure than having his partner's disabled brother sharing his home.

"Tristan, promise me you are one hundred per cent happy that I've asked Dom over later. Because if it's not okay, I'll tell him now. No pressure."

The other great thing about Lysander was I knew he meant it. "It's fine. Really. We've… we've mended our bridges."

"His driving has improved that much, eh?"

I thought back to yesterday's parallel parking incident outside the record shop. Thank God the Lexus had parking sensors. And that the lady we almost ran over quickly discovered she was a pushover for big handsome American guys.

Afterwards, I'd shared with him Maureen's first rule of parallel parking: to park somewhere else. We'd sat in the car laughing about it for about five minutes before I remembered I was supposed to be getting out.

"No." I smiled at him. "It's still shit. But he's genuinely sorry about the hot tub thing. He did something wrong, but he's also done a few things right since."

"Glad to hear it. At heart, he's a decent human being. I hoped everyone else would see that too." He raised an eyebrow. "I'm still working on Frankie."

Dominic wasn't above buttering up my brother with a little schmoozing. Lys must have told him Frankie was a sucker for flowers. The bouquet entering the apartment, a mile ahead of Dominic, was the size of a small family saloon. Even Milo and Mungo looked suitably impressed.

To my immense disappointment, Dominic had changed out of the suit. If naked swimming ranked as his best look, then future CEO-in-the-making ran a close second. At least now I'd be able to concentrate on my dinner, although the shower-damp hair, baggy-jeaned, Californian frat boy look was pretty special too. During the earlier car journey home, sneaking peeks at him, listening to his mellow accent, *and* the scent of his aftershave all combined, overwhelmed me. I'd stared out of the window instead, and hoped he'd not think me too weird.

Seeing him again now, my dick stirred. Christ, I needed to get laid.

I hadn't warned Dominic my friends would be joining us. As Milo cooed over the flowers, Mungo politely introduced them both. If you didn't know them as well as I did, you'd be forgiven for assuming they were unaware of the hot tub saga. Even if Mungo did throw a possessive arm around my shoulders, like a human shield, as he gave Dominic's hand an iron shake. Meanwhile, Milo's sharp gaze followed his every move, committing them to memory in order to file a police report later. When the time came to be seated around the dining table,

Dominic pulled out my chair and relieved me of my canes as if he did it every single night. A gesture not lost on eagle-eyed Milo.

"Dom joined us for the board meeting today." Lysander dished out heaped bowls of his unbelievably good hot pot. One of his mother's recipes, apparently.

"Don't you mean the monthly gathering of the Clan Corleone?" Mungo grinned. He worked for a law firm. His management meetings sounded like meditative yoga sessions in comparison.

"That's way too kind," laughed Frankie. "At least the mafia pretend to trust family."

Milo turned his attention to Dominic. "Flower, please tell me the Scottish cousins are not a figment of Frankie's overexcited imagination. I so want them to be real."

"Yeah, they're pretty real." Dominic gave a chuckle. "I got a hug from them at the end, which was… um… an experience. Like being cuddled by an octopus."

"Just be glad it wasn't Pauline," added Lysander. "Like being squeezed by a porcupine."

"And how are you finding London?" Milo continued. An innocuous enough opener although, inexplicably, my anxiety ratcheted up a notch. "Making *friends*?" He nibbled delicately at a hunk of bread.

"Sure, a few. Although working on the site is keeping me busy. I tend to come home in the evenings and crash."

"Yes," said Mungo, "I hear you've made good use of the facilities in the basement."

"I have. I've done a little exercise down there. The pool and the weights room are pretty cool."

Dominic threw me a nervous glance. He hadn't missed the not-so-subtle dig. It was to be expected, really. I was surprised Milo and Mungo had waited this long. "But mostly, I'm here to keep my head down and gain useful experience at the family firm. I'm a lucky guy to have that opportunity."

"And you use your nighttime swims help you to remember that, do you?" Milo, at his most waspish.

Dominic took a draught of his wine before addressing them both with a steely expression. "Listen, guys, you can cut the snide comments. I fucked up. I'm doing something about it. In my spare time, I'm helping Tristan get around. To make up for things," he added. "End of story. And Tristan and I are working things through."

A gaping silence followed, save for the scrape of cutlery. All we needed now was an argument about politics and religion, and we'd be able to write the whole evening off. I waited for Lysander to smooth things over, but instead, I opened my mouth, much to everyone's surprise.

"The only person Dominic owed an apology was me. He's done that. And if I'd known he'd need a coat of armour on tonight before he came up to join us, I'd have told him to stay downstairs. So cut it out, you two."

Wow, that *was* my voice. Milo's mouth opened, then closed again. He wasn't the only one taken aback. "I can fight my own battles, everyone," I added, "but I appreciate the support."

"You shouldn't have to fight any," Milo answered tartly, always keen to have the last word. "Especially in your own home."

"I *said* pack it in."

Another gap in conversation. Not daring to meet anyone's eye, I concentrated on my food.

"So, who's going to go through wedding invitation designs with me?" Frankie piped up, an unlikely ally for Dominic. Lysander threw him a grateful look. "The good news is I've narrowed the shortlist down to twenty-seven."

Mungo snorted. I sat back; I was off the hook. Getting him down to thirty-three had occupied most of last Sunday. Lysander began gathering plates. Having fallen on his sword for three hours last night, eliminating a further six, he was in the clear too.

"I'll help you with those, Lys." Jumping up, Dominic busied

himself collecting my leftovers and his own. Suggesting to Frankie the sparkly invite with 'Yay! We've got that *groom groom pow*' emblazoned across the front might not hit the right note with the conservative relatives could push their détente too far. He escaped after Lysander into the kitchen.

After he'd gone, I rounded on my friends. "Can you two shut the fuck up, please? You've made your point. He's said sorry, and he's being nice to me. This was supposed to be his first step into getting back to normal."

"We were only teasing him."

"Don't, okay? It's not fair. He's… he's younger than us, he's come to a new country to start a new job, and he's messed up. Give him a second chance. I'm going to." Wondering where this new assertive Tristan had come from, I gulped down the dregs of my wine. "Now, one of you needs to go and help Frankie, before he throws his toys out and picks the invitation with 'two queens make a pair' on it. My mother will have a fit."

I should flex a little more often. Seemed it got everyone's attention.

"Didn't you get an A in GCSE Art, Mungs?" Milo gave his friend a nudge.

"What the hell's that got to do with it?"

"Listen, flower, it's your turn. I had to sit though forty minutes of cufflink choices with him last Tuesday. At what stage does a phone call turn into a podcast? And anyhow," he patted my hand, "Tristan needs me here."

"Do I?" News to me. From the way he'd spoken to Dominic, frankly, I was ready for him to call it a night.

"Yes, flower. You do."

Reluctantly, Mungo heaved himself up. "Come and rescue me if I haven't reappeared by half past."

"We'll send Lysander in to flex his pecs at him, I promise."

Milo waited until the door to the study was closed, then turned to me. "Tris, my darling. All joking aside, I have the distinct impression Dominic is doing more than trying to make things up to you. However he felt about you the first time you met, I think his feelings have… um… moved on."

"Milo? I have no idea what you're talking about."

He laughed. "Oh, I think you do. Are you planning on putting him out of his misery any time this millennium? Or are you testing to see how long he can hold on, as some sort of punishment?"

"He's just doing what Lysander asked him to do. Which was to be nice to me."

"Don't give me that tosh." Milo tutted. "I know I look devilishly youthful for my age, but I wasn't born yesterday. Our handsome trust fund boy can't keep his eyes—or his hands—off you!"

"He's trying to get back in Frankie's good books, that's all."

Milo huffed. "Trying to get into your pants, more like."

"That's ridiculous."

"Not from where I was sitting, flower."

"And even if he was, then I'm just an option because he's bored. He has a wild time back in the US. I've heard all the stories from Lysander. Pole dancers, naked pool parties. Trust me, none of those tales featured a man like me."

"Well then, he's been missing out."

Towards the end of the evening, Frankie and Lysander became so nauseatingly lovey-dovey, I didn't have to wait long for them to disappear to the bedroom, allowing me to sneak out of the penthouse. Since the *thing*, I had avoided the hot tub, and my calves and thighs suffered as a consequence. Leaving my hearing aids beside the bed, I hauled myself to the lift and pressed the button for the basement, then sank against the back wall and let my eyes drift closed.

At a jolt under my feet and a rush of air signalling the doors sliding apart, my heart skipped a beat. The private penthouse lift only stopped at one other level prior to the ground floor and basement. My eyes flew open again. Dominic stood in the open doorway, dressed in nothing but colourful stripy boardshorts. A fluffy white towel hung around his bare neck.

A beaming, glowing, nipple-glinting, pleased-to-see-me Dominic, all tanned and smooth and perfect. And hot. So fucking hot. "Hey!"

I knew that's what he said—lipreading for beginners. I raised a less-than-enthusiastic hand in response. Although still fully clothed (thank God), I also had a towel draped around my shoulders, clueing him in to my destination. So his next utterance wasn't too difficult to deduce either.

"Hey, Tristan! Great minds think alike. Hot tub?"

I shook my head. "Potholing."

My weird deaf voice threw him a bit, although he recovered well. When I made a joke without my hearing aids, people were always discombobulated, as if I wasn't the same person with my disability unmasked. As if taking away my ability to hear also removed my humour and intelligence. I couldn't hear my deaf voice myself, just a vibration in my head, but I'd heard other deaf-from-birth people. Ever the helpful sibling, when we were kids, Frankie had informed me it was equally as jarring.

Dominic made an hourglass shape with his hands. "Funny man. I'm off to a pottery class."

The lift doors tried to close, and he stuck out a foot to prop them open. "Not wearing your hearing aids?"

He mouthed the words, pointing to his own ears and I shook my head. He then made further gestures with his hands. Basic signing, although I didn't recognise them. British and US sign languages were as similar as Spanish and Italian—some crossover, but not enough to exchange more than a rudimentary conversation. Having had implants from an early age, my own signing was next to useless anyhow.

"Better than me," I said, indicating his hands. "I don't sign."

"Do you want me to go?" He jerked his thumb back in the direction of his apartment. "I don't mind," he added. "It's cool. I can swim tomorrow."

A dilemma. My head told me of course, I had no right to tell him he couldn't swim. I'd retreat to the safety of the apartment and let him have the pool room to himself, sparing both of us the embarrassment of my clumsy flop into the hot tub without hearing aids, unable to smooth it over with conversation.

My heart—or, more truthfully, my horny little soul—pointed out I could take a brave leap forward, join him in the pool room, thus revealing my awful, mangled limbs, and allow him to assist me into the hot tub. The reward? Ogling his beautiful body as he swam up and down. Had he really flirted with me during dinner, as Milo had insisted? Had his hand rested on my shoulder longer than normal as he pushed my chair in for me? He certainly seemed happy we'd bumped into each other now.

Weighing the options, my eyes roamed over the smooth planes of his golden torso, the shiny glint at his left nipple, and the perfect sweep of his biceps.

Horniness won.

"Stay," I felt, rather than heard myself speak. "But I need to get my hearing aids."

His face lit up with pleasure. As heat whooshed up my neck, I was glad for my curtain of hair to hide behind. The effect he had on me was ridiculous. As if a guy like Dom would ever give me more than a cursory glance. Milo had misread him—he'd been showing Frankie he wasn't the arrogant, spoiled, trust fund boy my brother had pegged him for. That was all.

Light fingers tapped my shoulder. When I looked up, he addressed me again.

"I'll nip back and fetch them. I know the apartment code. Wait here."

"Go on. You have your swim. I'll... er... I'll be fine here by myself."

That awkward moment, when it hadn't occurred to God's favourite son a runt of the litter like me might not appreciate a side-by-side, visual comparison of our near-naked bodies. My willingness to risk damaging my stupidly expensive hearing aids rather than asking for his assistance spoke volumes.

"Yeah, I will in a sec. I'll just see you safely in, first. No rush." A quick flash of expensive American dentistry. "I'm crawling back into your brother's good books. I don't want to ruin it explaining how I let you crack your head open on wet tiles."

Which was how I found myself exposing every unappealing inch of my pasty concave chest and belly, a treat up until this moment solely reserved for close family and members of the medical profession. As I peeled away my T-shirt, Dominic stood patiently holding my sticks, pretending to find the bench, a cracked floor tile, and the instructions printed on the side of the tub sources of endless fascination.

I needed to be seated to remove my trousers. Fortunately, they were of a loose, elasticated sportswear variety, not that I ever engaged in sports. I'd already exchanged my boxers for swim shorts. A profound silence accompanied my excruciatingly slow striptease, and Dominic leaped forwards and turned on the tub bubbles. The rhythmic trickle of water crescendoed into full-on gurgling.

"Warming it up for you," he explained, all puppy dog, too-big-for-the-space again, especially now he held my body-warmed trousers, T-shirt, and sticks in his outstretched hands. An odd intimacy neither of us had anticipated or appreciated. As if scorching hot, Dominic dropped my clothes into an untidy pile on the bench.

"You can put my sticks there." I indicated to the useful corner triangle. Pushing myself off the bench, I rose to my feet, quite fluidly for me, and steadied myself against the wall, ready for the indignity of crab-shuffling my way into the tub.

A strong arm landed at my bare waist, curving around my hip, a mere inch above the waistband of my shorts. Every muscle in my body froze.

"Shout at me if you like, for helping you," Dominic gabbled, his eyes clamped on a random spot ahead and most definitely not on my wasted legs or pigeon chest.

Shouting was way beyond me; his skin sparking against mine had rendered me speechless.

"But I'm gonna do it anyhow. Just tell me if I'm doing it wrong, so I'll be better the next time." The long, tanned fingers I'd admired hugging a steering wheel now curled into the dip above my hipbone. Like a hot brand, Dominic's forearm pressed against the sensitive skin of my back. Only for a flash of time, barely long enough to store the feel of it in my memory bank, but long enough to plant both my own hands securely on the rim of the tub.

"Hang on. Don't move."

Some nights, the hot tub steps felt like a mountain too high to climb. Scaling them in one giant leap, Dominic grinned at me, oblivious to how easily he moved, oblivious to the hot water bubbling around him. Oblivious to the effect his graceful body had on me. The fabric of his wet shorts clung to his toned thighs, clearly outlining what rested between them as he offered out both hands, palms upwards. "Come. I'll support you up the steps."

We didn't actually grasp each other's hands, which was a mighty good thing, because if we had, then my legs would have turned to spaghetti, and the climb would have defeated me. Instead, we wrapped our fingers around each other's forearms. With a jerky motion, I progressed up each step, planting one foot, then the other, on each wet tile. Nearing the top, I transferred more of my weight onto him, until, for the slenderest of seconds, he almost held me in his arms.

And then I was down again, settled on my bottom inside the tub, hot bubbles swarming (and hiding) my ugly parts, like loyal old friends. Dominic beamed idiotically down at me, arms folded across his chest. Pleased as punch.

"What?" I tried to look cross and failed.

"I helped you, and I didn't fuck up."

Tipping my head back, sucking in a lungful of humid air, I

closed my eyes. Yep, I'd become best buddies with a fucking Labrador puppy. "Go for a fucking swim, Dom."

As he thrashed up and down the pool, I might have enjoyed an erection. The man had no right to so much energy at this time of night. Dominic's swimming style mirrored his approach to life; brash and enthusiastic and sometimes crashing into other people on his way. Anyone else sharing his water would have been mown down.

I had a sneaking suspicion he was showing off, in the way most cocky young men were inclined when they knew they had an audience. A suspicion confirmed when he exited the water at the farthest point away from me, maximising the length of his poolside strut. As if I'd had them closed the whole time, I slammed my eyelids shut, not opening again until he splashed down onto the opposite bench of the tub.

He spread his legs and arms wide, as if he owned it (and technically, I suppose he did, or at least his family did), taking up way more space than me.

"Do you ever go for a dip in the pool, Tristan?"

Still recovering from his wild exertions, the twin domes of his chest heaved above the bubbling water. I couldn't work out whether the silver bar through his left nipple was a mini dumbbell or a snake. Milo said sucking on nipple piercings tasted like car keys. I felt an overwhelming desire to confirm that opinion for myself.

"Not without floats and things." Muscles loosened, I stretched out a little myself. The outside edge of his foot carelessly brushed against mine. He left it there. "And someone keeping an eye. But I tend to get cold, just bobbing around, so I prefer it in here."

Neither of us spoke for a while. Savouring the muscle-pummelling, Dominic tipped his head back and shut his eyes, allowing me to openly admire his handsomeness. And his veiny hands. And the sweep of muscles over his broad shoulders. As much as I looked forward to catching up with Maureen on Monday, I'd miss our chaotic car journeys.

"What are all the scars on your legs?" he asked suddenly.

Even though the rippling water obscured my body, my gaze shifted down. "From lots of operations. From when I was a child and still growing. Tendon-lengthening procedures, to reduce spasticity. They helped, a bit."

He nodded and tipped his head back again. Surprisingly relaxing company.

"What are you hoping to get out of your internship?"

The jets switched themselves off. My skin had turned pruny, but I was in no hurry to leave. Dominic answered with a dramatic groan. "God knows. Ask me in a month or so. I might have an answer by then."

"That's not a very corporate, St. Cloud response."

"I'm not a very corporate St. Cloud."

Opening his eyes, he smiled at me, lazily, like a sun-warmed cat. His irises shone an iridescent green in tonight's muted lighting. Earlier, over dinner, I'd concluded they were a light hazel. "But let's see how I respond after a month of indoctrination."

"You don't sound terribly enthusiastic."

"I'm not." He sighed. "The internship wasn't exactly my idea."

"Working with the family at Cloud Ten isn't that bad, is it? Lysander's retained several human traits. Aside from his bizarre fascination with my irritating brother."

With his index finger, Dominic drew patterns across the surface of the water. His foot shifted against mine, if anything increasing the contact. Deep in thought, perhaps he hadn't noticed. He sighed again, lingering on a long exhale.

"Nah, not really. The board meeting was more interesting than I expected. I'm doing a business major back in college, and seeing some of that book learning in action was cool. Although after spending a few days on one of the construction sites, not everything I learn about in the classroom makes sense."

"In what way?"

He pursed his lips. "There's a disconnect. What happens on the top floor of Canary Wharf seems a hell of a way apart from what happens on the ground. I wonder if some of the folks up there have forgotten that when they talk about units and logistics and workforces, they are actually referring to people with real lives." He shrugged. "That's corporate structure, I suppose. Workers, pen pushers, and bosses, all doing their own thing."

Forehead creased in a thoughtful frown, he carried on. "Like this one guy, Jason, down on the construction site. He's super smart; he's mad keen on maritime history. He told me about these great big aircraft carriers you guys used in a war against Argentina. I didn't even know you'd had a war, and it was only, like, forty years ago! Jason sounded like one of my college professors. Yet some other guy with a smart suit and a clipboard came over to the site last week and wouldn't give his opinions the time of day. As if he had nothing to offer except his ability to dig a trench in a straight line."

"Just because he's an expert on the Falklands War doesn't make him an expert on building warehouses," I pointed out.

"No, it doesn't," he agreed. "And maybe the clipboard guy's views were valid. But I think it was the lack of respect that bothered Jason. That Clipboard Carrier dismissed him as just a construction worker with no inherent value other than to shovel a damned hole. Jason's a smart guy, but he didn't feel *seen*."

Christ, if anyone understood what that felt like, it was me. Some people pretended to listen when I spoke, but like they were doing me a huge favour. As if the only issues on which I could hold a valid opinion were related to my disabilities. Whereas really, they weren't listening at all, just waiting their turn to speak, to voice their own superior opinion. Even my friends were occasionally guilty—taking pot shots at Dominic, for instance, after I'd made it clear they didn't need to. That although I was disabled, I was perfectly capable of doing that all by myself.

"Anyhow, I'm not convinced Cloud Ten values its workforce as much as we think we do. It's like a game of telephone. Do you have that in England? Mangled messages. By the time the message from the top of the hierarchy threads its way to the bottom, it's unintelligible. And vice versa."

I'd heard Lysander bemoan a similar thing, although I hadn't expected Dominic to come up with such an astute observation. "Sounds like you're getting something out of your trip to London after all."

His mouth creased into an unhappy moue. "I guess. You've probably worked out coming here for a few months was not my choice. If it had been up to me, I'd have stayed in SoCal, doing everything I love." He shot me a quick glance. "Partying. College, the beach, football. Living the dream."

I nodded, as if fully comprehending the joys of his hedonistic lifestyle. "I'm surprised a spoiled trust fund brat like you lets people dictate to him where he goes and what he does."

With a brittle laugh, he shook his head. "No, you're right. But I took the partying one step too far, and my folks decided I needed to get the fuck out of Dodge for a while."

He drew even larger swirls across the water, big figures of eight, eyes focused down on his task. "They were probably right."

Water trickled into the filter behind me. Otherwise, a calm stillness descended over the pool room. A nosy bugger, I itched for the full story, but being the quietest triplet had taught me one thing: noisy extroverts always spilled the beans eventually. They couldn't help themselves.

Dominic was no exception. "I drank too many beers one afternoon down at the beach and... um... relieved myself against the side of a fire truck."

Okay. Not what I'd expected. Dabbling with drugs maybe, or flunking exams. Perhaps a stupid drunken prank. But being caught short after a few beers? Happened to the best of us. "So what?"

"Unfortunately, it wasn't just any fire truck, parked up and minding its own business. It was at a big funeral parade for a firefighter, and it was the dead firefighter's goddamned truck. The guy was killed in the line of duty, saving another person's life. He'd been someone's husband, someone's dad. All the roads through the centre of town had been closed for the event. Although I hadn't known jack shit about any of that. I was just on my way back from the beach and took a slash against a convenient upright. I was so smashed I don't even remember doing it."

We'd all experienced big awkward, cringey moments. What with my CP and deafness, mine could fill a book. But there were the little things, too, everyone encountered. Like last week, after a random shop customer leaned in close to point out my flies were undone, leaving me with the sinking certainty they had been that way for the preceding three hours.

A step worse were the interactions that still made you squirm with embarrassment, several years later. Like when I once plucked up the courage to ask a girl at the school gates if I could stroke the cute rabbit she was cuddling, to realise far too late it was a furry hand warmer.

But the thing about these moments, the thing that enabled you to move on and even joke about them, despite being forever humiliating in your own crazy head, was how everyone else had entirely forgotten.

Unless your faux pas was a little more public.

"We don't really have big funeral parades like that in the UK." A facile thing to say, to be fair, but the correct response eluded me.

"Maybe that's why they sent me here." Dominic threw me a wry, lopsided smile. "So I'm not tempted to do it again. Turns out I arrived in London and managed to fuck up another way, anyhow. And no alcohol to blame that time."

Abruptly, he stood, the sudden movement sending water sloshing over the sides. "Come on. You're starting to shiver. I'll help you out."

CHAPTER 10
DOMINIC

I don't know why I shared it with him. I hadn't planned on anyone knowing. But as I assisted him out of the tub and back onto the bench where he rubbed himself dry, I spilled the whole tale. How the local news station picked up the story after footage of me doing the deed had been caught on a panoramic camera shot. How the hunt for the perp focused in on a guy in a football shirt and a Chargers cap. How every other damn guy in San Diego dressed like that, but my mom's best friend had recognised me anyhow. Which meant lots of other folks would too. How, twenty-four hours later, strings had been pulled, and my dad—plus his expensive, smarmy lawyer—had swooped in. How I found myself on the next flight out of there.

I didn't tell Tristan sharing the hot tub with him had been the best evening since. How his quiet company turned down the volume on the loud engines inside my head, telling me to do reckless things. How he steadied me, how much I admired him—not for how he coped with all his shit (but that, too), but how he acted like he'd forgotten our first encounter in the pool. I didn't want to sound like some ableist insensitive jerk.

"Must be nice being so rich you can pay all your mistakes to go away."

Not all of them; no amount of money could nullify my behaviour towards Tristan.

"I kind of asked for that, I guess."

With no perp, after a few op-eds in the local rag about disrespectful youth, the city's growing degenerate drugs-and-alcohol culture, the menace of college kids, blah, blah, the story died a death. My mom and dad, briefly united in their condemnation of my shameful behaviour, read me the Riot Act. Nobody asked me how I felt about what I'd done. Nor what I felt I should do about it. Nobody cared. I didn't have a right to an opinion.

"Yeah. They are still thrashing out the details, but... yeah, my dad is making it all go away."

Tristan took an age to wrestle his legs back into his sweatpants. I tried to make out like I hadn't noticed or wasn't waiting by taking an inordinate length of time to dry between my toes and fiddle with my hair.

"Let's just say, by the time my dad's lawyer has done his job, the guy's widow won't have to worry about a college fund for the kids. She won't have a mortgage for much longer either."

Eyes narrowing, he studied me from the bench. "What about you? Has the experience changed you? Have you learnt anything from it?"

"Well, I won't get quite so shitfaced on the beach in the middle of the afternoon anymore."

A glib answer, and a lie. Once we were reunited, I probably would go on a drinking spree with my buddies again. Not to those lengths, though. Not so much that I lost all sense of control.

"It haunts me," I confessed, seeing as Tristan was still waiting for a real answer. "I fucked up. Looking back, I... I'd like to have had the opportunity to apologise—maybe even faced the consequences?"

He raised a challenging eyebrow.

"Well, maybe not *all* the consequences. I mean, I'd have been kicked out of college and gotten a criminal record. Stuff like that carries a possible jail term, but my dad's lawyer reckoned he'd have gotten me community service. And my family's name would have been dragged through the papers, of course, including my relationship to Lysander. I think that meant more to my dad than me getting off, to be honest."

"You think?"

"Actually, I know for sure." I passed him his sticks. "So I'm glad I escaped all that, and I'm glad the dead guy's family have had their futures made easier for them. It won't bring him back, and it won't erase the image of a disrespectful dumb kid pissing against the side of their dad's fire truck, but I guess it's something."

I felt better for offloading. I hoped he wouldn't tell Frankie, who probably thought his opinion of me couldn't descend any lower only to discover a whole new level. As we slowly meandered back to the elevator, I mulled it over. I'd grown accustomed to walking at Tristan's pace. It gave more time for talking and thinking.

"You could still say sorry, you know," he observed as the elevator ascended. "In private, when you go back. It's never too late. Your dad doesn't need to know. You don't need his permission."

"Yeah. You're right. I think about doing that sometimes. Not sure how to go about it, though." We arrived at my level with a smooth bump. "Do you need my help getting to the next floor?"

Over the last two weeks, it had become our daily joke, since I'd asked him that dumb question on our first day. I was going to miss the sweet smile it elicited. Making Tristan smile somehow made me feel like a better person.

"You could just knock on her door and tell her how sorry you are. When you get back to the US."

I scoffed out a strained laugh. "Knowing me, I'd balls it up. My dad's lawyer advised me to keep the hell away from her."

Tristan pursed his lips. "So? You're twenty-one. You don't have to do everything your parents and their lawyers tell you."

"Maybe it's time I did. Keep me out of mischief. Although I

often think of doing exactly that. Standing on her front porch and telling her it was me. Then offering to mow her grass or something."

Checking he had his towel tucked securely under his arm so it wouldn't fall, with a salute, I turned to go.

"You're not so bad, you know," he called after me. "For a spoiled trust fund brat."

"Try telling your brother and your friends that."

For the duration of my hastily-put-together internship, I'd been assigned as my Aunt Pauline's bitch. No doubt another of Frankie's little jokes at my expense. Now divorced from my Uncle Paul, I wasn't sure if, strictly speaking, that still made her my aunt, but here she was, settled in a spacious prime corner office and an ongoing, integral piece of the company jigsaw. Once a St. Cloud, always a St. Cloud. Lysander had warned me about her sharp tongue, but at the board meeting last week, she'd been surprisingly tame. Maybe she missed her usual sparring partner.

We spent the first hour of the day facing each other across a low table, sipping decent coffees and bitching about my Uncle Paul. Tottering on a pair of heels, more attitude than footwear, his PA, Natalie, sashayed in and out a couple of times, so we spent the second hour bitching about her. To be honest, from where I sat, I could see very little wrong, and, from the suggestive looks she tossed my way, the feeling was mutual.

Once we got down to business, it soon became clear why my sourpuss aunt retained her position on the board. I wasn't a believer in photographic memories, but Pauline did a damned good job of convincing me otherwise. The woman could recite the small print from every financial transaction the corporation had ever undertaken. And, instead of shooting covert glances at the clock and counting down the minutes until the day ended, I... kind of dug it.

Midafternoon, she sent me across to Lysander's office to go

through some recruitment bumf with him. A low-level project she wanted to steer in my direction, a data-collection mission, examining the financial packages for middle-management career advancement and a comparison with our competitors. Nothing too complex, but nevertheless, a mini-project of my own, and on my first day too, was kind of cool. I hoped Big Bro would give me some pointers enabling me to impress her.

When I arrived at his office, though, my brother was nowhere to be seen. My initial disappointment was offset by a most beautiful pair of long, slim legs disappearing under a thigh-hugging pencil skirt. Whether still dreaming of the beaches of So-Cal or not, I had to hand it to the family: so far, the St. Cloud office scenery had been on point.

The blonde owner of the endless legs had her back to me, picking the most delightful moment to bend over and rummage through a filing cabinet.

"Be with you in a sec," came a muffled voice.

I was more than happy to wait and admire the view. "No worries, you just take your own sweet time."

She reached across for a file, and I drank in the sight of thin white cotton stretched taut across her shoulders. No bra straps. A lean, well-toned back, a trim waist, and a very tasty, bouncy ass. Bloody hell. Totally wasted on Lysander since he'd crossed over and gotten himself shacked up with a guy. On the right woman, the no-bra look was one of my favourites, fabulous when the air con temperature lowered, and even more so on a woman like this, with a small, pert pair of—

"Dominic. Petal. Your attention is terribly flattering, but a little peculiar, don't you think? Given our… ah… impending relationship to each other?"

The mystery person's front view wasn't quite as beguiling as the rear. Well, in some ways it was, because Frankie Carter was a fucking gorgeous guy, even wearing a skirt. But he was my big brother's fucking gorgeous guy, and, since the Tristan debacle, regarded me like something the cat had dragged in.

"Um… sorry, Frankie. I wasn't at all. I… um… I."

He coolly arched an eyebrow, above an eye the same brilliant shade of blue as Tristan's. When would I do something *right* in front of this man? Instead of coming across as a rude, incompetent, overgrown teenager?

Tutting, he slammed shut the filing cabinet behind him with an elegant high-heeled kick. How the hell had I managed to forget Frankie felt a little genderfluid every now and again? When was I going to start paying attention to what people told me about their lives, instead of being exclusively wrapped up in my own?

Lysander had confided in me about this, pouring his heart out for hours down a phone line. Just like he'd explained to me about Tristan having CP and being deaf. And in return, I'd paid him the scantest lip service, too busy amusing him with my own immature exploits and highjinks. Lysander had given me real life; I had returned the favour with trash talk and bravado.

Heat flared in my cheeks. "Okay, you got me. I was totally checking you out. I'm sorry. I thought you were, you know…"

"I know what you thought," he replied in an icy tone. If I imagined dressing in a more feminine fashion would soften his stance towards me, then I was sorely mistaken. "Lysander's not here. He's conducting a site visit and won't be back this afternoon." With a prim gesture, he smoothed down the skirt. "Is there anything I can help you with?"

"Um… the quickest route out of this office? The key to the French windows?"

Frankie's hard gaze slid to the door, as if seriously contemplating it. Feeling brave, I held my ground. Maybe catching Frankie alone was an opportunity for us to have this thing out once and for all.

"Hey, listen, Frankie. What I did to Tristan. You have no idea how sorry I am about that. Truly, I am. I've tried to make it up to him, and I'll continue to do so, any which way I know how."

Frankie sucked in his top lip, perusing me with narrow-eyed scrutiny. So like Tristan in so many ways, and yet so different.

Harder than his brother, but fiercely loyal too, to his friends, his siblings, and, of course, Lysander. The kind of guy you wanted in your corner, rolling up his sleeves when times got tough.

Time stood still. Maybe I'd head back to Pauline's office anyhow and try to fathom the data-collection exercise on my own. Some guys held onto resentment forever. I turned to go.

"My opinion of you, Dominic, after what you did to my brother, sank lower than my mother's pelvic floor after carrying triplets."

I turned back, to see a hint of a smile playing on his lips.

"Believe me, that's pretty bloody low. Maddie was all for insisting Lysander send you back to the US. Mungo was just going to cut off your balls." As shame flooded through me, he ran a delicate hand along the line of his smooth jaw. "Lysander and I had a serious falling out over you. He probably hasn't told you, has he?"

Of course he hadn't. One of life's good guys, my brother would never burden me with that kind of guilt. I shook my head, even more humiliated.

"He defended you. Tried to tell me all your good points, which I wasn't open to hearing. I was upset, as you can imagine. You spoiled one of the happiest weekends of my life, right at the end. It was our first proper row, and I hated you for causing it."

"I'm so sorry." Jeez, I found that word on my tongue a hell of a lot these days.

Frankie shrugged, taking a crisply indrawn breath. "Your brother is hard to rile, but I succeeded, enough for him to remark that wasn't quite true. He reminded me we'd had the mother of all blazing rows in the middle of a park in London after I confessed I was a gay man pretending to be a woman in order to advance my career. He pointed out I'd not cared a jot about the effect my little joke would have on people around me, especially him. That argument was a nadir in our relationship, as you can imagine, even though it became the starting point of an even better one. At any rate, I'd hoped we'd never have another like it."

Meekly, I adjusted my view downward, seeing nothing. Waiting for the part when he asked me to fuck off back to the US, to stay away from him, my brother, and Tristan.

"Lysander also pointed out that I'd massively fucked up by leaving it so long before I told him the truth about me. I'd made a monumental mistake, but he'd given me a second chance. We'd given each other a second chance. And look where that led us."

He glanced around the room, as if taking in and cataloguing his surroundings. "We couldn't be any happier if we tried."

His gaze landed once more on me. "And since your twattish behaviour, you apologised to Tristan, and he accepted it. Whatever you said must have been bloody good, by the way, because Tristan's a difficult bugger."

"I think he's amazing," I blurted. It was the freaking, simple truth. "Honestly, he's incredible."

Frankie smiled properly, even though he scoffed. "I wouldn't go that far, mate. Try living with him for twenty-five years."

Walking over to his desk, swishing his ass in his high heels with even more sass than Natalie—although I pretended not to notice, because like... no—he daintily took a seat behind it. "I gather Pauline's stopped bitching about her ex and given you a job to do. Can I help you with anything?"

"Yes, as a matter of fact, I think you can. Did you know construction workers have three times the UK suicide rate average?"

"Yes Dominic. I'm Frankie." He threw me a look as if that explained everything. "It's my job to know everything about people who work in the construction industry. And?"

"And it has nothing to do with the task Pauline has set me, but I think it's more important, don't you?"

I'd unearthed this horrifying statistic after relating to Tristan my observations about Jason, Mick, and Dick. Jason had his naval passion to occupy his lively mind, and Mick had a big busy family. Overall, despite his money worries, he was a cheerful chap. The quietest of the three had been Dick. Middle-aged and divorced, he lived alone, his main source of amusement found staring at the bottom of a pint glass, as far as I could tell. Though he joshed as much as the others, I'd caught him staring into space a couple of times, and… it was hard to put my finger on, but something was brittle about him, like he was going through the motions, rolling from one thing to the next, but not caring whether he was in the present or not.

I endeavoured to explain all this to Frankie, while he tapped at his keyboard, efficiently downloading everything useful to complete Pauline's data collection exercise. I didn't know how relevant it was to the top corridor of the Cloud Ten machine, only that I needed to offload it onto someone.

"It's a shame Lysander's not here to listen to you," he remarked after I'd finished. "Because everything you've said mirrors his thoughts exactly. And while he's the figurehead of our *green is the scene* agenda," he made a face at this, "he uses that as a means of travelling around, listening to the ground crews and improving the services they can access."

Finished typing, he sat back and folded his arms. "People groan when they hear the phrase 'Health and Safety'. Lord knows I'm one of them. But we're trying to change that image, to make the 'health' part actually have valid meaning to our employees. To actually offer them relevant health advice and support, not only a list of do's and don'ts to avoid workplace injury. Stick around long enough, you could become involved."

CHAPTER 11
TRISTAN

Things I loved about the penthouse: part 7: a hot guy had moved in one floor below.

"I won't be here tomorrow," began Maureen, as I sorted out my seatbelt. "Baby Chewbacca is misbehaving, so our Gina's going into hospital to be induced into labour."

I concealed my slight shudder. Maddie had been quite graphic with her account of recent childbirth; I wasn't ready for another.

"That's exciting." I hoped I sounded like I meant it. Thanks to Maddie, I also knew how these types of conversations were expected to go. "Has she got any baby names lined up?"

"Phyllis if it's a girl and Nigel if it's a boy. Or maybe Keith, depending on whether he looks like a Keith."

In my mind, Keith was pushing sixty, had a combover, and worked as a pedantic school's inspector, so I doubted Chewbacca would. And Nigel was—oh my God, who on God's green earth called their baby *Nigel* these days?"

"Or Clive. Her boyfriend likes Clive. And Geraldine if it's a girl."

"Nice," I managed weakly. Given those choices, I'd stick to Chewbacca.

Maureen slapped me on the shoulder. "Only kidding. It's

Olivia for a girl or Jack for a boy, you daft sod. You should have seen your face!"

"You've been checking the clock for the last twenty minutes," observed Irene. "It won't make the hands tick round go any faster, you know. Got a hot date?"

"No." I blushed. She'd rumbled me. At two o'clock that afternoon, Maureen had become a proud grandmother to a healthy, not excessively hirsute, baby girl. Chewbacca was now Olivia, weighing in at nine pounds one ounce. More than Frankie, Maddie, and me combined! The point being Cloud Ten would send someone else to pick me up, and my horny little soul was praying for—

"There's a very tasty bloke enjoying a coffee out the front." She smirked. "Although I did catch him skimming through the Shania Twain half-price rack before he sat down. But hey, you can't have everything."

Did we judge our clientele on their musical tastes? Absolutely.

"And by the way, like you, he's also staring at the clock every two minutes."

My heart gave an insane little jump, even if I did try to play it cool. "If it's Neil, I'm not here."

"Neil would rather eat raw veal from an ivory fork inlaid with blood diamonds than be caught anywhere near the easy listening section. He'll have to get used to it, though, because I've invited him to Emily's fortieth. She's going for a 90s disco theme."

Deep joy. She'd presented me with two solid reasons to "accidentally" leave my hearing aids behind. "Great. Thanks for the heads up. Gives me time to prepare myself for another discourse on the negative role of male white privilege in the underground Cuban reggae scene."

She laughed. "Relax. It's not Neil out the front. It's your other admirer. The Californian eye candy with the cowboy accent. Who looks at you, young man, as if you're perched right on the top of his 'to do' list."

I blush-snorted, if that was a thing. Mostly, Dominic looked at me with a slight sense of trepidation. As if one wrong move and Frankie would leap out from behind a stack of records to accuse him of assaulting me. It was high time Frankie chilled with the whole protective, three-minute-older brother thing. Dominic was not the enemy. Far from it.

Irene made a lewd noise. "And you'll be pleased to hear he's treating us to The Suit again."

My heart danced a two-step. The Suit had featured heavily in last night's dreams, and I'd woken up all kinds of sweaty. "Are you sure you're a lesbian?"

"Yes, but I can still appreciate an alpha male, Tristan! When he's all dressed up in that expensive Italian number, Emily thinks he looks like a hungry panther—ready to pounce on you. Or a rutting stag."

Another thrill buzzed through me. "Didn't the Rutting Stags headline the pyramid stage at Glastonbury in 2007?"

She giggled, making all her jewellery rattle. "Yeah, warming up for the Pouncing Panthers. I've invited him to the party too, by the way. That way you'll have someone to drive you over."

"What?" The thrill made itself at home in my lower belly. With a couple of clicks on the keyboard, I logged out for the day and gathered my satchel and sticks. "Don't tell me he said yes."

Her eyes twinkled mischievously. "After I mentioned you were going? What do you think?"

As I shuffled into the store, the music switched to Bowie's "Young American." No way was that a coincidence. My ad hoc chauffeur rose, adjusting his silver cufflinks as he waited for me to hand him my satchel. Pale pink shirt cuffs poked out from the sleeves of his navy suit jacket, contrasting beautifully with the tanned skin of his hands. The beginning of a dark five o'clock shadow painted his lower jaw. Ugh.

"I've spent the afternoon with Frankie!" Mighty pleased with himself, he helped me into the car. "He's a sweetheart once you get to know him, isn't he?"

"Is he? Then I'm not as well acquainted with him as I thought." Lordy, the way his hands encircled my calves was positively criminal. "You might revise that opinion if he catches you failing to stack the mugs in the dishwasher to his exacting standards. God knows how Lysander lives *and* works with him."

"He was unbelievably helpful," continued Dominic. "Gave me a brilliant impromptu tutorial on Excel spreadsheets. Amongst other things."

Oblivious to the red Ford Focus slamming on the brakes behind, he pulled out from the kerb. His long slender fingers drummed on the steering wheel. Not that I was staring or anything.

"I have to prepare a fifteen-minute presentation to the board before I leave." He flashed me a quick smile. "They make all the interns do one. Frankie gave me some pointers. Most interns have six months or a year to build up to it. I hoped I'd dodge it, being here for just a few months, but Daphne has 'high expectations' apparently."

"What's the presentation about?"

The thought of Dominic's few months coming to an end chilled me. I'd miss our occasional car journeys. And I'd miss knowing he might join me in the hot tub, even if that did mean he saw me nearly naked.

I tried to imagine sharing a hot tub with Neil. He'd probably refuse on principle, citing a lack of eco-friendliness.

"Pauline has given me the title '*A change I'd implement if I was CEO for a day*.'" He threw me a knowing look. "Typical of the St. Clouds. It's a smart choice. I'll have to come up with a suggestion that's achievable, innovative, and yet doesn't come over as highly critical of the current regime." His eyes were back on the road. "I'm not worried. I've a couple of ideas knocking around."

Not worried? I couldn't imagine much worse than standing in

front of a bunch of high-flying execs, facing ridicule. "Lysander hates doing that kind of thing."

"I know," agreed Dominic. "But I'm not Lysander. And he's better at it than he realises, although I don't think he'll ever want to do it regularly."

"If only he had a super confident younger brother to present his ideas for him," I teased. "You'd make a great team. 'Cloud Ten—to infinity and beyond' or whatever your logo is."

"It would be a team of three." He chewed his top lip thoughtfully. "Him and Frankie were made for each other in the workplace. Frankie translates Lysander's ideas into a coherent strategy and five bullet points. Your brother looks great in a skirt, by the way. I'd never seen him dressed like that before."

"He's always felt a little different," I acknowledged. "It's good he can express it without feeling judged."

"Talking of different," he went on, "I'm taking you to Emily's party. A fortieth! I must be growing up! What happens at those?"

"Same as at any other. People stand around drinking way too many cocktails in the hope other people will start to sound more interesting. And after one vodka cranberry too many, they make bad decisions."

Briefly, Dominic took his eyes off the road to smile at me. I braced as the car wobbled out of its lane. "A fan of parties, are you?"

I shrugged. "They're okay. But lots of people all talking at the same time interferes with my hearing. Don't feel obliged because Emily asked. I won't be offended. And it's Saturday night, so I'm sure you have much better things to do. Honestly, you could just drop me off, and I'd get a cab home."

"I know all that. And I don't feel obliged. I'll have plenty of other Saturday nights. Lys and Frankie are busy schmoozing clients this weekend. And my internship buddies are out of town. It's cool. Plus," he gave the steering wheel a fond pat, "I've... I've missed driving the Lexus."

"The Lexus hasn't missed you."

As if to underline my point, a taxi joining the stream of traffic beeped at us for not giving way. The Lexus juddered for a few metres as Dominic pressed a little too enthusiastically on the brake.

He looked at home behind the wheel, though. Dominic's days now revolved around smart suits and long meetings. Trying to act and think like the future of Cloud Ten instead of ferrying me about dressed as a lumberjack. As I listened to him chattering on, he was clearly enjoying his internship a hell of a lot more than he expected, even if he hadn't realised it himself yet. I had a feeling my occasional chauffeur was a future CEO in the making.

He drummed on the steering wheel again. "And what about the Lexus's Very Important Passenger?" he asked lightly. "Has he missed me?"

His question was timed to perfection. We slowed for a set of traffic lights, enabling him to transfer his gaze from the road ahead and properly over to me.

"Can I… can I do something, by the way, Tristan? It's something I've been wanting to do for weeks."

With a quick movement, his fingers left the steering wheel. Carefully, almost tenderly, he tucked a few long strands of my hair behind my ears so I couldn't hide behind them.

"Much better. I can see you properly now."

His dark, velvety accent washed over me, like a warm caress. A kaleidoscope of butterflies took flight in my stomach, and my cheeks felt as red as the stop sign. If I moved my face an inch to the left, those fingertips would be at my mouth, and I'd be able to show him exactly how much I'd missed him.

"You haven't answered."

With a roll of my eyes, I shook my future brother-in-law off. "Just drive the bloody car, Dominic."

CHAPTER 12
DOMINIC

Things I hated about London: crosswalks named after freaking birds. Puffins and pelicans and toucans. It was most definitely not cute.

I'd been in the thick of some wild parties at college. In the frat house especially, thirty ambitious high achievers with deep pockets and feckless brains trying to outdo the frat next door. Pole dancers, strippers, champagne fountains; you name it, we'd provided it.

Needless to say, Emily's modest house party took a different slant. She shared a dinky old row house with Irene. Here, they were known as terraces, hers identifiable from the twinkling lights and birthday balloons strung up outside. No steps up to the front door, just a smooth slabbed path. Funny how I'd automatically begun to scope for these things. And the music wasn't blaring, at least not from the sidewalk—sorry, *pavement*—which would make Tristan's evening easier.

Not that I automatically found myself considering stuff like that, either. But I liked being a part of Tristan's understated life, and I'd miss it when I headed back to the US. Tristan, and his accepting, calm way of dealing with his personal challenges had crept under my skin.

Despite attempting to blend in with Tristan's crowd as much as possible, I still looked like a fish out of water. I had an outdoorsy Californian build—and tan—and my jeans and button-down were expensively made and smartly pressed. In a sea of sturdy Doc Marten boots, my brown leather loafers hit a jarring note. I was the only attendee not flaunting an ironic band T-shirt. Tristan's was vintage, from an old Stone Roses gig, which on him looked cool. On me, it would have been a tragic attempt at trying too hard.

Not that it mattered a fig; I could have come dressed in a garbage bag, seeing as no one paid me the slightest attention anyhow. After all, I was escorting the most popular guy in the room.

Briefly, I had Tristan to myself while one of his admirers went in search of a chair. At some unseen moment over the last couple of days, a need to hold this man close and find out what his lush soft lips tasted like had slipped into my mind and lodged there. It was high time I stepped closer to finding out.

Lowering my voice, I spoke into his ear, inhaling the clean scent of freshly washed hair. "Are you going to show me how you do that trick?"

Hey, I was American, born and bred. We didn't do subtle.

He looked puzzled. "What trick?"

"The one that make everyone want to be your friend. That makes us all fall for you."

Colour pinked his cheeks; Tristan's gaze shyly flirted with mine through a film of hair. Reaching up, I tucked the soft-as-silk golden strands behind his ear, as I'd done in the car.

That time, he'd pushed me away, embarrassed, but now, he moistened his lips with the tip of his tongue, those stunning eyes never leaving mine.

"I get it now," I murmured. "That's how."

The urge to dip my mouth to his took hold. As did the realisation my cheesy pickup line hadn't been cheesy at all, but God's honest truth. Blood pounded giddily in my ears, and words queued up in my throat, inappropriate words, words I'd never felt a desire to say to anyone else.

"Tris, I found you a stool from the kitchen."

A woman I hadn't seen before but who knew Tristan well enough to abbreviate his name began fussing around him. His gaze slid away from mine, and the moment passed. Another woman joined, greeting him with air kisses. On the periphery, I wandered off in search of a drink, preparing myself for a long night.

A while later, still nursing a single bottle of beer, I found myself hugging the wall and watching with amusement as a crowd of partygoers hogged Tristan's attention. One guy was a customer from the record store. Neil, if I recalled. According to Tristan, he played in a band and penned clichéd, adolescent lyrics about giving peace a chance and saving the planet.

Neil circled back to Tristan two or three times, keeping almost as close an eye on my cute friend as I did. If contrived dreadlocks on a white guy were your jam, then Neil had conventional good looks, although it wasn't my preference—at least not anymore. These days, my jam hid his pretty features and startling aqua eyes under a shield of blond waves and sometimes permitted me to hold his bag and lift his legs into the car for him.

"I see you've become the latest member of the Tristan fan club," said a cheery voice at my shoulder. "I should start selling tickets. It's becoming quite unwieldly." I turned to find Emily, the birthday girl, peering up at me, her lips quirking in a knowing smile.

"Don't worry, I'm good at keeping secrets." She jerked her head in the direction of Neil. "You're not alone here tonight." Leaning a little closer, she lowered her tone. "It might interest you to know that Neil's taken Tristan out for a drink a couple of times. Don't let him get the jump on you."

I stared at her, the swirl of jolly folk around me fading into a blur of background noise. I could have lied and denied, but, as if magnetically drawn, my gaze flicked back to Tristan. Neil was handing him a plastic beaker of wine, fingers touching his. A flash of irritation grabbed me by the jaw.

"Don't leave it too long. Neil's been hankering after Tristan for months."

"And he hasn't got anywhere?"

Emily shrugged. "Nope, I don't think so, not really. But he's very persistent. And he's nice enough."

I looked over again. Neil leaned forward, saying something meant for Tristan's ears alone—speaking directly at him, enunciating so Tristan could decipher his words above the song blaring from the stereo. Either that, or Neil was using his compromised hearing as an excuse to sidle even closer. No more than half an inch separated his face from Tristan's.

I clenched my fists. We'd reached the stage of the evening where alcohol had been imbibed and inhibitions had loosened; Neil's too perhaps. Someone had cranked up the volume on the stereo. A sofa had been pushed back, and several couples were on the makeshift dancefloor, doing their thing to a cool disco vibe I didn't recognise.

Tristan laughed hard at whatever Neil said, his delicate features sparkling with delight. Following up with another comment, Neil rested a possessive hand on his arm and took a long, satisfied draught of his own drink. His bony Adam's apple bobbed with every gulp.

My whole body itched to stand between them. No, more than that—to elbow Neil out of the way and take his place. To be the one whispering sweet nothings into Tristan's ear, If we'd been in a dark club, and Tristan had been anyone else, I'd have cockily cut in and hauled him off, on the pretext of wanting to dance.

"I can't just march over there and interrupt, without an excuse. It's not as if I can drag Tristan onto the dancefloor. If I do join them, I'll find myself standing around like a lemon, as they carry on their conversation. Or rather, as Neil carries on sliming all over him."

Admittedly, Neil wasn't sliming. Ten minutes earlier, he'd sought out a drink to save Tristan the bother of walking to the kitchen, like the decent guy he probably was. And didn't he have as much right as me to make a play for Tristan? They were single men with shared common ground. Emily threw me a puzzled look.

"Why can't you ask Tristan to dance? Do you have two left feet or something?"

"As a matter of fact, yes, but that's not the point. Tristan..."

"Don't make assumptions," she interrupted while I was still trying to come up with a polite way of alluding to Tristan's physical disabilities. "Tristan dances when the mood takes him. We often have a little boogie in the back room of the shop when something good comes on. But I warn you—he's had a glass of wine, so his balance might not be all that." One of her eyebrows winged up in a knowing look. "He might need someone to hold onto him, so he doesn't fall. A big strong man like you could manage that, can't you? Otherwise, I'm sure Neil will oblige."

The flash of irritation swelled into an ugly, green-eyed monster. "No, he damn well won't."

I'd seen and heard enough. Neil leaned in again to whisper even more sweet nothings. His body language, hand still glued to Tristan's arm, semaphored he was on the cusp of making his move.

What the hell was I waiting for? I wasn't a freaking wallflower. Dreadlocked, pretentious Neil had his hand on something I badly wanted. And I was a St. Cloud, descended from six generations of empire-building St. Clouds. Our methods hadn't always been pretty, but if we wanted something? We damn well took it. Swigging back the last few drops of my tepid weak beer, I handed the bottle to Emily, then straightened my shoulders and wiped my mouth with the back of my hand.

"Hey, Tristan."

"Hi."

"Just checking you're okay?"

I received a well-deserved sardonic eyebrow. "Yeah? I guess? You, like, last checked in on me about twenty minutes ago? And you've watched me leaning against this wall since."

"I know, I… just… I…"

After a large glass of wine and in a warm room packed with people, Tristan's cheeks glowed a delicate pink. The teasing sparkle in his eyes and perfect sweep of eyelashes above rooted me to the spot, uncharacteristically tongue-tied. Less a lemon, more an oversized, clumsy fanboy.

Bedroom eyes, that's the name my mom gave them. Seductive and dangerous. Before coming to the UK, she'd issued me all sorts of warnings: don't look the wrong way when crossing the road, biscuits were sweet not savoury, and my Uncle Paul was a snake not to be trusted. She'd even warned me how the first floor meant the second floor and the ground floor was the first floor—and no one would know what I meant if I asked for ranch dressing in a restaurant.

But she'd utterly forgotten to warn me about the perils of beautiful blond Englishmen with canes and hearing aids and bedroom eyes. And about falling in love.

"I'm Neil. You're the driver, yeah?"

The bedroom eyes glittered with amusement. "That's a very loose description of what he does behind the wheel, yes." Tristan treated me to a sly smile, and my stomach flipped. "When he's not slaving away for mere *pennies* in an office, living hand-to-mouth, he's an occasional fill-in for Maureen." I rolled my eyes at him, which he ignored. "And now he's checking up on me and stepping into the role of my dad."

Freaking hell, if only he knew. Right now, my thoughts were a hell of a long way removed from paternal.

Neil stuck out his hand in a lazy fashion, and I took it, barely registering. "Something like that, yeah."

Up close, Neil was even better-looking. Like a white Lenny

Kravitz. An inch or so taller than me, too. The handshake turned into a weird kind of fist bump. Even I, coming from the country that popularised them, found it a little cringey. He threw me an almost pitying look.

"Office job, yeah? One of the worker ants funding the capitalist dream, yeah? So the guys at the top in Armani suits can buy more Armani suits. Anarchy, yeah? We should get together. We should fight as brothers to overthrow fractured democratic ideologies and restore the ordinary people to their rightful place."

Fortunately, the dim lighting of Irene's living room was on my side. My boxers were Calvin's, my shirt Ralph Lauren, and my jeans Armani. Or perhaps Tom Ford. Who cared? Both pairs were similar. Tristan's temporary driver was a walking, talking, good 'ol product of the American capitalist dream.

Tristan's naughty expression said he may not have caught all of Neil's words, but he got the gist and was gonna fuck with us both. "Neil, I didn't realise you two hadn't met. This is Dominic. Dominic St—"

"Can we dance, Tristan? Like, right now? I mean, do you dance? Would you like to dance… with me? Is your dance card full? Is there room for my name on it?" A quick glance at Neil. "But just my first name, and not my surname, because then…"

Tristan casually raised his shoulder, glancing me up and down as if assessing my suitability as a capable dance partner and concluding it would be on a par with my driving. Breath snagged in my throat. "Sure," he said eventually. "This is a solid tune. Let's go."

Abandoning his canes to a suddenly disgruntled Neil, with a brisk nod of his head, Tristan allowed me to lead him all of three paces into the middle of the lounge carpet. My arm slid around his waist and stayed put, because no way would this guy take a tumble on my watch.

When assisting him into the hot tub, I chastely grasped his narrow wrists, and he grasped mine. Like a professional carer might. Here in Irene's living room, one of his hands was glued to my upper arm, and the other clasped my shirt for support. My free arm remained surgically attached to his waist.

"I warn you, I've never danced sober before!" I shouted. He grinned back.

"Why does that not surprise me?"

It proved to be a novel experience. Alcohol and clubs went hand in hand for good reasons. Hitting the bars of San Diego, with half a bottle of tequila inside me, I moved like Justin Timberlake, except twice as good-looking. Whereas limit me to a few swigs of warm beer, and I transformed into Pinocchio's even jerkier jerk of a brother. Add a tipsy deaf bloke, whose balance wasn't the greatest at the best of times, and we made quite a team.

Laughing eyes gazed up at me. "I'm wondering if you've ever danced at all!"

Not with anyone as pretty as you.

We danced close, closer than all the other couples, his head brushing against my chest, hips bumping. I didn't recognise the bass-heavy song, no doubt some ultracool British band. Not that it would have mattered. Because me and Tristan clumsily gyrated together to the beat of a very different drum. Whoever claimed dancing was the body's expression of your heart speaking... was totally wrong.

Sure, my heart was serenading him, but my freaking legs? Jeez, I'd seen better choreographed footwork in desperate queues outside a nightclub bathroom. We owned two pairs of feet between us; we might as well have been coordinating twelve.

"It's the carpet!" I yelled, bending towards his ear after stepping on his toes for, like, the hundredth time. "I'm not used to dancing on carpet."

"I can't decide what's worse, your dancing or your driving!"

Rich coming from him, but at least he had a decent excuse.

"Wait until you experience my cooking!"

CHAPTER 13
TRISTAN

Thank God Irene had dimmed the lights. A determined erection was trying to fight its way out of my jeans, and every time Dom's upper thigh brushed against my lower belly, it came a little closer to claiming victory. And this was *despite* Dominic jigging around with the grace of a hippopotamus, at least diverting our rapt audience's attention away from my own fancy footwork.

My legs felt even weaker than normal as I clutched at his strong bicep. My face sat snug against his chest. Naturally, a rich boy like him smelled fucking divine. With every bump of my nose against his expensive shirt, I inhaled a lungful of fancy washing powder mixed with fresh masculinity. His palm rested spread across my lower back like a hot brand. When I undressed later tonight, I expected to discover a hand-sized scorch mark there.

Someone flipped the music to a slow song—I'd lay money Emily had a hand in it. The bloody Spice Girls began crooning a cloying, sentimental ballad, and I snorted back a laugh. "Viva Forever."

No way would Irene ever play that in the shop, but here, the sugariness fit the moment. Taking Emily's hand and to the cheers of our friends, she dragged her into a romantic embrace in the middle of the lounge carpet. As the tempo dropped,

Dominic's chuckle rumbled through his chest, and a low and pleasant hum warmed my blood. What could have passed off as two friends dancing together—one holding the less physically abled up—had turned into a full-on, end-of-school-disco smooch.

"I haven't done this since eighth grade!" he murmured, his breath tickling my ear. "Not since Madison Miller grabbed me at the end of a Halloween party because her best friend Ashley Simpson dared her. I tried to kiss her when the song finished, and she ran away screaming."

I smiled at the humour, but there were no Madison Millers in my childhood. No fun recollections of awkward adolescent slow dances either. This one with Dominic was my very first. Some aspects of school were brutal to kids like me.

"Are you going to run away screaming, too?" He squeezed me tighter as if I might be contemplating it. "If I try the same on you?"

Considering my thoughts were refusing to line up, my answer sounded surprisingly coherent. "You may have noticed by now that running is not within my repertoire."

In a perfect world, we'd all dance in time, but this was reality, and I was at a party in the arms of a hot guy. No complaints here. We shuffled unrhythmically from side to side, and I chanced a look up. Still smiling at his fond memories with that perfect, all-American smile, Dominic had no fucking clue the only people who'd ever held me this close were my parents.

"That's good, Tristan, because I don't want you to."

His guileless eyes—hazel again tonight—locked onto mine and held. The eyes of a twenty-one-year-old college boy with the world at his feet. Maybe this dance was another way to make up for his shitty past demeanours. And, in the process, unwittingly perpetrating multiple further crimes. Because as he shuffled next to me on that ragged carpet, Dominic St. Cloud stole each of my senses, one at a time, filling them up with only him. His dark handsomeness blinded my vision, his delicious scent pervaded my nostrils, his drawling accent melted my soul. The touch of his palm at my back rendered me weak.

One sense remained. Taste. If he pinched that too, he'd own the entire set. For the sake of completeness and with an out-of-character reckless stupidity, I tilted my head up and kissed him.

Thank fuck he kissed me back.

It wasn't my first kiss, although I'd not shared many, but easily the best. Like a record stylus dropping lightly into a vinyl groove, his lips brushed softly against mine. He licked a line along my lower lip before delicately lapping at my tongue, and a tingly shiver ran from the top of my spine to the bottom. He might not have been much of a cook, a driver, or a dancer, but credit where it was due—the boy knew how to kiss.

I hadn't needed to kiss a few women to confirm I preferred men, but if any doubts lingered, then this kiss sealed the deal. Our feet stilled, pleasing my poor bruised toes. His hand, resting at my hip, slid around to join the other on my back, but higher, closing the last of the gap between our bodies and mouths, deepening the kiss. Our mouths melded. With a low noise in his throat, his featherlight touch grew into a firmer discovery.

Time passed. Geri, Sporty, and Co. stopped singing, and we pulled apart. But just a fraction. Only far enough for Dominic to line up his kiss-damp lips against my ear. "How about you and I get the fuck out of here?"

"When?" I responded because I was so fucking new to this game.

Laughing, he rocked his groin up against my belly. No misinterpreting that, even for an amateur like me.

"What do you mean when? How about right the fuck now?"

I'd watched plenty of movies; I'd read plenty of books. So I recognised the moment when the desire to ram my tongue into someone else's mouth led to an urge to clamber all over their body. As a matter of fact, that urge hit me right now.

Except, unlike in films, I had fluffy carpet, rugs, a doorstep, and a garden path to negotiate first, not forgetting the twin chores of settling myself in and out of a car. Plenty of time for Dominic to cool down and ask himself what the hell he thought he was doing. Plenty of time for me to calm down and rationalise, too. To gulp the clean night air and clear my head. To steel myself against rejection.

By the time we reached the car, my legs were ready to give out. After an evening spent standing around chatting, dancing, kissing(!), and now walking, my calf muscles complained as if a pair of gnarly cricket balls were stuffed under my skin. For the last few steps, my hip flexors joined in too, screaming their unhappiness with every jerk forwards. Which kind of killed my erection.

Dominic swung my legs into the footwell for me. Not seeking permission, not even raising a questioning eyebrow. He just fucking did it, crouched on the tarmac next to the car. Scanning my face speculatively, with gentle fingers, he pushed my hair back from my forehead. "You're a lot of fun after a glass of wine, Tristan."

"You should see me after two. I do that breakdancing thing where they drop to the ground and spin on their heads."

Leaning in, he planted a soft kiss on my lips. "And you're very pretty, too." Another kiss, this one lingering. His fingers cupped my jaw, cradling it tenderly, as if made from bone china. His other hand drifted down my calf, massaging through the denim. I stifled a moan of relief. "These feel tight, babe."

Out of jokes and out of energy, I nodded wearily. With a final kiss, he straightened and glanced up and across the quiet street before dropping his gaze back down at me. "Which means tonight I'm gonna have to see you right to your bedroom door."

I bloody fell asleep in the car. A high-risk manoeuvre with Dominic's crazy driving. God knew what near misses I'd dodged, but when he woke me with a gentle shake as we bumped down into the underground carpark, the car still intact, he looked mightily pleased with himself. "I drove down Mincing Lane!"

God, he was such a child. Rubbing my eyes, I tried to focus. "That street isn't on the way home, is it?"

"I know!" A delighted grin broke across his face. "I went the wrong way! But hey! I took a photo of the sign to send to the guys back home. How are you feeling?"

I wasn't entirely certain. Sore and confused. Tired. Horny. Wishing I had normal legs.

On reaching the level of the sub-penthouse, the lift didn't stop. Seemed he was making good on his promise. I hoped to God Frankie and Lysander were still out or had already retired for the evening. From the silence and dimness of the sitting room, I was in luck.

At my bedroom door, I turned, ready to wish Dominic an awkward goodnight. And found I didn't know the man as well as I thought.

"Nah." He shook his head and pushed open the door, ushering me through. "You don't get rid of me that easily. I'm tucking you up and giving you a goodnight kiss."

So, here's the thing. People, in general, didn't get to decide what I did and didn't do because it pissed me off. Stripped me of my sovereignty. Ableism at its very worst. From time to time, Frankie and Maddie had a go, thinking they knew better, but, on the whole, my personal space and autonomy was rarely encroached upon. So either I wasn't radiating my usual stern vibes, or Dominic had chosen to ignore them.

From the way he manoeuvred me backwards onto the bed, my canes clattering to the floor, I concluded he'd chosen to override them. And when his lips landed on mine again, I no longer cared.

CHAPTER 14
DOMINIC

I wished Tristan could see himself through my eyes. For a fleeting moment, I worried I'd gone too far by pushing him backwards onto the bed—part of me was already convinced I'd gone too far finagling my way into his bedroom. The guy radiated wariness like a San Diego summer radiated heat. But as he sleepily peeked up at me from under those fucking eyelashes, blond hair spilled across the pillow behind him and kiss-swollen lips parted, no way was I returning to my place without a little light relief first.

To cool myself down, I crawled up the bed and cupped a hand around his ankle. Lifting one of his legs a few inches into the air, I eased off his shoe and sock, tossing both onto the floor, and repeated the action with the other foot. I kneaded his calves through his jeans, gently at first and then with more vigour, trying to ignore the appreciative sex noises emanating from my sweet man's throat.

"That good, eh?"

It felt a hell of a lot more erotic than rubbing our linebacker Sam's cramp in the middle of the endzone. For a start, Tristan's calves were daintier. And Sam didn't have such goddamn pretty little feet. My advice to anyone employing calf massage as a strategy to calm the fuck down? A hard avoid. Thanks to the guttural sighs building around me, my cock was hell bent on climbing out of my shorts all by itself.

I didn't know how Tristan negotiated these things, but I'd be over or under someone by now. Not knowing how straight or spread his legs would go, I played it safe and rearranged him, so we lay side by side and faced each other. With my own leg over his hip so his knees nestled in the space created between mine, this got us close. By the time my hand snooped up the back of his shirt, we were even closer.

Stroking his knobbly spine with my thumb, I explored the corners of his mouth with my tongue. With a hell of a lot more natural rhythm than my efforts at dancing, my cock pushed up regularly against two layers of denim. All in all, things were pretty damn cosy.

"Calves better, babe?" I skimmed my lips along the sweep of his cheek. Tristan melted into the mattress, all his hard planes loose and liquid, so I reckoned I knew the answer.

We kissed a little longer, Tristan's hand content to sit on my hip. Which was all well and good, but for the last few minutes, my cock reminded me with increasing urgency it had usually joined the party by now. Abandoning his spine, I gave myself a reassuring squeeze.

"Rubbing your calves has kind of worked for my friend down here, too." I said with an apologetic laugh. "Wouldn't you know, all that pent-up hardness in your muscles has somehow transferred itself over to me."

"Yeah?" Voice breathy, gravelly, he ran his tongue over the edges of his teeth. A light mist of sweat painted his forehead, a few strands of gold plastered to it. I knew this look; my pretty man was turned on and hot as fuck.

I wasn't ready for a conversation about the mechanics of sex with Tristan. I guessed he fully functioned down there, but I needed to be certain of some details before blundering in. Google, outlining a whole spectrum of possibilities, had been no help at all. For sure, I was gonna taste the goods someday. From the second Neil laid his grubby mitt on Tristan's arm, I'd already made up my mind about that. But forewarned was forearmed. Frankly, reaching first base had been a miracle in itself, considering our inauspicious beginnings.

Tonight, unless Tristan made the moves, I'd confine my roaming to above the waist. He didn't have to, though, and a young horny guy like me had needs. Pressing needs.

Holding his fingers in mine, I unsubtly dragged his hand from my hip around to my fly. "There's a sachet of lube in my wallet, but I'm happy with spit if you are. I like it a little rough."

For a split second, Tristan looked as if he was considering pulling away. The hand gripping mine tensed; his eyes grew impossibly wider. "I'm... um... this hand isn't very good with buttons."

Not an insurmountable obstacle. "Then I guess I'll be sure to remember to wear my best loose sweatpants next time."

Nuzzling into his neck, I made chobbling sounds as though I was eating him. Giggling and squirming, the tension left Tristan's shoulders, and my own fingers made short work of my fly.

I couldn't give a flying fuck about buttons, because his fine motor skills proved just sweet and dandy around my cock. Plenty of juice kept things slick; he licked his palm, and I'd been steadily leaking like a faucet anyhow. Keeping in mind how I liked it rough, his thumb dipped into my slit like a champ, giving me a little twist on the upstrokes.

I rocked up into his fist with a moan. "I'm not gonna last, Tris. You're so fucking good at this."

I stopped kissing him to appreciate the full satisfaction of his hand on my cock and to watch his pretty face as he brought me off. His flushed cheeks and sweet breath, hot little gusts mingled with mine, showed he was almost loving it as much as me.

"You're circumcised," he whispered, almost with wonder. "God, I like the feel of that."

"And you're not?"

"No. Not many British men are."

Uncut. Dear Lord. I groaned as my cock pulsed, needy and wet. He had an *uncut* dick, a *hard* uncut dick, hidden inches away from my fingers. A rarity. A precious jewel. Fuck my plans to take it steady—I needed to find out what that felt like right now. To peel him back, expose that hidden tip and discover for myself how sensitive these mythical intact guys really were.

"Oh, God, can I see, Tristan? Would you let me see?"

His hand on my cock stuttered, bringing me back from the edge, and his eyes slid away from mine. Oh, fuck, I'd blundered straight in as usual.

"Hey, babe, it's okay." I stroked his hair back from his forehead and planted my lips against the smooth damp skin. The last thing on earth I wanted was making this sweet man feel awkward. If that meant the end of the awesome handjob, so be it. "It's okay if you don't want to. I don't mind. I was just... being me, you know? The usual, thoughtless and impulsive. I'm pushy, too pushy."

His hand, still on my cock, slid up and down the shaft, more of an absent caress than anything purposeful. But at least he hadn't let go. "I should have... we should have talked about stuff, Tristan. I guess I wanted it too badly to stop and think."

Another slow sweep up and down my shaft. This guy had some serious hand game, and I bet he hardly knew. His eyes landed back on mine, and he gave me his shy smile, the one I'd fallen for spying on him talking to folks he liked in the record shop.

"You can touch me, Dom." Letting go of my cock, he took my hand in the same way I'd taken his earlier, guiding me to the hard knot straining at the zipper of his jeans. "But this is a big deal for me, letting... letting you in so close. Much bigger than for someone like you. You need to know."

Fuck, even a crass young idiot like me realised that. Being this close to him? Touching him? A fucking privilege, one I didn't deserve. He wouldn't thank me for saying those things, though.

For once, I managed to keep my big mouth shut and simply nodded before carefully undoing his fly.

"And just so you know?" He threw me another of those bashful smiles, and my cock throbbed with need once again, "I'll apologise now if my body doesn't have the coordination to come and get you off simultaneously."

My palm found his shaft, hot and so freaking hard for me. Testing the give and slide of his slick hood, I made an involuntary noise, somewhere between a gasp of pleasure and an urgent growl. I rolled the thin satiny layer of skin up and down again, experimenting with the slippery damp glide. So freaking beautiful. "Come *and* jerk you off? Way too complicated. Right now, Tristan, my body is battling to coordinate itself to freaking breathe."

For someone allegedly struggling to jerk my cock while having his own needs tended, Tris was doing an awesome job. Who was gonna come first was a close-run thing, but I raced into the lead from the second his slick velvety tip nestled in my fist. One more pull and I spilled into Tristan's hand as if he'd tugged on a frayed edge and the whole sweater unravelled. Right after me, with one more squeeze of my palm around his slippery hood, Tris tipped over the edge, too, curling in on himself and crying out with a tiny note of something fucking glorious, even wringing a few more drops from me. I smothered the noise in a kiss, babbled a load of embarrassing shit about how freaking delicious he looked, and then we were both done. Thank God, because my eyes had rolled back into my head and my lungs threatened to implode.

"You good, Tris?" Panting, I lurched to an elbow. "Are you comfortable?"

He nodded, chest heaving, and arms flung across his face, pancaked in the middle of the bed like he might never rise from it again. I grabbed us some tissues, wiping his hand for him and giving an impersonal quick one around his shrivelled dick as if I didn't want to turn the overhead light on and study it properly.

He barely stirred, his eyes shut tight. Oh, fuck, were we gonna be awkward now?

"Are you sure, Tris? Are you sure I can't get you anything?"

Rousing himself, a weary but contented smile climbed his cheeks. Thank God. He shook his head. "I'm good. Really good. Just…tired."

One eye opened too, but only a fraction, like he was in the mood to sleep for three years. I'd have been happy to watch over him. A big deal, he'd said. Exposing himself, opening himself up to someone. And I was going to respect that. So instead of lying back down again and cuddling up, a hitherto unexplored mature portion of my brain told me it was time to take my leave. And surprisingly, the rest of my brain took note.

CHAPTER 15
TRISTAN

Things I liked about the penthouse: part 8. On Sunday mornings, I had space to laze in bed, snug in my ironic Scooby Doo onesie (thank you, Maddie), and wank myself to death. Without fear of interruption. My bedroom door also had a lock, so for an added bonus, I didn't need to bother with hearing aids.

Despite last night's spectacular orgasm, I was horny again and indulged enthusiastically, eyes screwed tight, trying to recapture the sensation of Dominic's thick knob in my hand and the emotions running across his face as he came. Putting him in that state myself already made the evening stellar. But then he'd held me, too, vigorously bringing me to climax, not caring when my hips spasmed into flexion at the end, trapping his wrist in an awkward position. He'd just kissed away my panic, told me my eyes were gorgeous—again—and cleaned us both up. The non-nonsense ending, followed by him sneaking out, had been much appreciated. My head was overloaded already. Chat and cuddles and promises of more would have made it explode.

With most of Sunday gone (some days I liked to lay around in bed—don't judge me) and my sexual needs temporarily satisfied, I emerged, blinking, into the land of the living to forage for food. Frankie was cuddled up to a snoozing Lysander on one of the sofas, a tidy pile of folders and a row of highlighter pens within reach on the coffee table.

"Afternoon." With a half-hearted wave, I shambled on.

"Hey."

I stopped in my tracks. Since when did Frankie say 'hey?' More to the point, since when had he developed an American accent? And not just *any* American accent, but a low growly one that turned my knees to jelly and managed to stretch that single syllable, banal greeting into a smoky invitation to let my imagination run wild?

I raised my eyes from the floor, and there he was. God's favourite son, in all his grey sweatpant-ed, white Henley-shirted, frat boy glory, sprawled opposite Frankie and Lysander. Long legs casually draped over the arm of the sofa and exceedingly pleased with himself.

Around this moment, I remembered I was still shrouded in my Scooby Doo onesie.

"Finally!" Frankie chided. "We've been waiting for you and your expertise to finalise the wedding reception playlist. Dom suggested we throw a little Spice Girls into the mix—to give it a retro vibe and get everyone on their feet. What do you think?

Goodness me, onesies could be hot and itchy. *I think I'd like to go back to bed.*

"Can't you leave that up to the DJ to judge?" I muttered.

"I think you know me a little better than that."

Frankie being Frankie, demanding everything done yesterday, had fixed the wedding date for six weeks' time. Not because he worried Lysander was having second thoughts, but because the usual obstacles of cash and finding a suitable available and affordable venue weren't a problem for the wealthy St. Clouds. And my brother had his wedding day planned down to the last teaspoon since he'd kneeled on the floor as a young boy, playing husband and husband with Action Man and Ken. As much as he enjoyed overseeing the minutiae and making us suffer, in reality all he had to do was hit the launch button.

Sighing, he rolled his eyes at Dominic. "We won't get anything out of him until he's had a cup of tea. I can be patient, Tristan. Your lack of enthusiasm will not diminish my zest for this wedding."

Ferocious glares were difficult to pull off dressed up as Scooby Doo. Chances of styling this out? Zero. Why the hell did Frankie's détente with Dominic have to bloody start now?

Escaping to the kitchen, I made myself a cuppa, churlishly not offering anyone else one. As I waited for the kettle to boil, I plotted a convoluted, heroic route back to my bedroom which avoided the living room. Needless to say, trekking via the utility room, the dining room balcony, the spare bedroom balcony and the spare bedroom, while balancing a cup of tea and two slices of toast and marmalade, did not play to my strengths.

"Hey, do you want me to carry those for you?"

Captain America leaned casually against the kitchen doorframe. Resolutely, I met his gaze, because if I stared any lower, it would be at the outline of his dick in those damned grey sweatpants. A dick I'd held in my hand last night, rocking my vintage Stone Roses T-shirt and not my, you know, comfiest ancient *loungewear*.

"Uh, yeah. Thanks."

He swept up the mug from the counter but, instead of leading us back to the living room, blocked my path, his grin stretching from ear to ear. "So this is what the cool kids look like on their day off."

"What can I say? I'm a flamingo in a flock of pigeons."

Chuckling, Dominic tucked back my hair. I fucking loved it when he did that, and couldn't help a small smile. "You're freaking adorable, Tristan, that's what you are."

"Freaking adorable and horribly embarrassed. What the hell are you doing here?"

"Helping with wedding preparation, of course! Letting your brother see what a thoughtful, mature, enthusiastic guy I am. And checking that I didn't overstep with my favourite ray of sunshine last night."

Before I realised his intention, he silenced my thoughts with a kiss, the briefest sweep of his lips before pulling away. His decadent gaze dropped to my mouth, and he gave a quick decisive nod. "No, I didn't. I thought not."

For many years, my biggest concern about sex, quite simply, was whether I would ever experience it. In my mind, this was a totally legitimate question but one I had no clear answer to, only hope. Since last night, however, and from the hungry looks Dominic threw my way as I painstakingly created a playlist meeting Frankie's exacting standards, I'd taken a big leap forward. Sex was now on the table.

I imagined most people were unsure and insecure their first time, but I had additional concerns thanks to my CP. Would I be able to do everything? What if I needed a wee halfway through? What if I developed spasms or cramps in the middle of it?

Well, I'd spasmed towards the end of the handjob, exactly like I had wanking in bed this morning, in private—I normally did—but Dominic hadn't cared. I had needed to wee last night afterwards, too, rather urgently as it happened, but Dominic left before I'd been forced to mention it.

Bottoming would be easiest. Fortunately, when I watched porn, I always got off imagining myself receiving. Dominic was bi, so I hoped a preference for topping extended to his male partners too. And bottoming wouldn't put my fine motor skills to the test with a condom in front of an audience. My right hand was fine, my left less so. Although Dominic knew as much now anyhow.

Another niggling concern had nothing to do with the physicality and logistics. *Feelings*. Inconveniently, I'd developed a considerable store of them for Dominic. More sex with him would add to their number. The guy was gauche. He jumped straight into everything, feet first—left feet at that. He was brash, loud, and clumsy. He drove the Lexus like a three-year-old at the peak of a sugar rush, oh my God. And did I mention his youth? Five years younger than me. The guy already had plenty under his belt, but if my brother and my friends were any yardstick, then he was still warming up, collecting notches on his bed post.

Sure, he wanted me now. His blown autumnal eyes and his hard dick in my hand made that extremely obvious last night. But in a month's time? Two months? Three? Before I knew it, he'd be back in the US, and I'd be trying to muster up enthusiasm for a man like Neil while attempting to blank out Lysander's regular updates on Dominic's latest sexcapade.

Oh, and had I mentioned the guy was about to become my brother-in-law?

So, yeah, feelings. If only I had someone I could ask for advice.

After ruminating, I acknowledged I had several someones. Strictly speaking, three, but one was out of town (Mungo). One was of the wrong sex and generation. Maureen would confront Dom over his intentions towards me and finish by quizzing us both about the new scuff to the Lexus's right rear bumper. Frankie and Maddie didn't count—their advice came unsolicited at all hours of the day and night anyhow, and I had no desire to share the ins and outs of my sex life with either of them.

Which left shrewd, calculating Milo.

On Monday morning, I slipped into the Lexus as nonchalantly as possible. Which, with my legs, meant not very nonchalantly at all. Maureen eyed my blank face with suspicion.

"How was the party? Was that Neil there? Please tell me you didn't go home with him. Beware the thin-lipped man, that's what Shakespeare said."

"I have a degree in English Lit., Maureen. I'm pretty sure he didn't." As she pulled away from the kerb, I fastened my seatbelt and pretended to be engrossed in my phone.

"And don't you give me that look, young man. You know I'm right about him."

"Who, Shakespeare?"

Maureen had eyes in the sides of her head, never mind the

back. And a voodoo doll of poor Neil. I agreed with her about his lips, though. On Saturday, I'd studied them as he droned on about energy-saving kinetic dance floors. They were like a knife slash. Unenticing. Whereas a certain other young man had lips I could...

"Oh Lord. You did, didn't you? You're looking right pleased with yourself this morning."

The remembered taste of Dominic's mouth scurried through my belly, and I almost giggled. "Yes, Neil was at the party and no, I didn't go home with him. At the end of the evening, I went back to my own home."

We slowed for a set of traffic lights, and Maureen briefly took her eyes off the road. As a casual throwaway, I added, "Dominic gave me a lift. You know, Lysander's brother, who helped out when you were in Ireland."

"Did he give you more than a lift? He did, didn't he?"

"Bloody hell, Maureen! Get right to it, why don't you?"

"But did he?"

Oh my God, I was sharing my sex life with someone's grandma. "Yes, as a matter of fact he did. The lights are on green, by the way."

The car didn't move. Someone behind us beeped their horn. "Young man. The lights could be flashing pink-and-yellow hearts at me right now for all I care. You cannot spring news like that on me before eight o'clock in the morning! Did you take precautions? Do I need to have a talk with you about wrapping the postman up in parcel tape before he uses the letterbox?"

For fuck's sake. "The lights are still on green, Maureen."

"Yours better hadn't have been. Not without taking a copy of his full medical records first. You keep him dangling on amber, young man, until you can be sure of his intentions."

When I arrived at work, a mug depicting the stars and stripes of the American flag was parked alongside my Little Lord Fauntleroy mug. Tom Petty blasted out "American Boy" through the shop sound system. Bastards.

I told myself there was nothing unusual about texting Milo to see if he was free for a drink after work. We did this together sometimes. He could always be relied on to tell it to me straight. We met in a grotty pub around the corner from the record shop. Neil brought me here a couple of times. Drinkers of all shapes and sizes wandered in and out of this place, so I felt comfortable.

"I do think Dominic is rather tasty, flower. I've decided to forgive him."

"He'll be thrilled to hear, I'm sure."

Milo put his hand over my wrist, fluttering his eyelashes at me. He hammed it up in public. "But I shan't fight you for him. I like my men like I like my tea: hot and British."

I almost pointed out Mungo was hot and British, but then I'd have had to listen to ten minutes of him claiming Mungo would only ever be his best pal, when every man and his dog knew that wasn't the case.

"And I'm so glad Dominic's rescued you from a lifetime of purgatory," he drawled after we'd ordered a vodka tonic each. Milo sipped his through a straw, hollowing his cheeks suggestively at the good-looking barman, just because he could.

"Although Neil will be dreadfully disappointed when he finds out," he continued. "He had designs on you and him conquering climate change together, one bowl of organic quinoa at a time." Pursing his lips with disdain, he added, "He always puts me in mind of a chap hoarding a top drawer full of bandanas."

Neil liked nothing more than to tie his culturally misappropriated dreadlocks back with a colourful bandana, but the poor guy had received enough of a hammering today already, so I let it pass.

"Can we talk about Dominic please? This is kind of important."

Milo eyed me shrewdly. Underneath the drama hid a solid, dependable friend.

"I'm... um... planning on having sex with him. Real sex. You know."

Yep, he knew. Was thoroughly, thoroughly acquainted with the subject. Which was why he was a good choice for this little tête à tête. My face burned, but I ploughed on anyhow. I couldn't do this on my own; I had no frame of reference. If a manual existed for gay men with CP having sex with their future brother-in-law, I hadn't unearthed it yet.

"Okay." His voice was brisk. "Define sex. Just so we're on the same page here."

"You know." God, was he really going to make me spell it out? "Sex. Clothes off. Um… penetration. Probably." *Hopefully.*

Blushing furiously, I outlined Saturday night. Frankie and he used to have thorough debriefs like this all the time, without a shred of embarrassment. I was rapidly discovering I was not my brother.

"I'm struggling to see the problem." Milo paused. "Unless he…doesn't want to have sex with you?"

I could list a million problems, starting with the physiological and logistical ones and finishing by pointing out the hundreds of thousands of gay men in London Dominic could choose from, the vast majority of whom didn't have CP and were probably uncircumcised too.

Instead, I threw him a helpless look as he took a long draught of his drink. "Although from the way he pandered to your needs at dinner, I'm fairly certain he's game."

My cheeks heated. "I'm fairly certain he is too. We… um… kind of established that on Saturday night. And he wasted his entire afternoon yesterday helping Frankie with wedding planning, in the hope I might put in an appearance. If that's any indication."

"Then he must be totally besotted. I'm still struggling to see any issues, flower. Unless it's because of your cerebral palsy."

"No. It isn't. Not entirely, anyhow."

I loved the way Milo happily pronounced *cerebral palsy*, without hesitation or hedging. Not a lot of people managed that. And I loved that he hadn't assumed all my reservations stemmed from my CP either. Because, as if my disabilities weren't enough to contend with, I had insecurities about other mundane stuff too, like most people. Such as being too fem, or the reactions of big straight men when they found out I was gay, or that my dick was too small, or my hair thinning.

"First of all, he could be going back to the US in a few weeks, and I... I don't want to fall for him, but I really want to have sex with him. Separating the two is hard. But I've never done much with anyone before, and I feel this is my chance."

As he nodded at me thoughtfully, the twink giving the come-on to the barman faded. The analytical smart lawyer took over. "To summarise: so far, you have played around together, and you feel sufficiently comfortable with him to have anal. Bottoming to begin with, I presume?"

My gaze darted around the bar. "Um... yeah. If that's something I can do. I'm not very... um... flexible, and I don't know whether my spasms will behave, so we might have to try other things too."

"Trust, flower. If there is a will, then there's always a way."

"Yes, I know. I think it will be fine, actually. But if not, then we can... do... um... other stuff..."

A naughty grin split Milo's elfin features. "Sometimes the other stuff is just as good, if not better." Like a bank manager about to lay out my mortgage options, he clasped his hands together and leaned forward. "Are you worried about explaining all that to him?

"No." I didn't hesitate. "Not anymore. He's seen me in the hot tub anyway, so he's seen most of my body already. We've become quite close."

And there lay the real problem. I'd had in mind an uncomplicated interlude. Popping my cherry with some good sex and then waving Dominic off on his way. But it wasn't to be. Sex with me could never *be* casual, from negotiating a flight of stairs up to a man's bedroom to explaining why I couldn't straighten my legs out or hook them around his waist. By default, I'd have to feel close to whoever I had sex with, leaving my heart exposed with a person who might not necessarily feel the same way. Hoping they wouldn't move on to the next, just because they could. Especially when that person was twenty-one and a temporary British resident.

After a fortifying swig of vodka, I blurted all this out to Milo.

"Unfortunately, you're suffering from a severe case of honest feelings and bad timing. A painful combination. You're worrying that when he goes back to the US, you'll be left heartbroken? Yes?"

"I don't know about heartbroken, but yeah, something along those lines." I nodded with relief. Typical Milo—guaranteed to spear the heart of it. His clinical, practical approach lessened my embarrassment by the second; we could almost have been discussing a shake-up of my fantasy football squad. "It's not just his looks. Dominic is funny, too. And I trust him to... to see me like that. Which is a big deal. And the real pisser is that when it's all over, he'll still be in my life—on the periphery anyhow. Because he's bloody Lysander's favourite brother."

"I know, flower."

Milo didn't do tender, but I was almost the recipient of something approximating it. He swirled the melting ice at the bottom of his glass. "For what it's worth, in my opinion, you should just go for it. Let the guy fuck your brains out. Enjoy everything he has to offer."

"I think you missed the bit where I said I'd end up very fond of him and then he'll be going back to the US?"

"Nope, I got it." A dramatic pause while he finished his drink and crunched the ice cubes. A mischievous curve played at his lips. "You haven't asked yourself the vital question, flower. But I think you know the answer anyway. Is the lemon worth the squeeze? Is sex and fun times with Dominic worth the misery after he's gone?" He lifted a shoulder carelessly. "Sounds like it to me. Dominic roots, shoots, then leaves? Fine. Enjoy. And we'll deal with the fallout later."

He threw me a full-on, naughty grin. "At times in a queer

man's life, Tristan, he's not looking for a relationship. We're programmed differently to everyone else. I don't know about you, but I'm not expecting a mortgage, two kids, and a pension scheme out of every guy I hook up with. A blowjob and a couple of orgasms will do just fine."

A valid point, although to be fair, even if I'd been straight, I'd never have assumed any of those. "So what are you saying? Neighbours with benefits?"

"Absolutely! I'm saying, my darling, sometimes we want nothing more than to go out and get our arses licked by a hot masc guy." He spread his arms expansively. "So why don't you put on your big-boy pants—and then take them off, obvs—and dive into this with the express aim of getting your rocks off? Make riding his dick your daily work out. Forget about the future. Do it for fun. Not for feelings or relationships or any of the other Hallmark heterosexual bullshit."

On a roll, his hand landed on my arm. "Dom's a hot bloke. You're a hungry flower. What have you got to lose? Neighbours with benefits. Park the rest for now, and, as I said, we'll scrape up the pieces afterwards. If there's any left by the time he's ploughed you into the mattress. You're rather scrawny, Tristan."

CHAPTER 16
DOMINIC

Thinks I hated about living in London: locating eggs for breakfast. Eggs are inexplicably not refrigerated and hidden in the regular food aisle of the grocery store next to the fucking yeast and some black, tar-like sticky shit called Marmite. Wtf?

A week passed without seeing Tristan. I didn't want our unexpected makeout session in bed to be a one-off, and after I'd kissed him in the kitchen, I'd got the impression he didn't either. Regularly, I reminded myself we had zero future and I shouldn't let this thing between us grow into more. And then pushed that thought aside every time I replayed the wet slide of his delicious cock in my hand.

We'd texted, at least. He'd been cautious at first and then more often. He had a Twitter following of several thousands (not that I was stalking his social media). I wasn't surprised; his pithy one-liners had fast become the highlight of my day.

I thought about him plenty, but my aunt Pauline had a deadline to meet, bidding for a large plot of land outside of a town named Cholmondeley, not pronounced remotely how it was spelled, and we were all hands on deck. *Proper preparation prevented piss-poor performance.* Pauline's mantra. Every detail of the financial report was scrutinised and considered from every conceivable angle. Her divorce from my uncle Paul (marrying him arguably the only wrong calculation she'd ever made) ran down similar lines, and he still whinged about the settlement to his lawyers even now.

Her pernickety approach could be a result of wisdom and experience. For all I knew, when she was my age, she ran around Marble Arch naked, belting out hits from her favourite musicals. I doubted it, somehow. The woman's every move was calculated to bring about desired results, but people could be surprising.

In complete contrast, my own life unfolded as a series of unexpected events, several of them unfortunate. Looking back, many had been a slow car crash waiting to happen. The fire truck incident, for example. A spoiled, out-of-control, moneyed brat thinking he could do whatever the hell he liked. My arrogant, entitled behaviour towards Tristan that first time we met. The latest plot twist, however—losing my heart to him—I hadn't seen coming at all.

"How do you like to spend your free time, Dominic?"

Pauline's brusque tones dragged me back to the here and now. We were journeying north, to Cholmondeley, which everyone insisted on calling 'Chumlee'. It had taken me forty-eight hours of working on the project to realise they were one and the same.

For the first half of the trip, she'd gone through some aspects of the bid I hadn't understood. When we weren't discussing the project, we bitched about Paul's misdemeanours and very little else. How I amused myself out of hours had never come up.

I searched for a suitable, mature response. *Crafting what I hoped were terribly witty texts to a guy, with the header Dear Rumpleforeskin? Pondering how I could persuade said guy to have more sex with an immature idiot like me? Deleting every Coldplay track from my Spotify playlist and replacing them with some random cool shit to impress him when I invited him over?*

"Um… I like sports, I guess? Swimming?"

"I expect you are making the most of the London nightlife, aren't you? I remember those days. Out until four and hauling myself into the office five hours later stinking of alcohol and cigarette smoke."

Okay, so maybe my Marble Arch theory wasn't wide of the mark.

"Um... a little?" Tristan's breathy, high-pitched moan as he spilled into my hand flooded my brain, and my cheeks turned red. "But not as much as I thought. I've been... um... hanging out with Frankie's brother?"

She beamed at me. "Oh, well, if he's anything like the lovely Frankie, then I'm sure you'll be having a blast. Lysander was telling me he's one of triplets!"

I hadn't yet been exposed to Frankie's lovely side, but I waited in hope; his attitude towards me had promisingly shifted from permafrost to lukewarm. "Yeah, Tristan looks like Frankie, but... um... he's different. He has cerebral palsy, so his mobility isn't very good. His life is a little quieter. He works in a record shop. He's... nice."

"Oh, yes, I think Lysander has mentioned him once or twice. Talking of Lysander, has he given you some input into the pay scale comparison report?"

Small talk over. The minutiae of pensionable contributions and tax-deductible benefits in kind took over the next half-hour. During conversations like these, I felt way out of my depth, as if I'd gone from bouncing on my mother's knee to a Wall Street trading pit, skipping college altogether.

But, as we went along, Pauline patiently explained everything to me.

"When you take your seat on the board, you'll find that, at Cloud Ten, we're happy to cross-check each other's stats and figures on bigger acquisitions. It's time-consuming and hard work, but that way we minimise errors and have the advantage of in-house second and even third opinions. That's assuming you will want to take your seat on the board after finishing college, of course."

"Yes. Yes I do."

Wow. Where the fuck had that come from? Was I just sweet-talking my way into her good books, saying the right things? Or was it because I'd caught Tristan eyeing up the suit and wanted to wear it more?

I pondered that for a second. No, although he could eye me up in a suit all he wanted (strip me out of it too). But right now, poring over the incentive remuneration and bonus packages for subcontractors in Cholmondeley, Cloud Ten was what I wanted. My life's direction of travel. With one glaring exception.

I'd take my seat on the board one day, but when I did, it wouldn't be how the fam planned it. Not as a sniping silent partner like Cousin John and not dumped in my lap like Lysander.

"Pauline, don't you think it's wrong how someone like me has open access to step right into the top of this company, whereas other folks claw their way toward the top and often never make it? Just because my name happens to be St. Cloud?"

She side-eyed me thoughtfully. "Yes, of course. It's morally wrong and abhorrent on every level, and it shouldn't happen. If it was up to me, I'd have you emptying the bins and scrubbing the floors for six months."

Huh. I supposed it was my fault for asking a question I didn't already know the answer to.

"But that's the way a limited company, family firm works," she continued. "And one of its strengths, as well as a potential weakness. Despite the ups and downs, we're a tightknit team, because we mostly only allow family to sit on the board."

"Weren't you tempted to leave when you got divorced?"

Pauline shook her head. "No way. I spent five years in the secretarial pool before I became a PA, let alone a director. Attended night school, wasted countless sunny weekends studying for exams. Missed out on having children. And just to be clear, nepotism didn't get me my seat on the board. I made it this far despite being married to your uncle, not because of him."

"This is exactly what I mean." I nodded rapidly. "Next to that sort of effort, I feel like a fraud when I put on this suit every morning."

"Good! That gives Daphne and I hope for the future. You're very pleasant and smart, Dominic, for a pampered over-privileged child, but it irks me that you don't have to graft the hard way. And probably irks all the folk on the lower rungs too. Gaining their respect will be ten times harder."

Not one to mince her words, my Aunt Pauline. She hadn't been born a St. Cloud, but she fitted right in. "Is that how you feel about Lysander, too? Is that how everyone feels?"

She shrugged. "Lysander was always going to be an asset, from his previous career and life experiences. He just didn't know it. And he was older than you. Wiser. He already knew the meaning of strive. You're going to have to work twice as hard to prove your mettle."

I was about to sound like a turkey voting for Thanksgiving. "After I finish my business degree, I want to join the company. But... at the bottom. Do you think the family will let that happen?"

She smiled. "I don't know. But have you come up with an idea for your presentation yet? Daphne takes the ideas suggested by the interns very seriously because it's an opportunity to hear the views of someone experiencing the firm with fresh, youthful eyes. Usually, the interns offer tech or social media angles us oldies haven't considered, but you could put a more personal slant on it."

I got back from Cholmondeley with barely time to shower, then raced around the apartment trying to create a state of cool professional sophistication instead of the college-boy dump it had morphed into. Satisfied, I invited Tristan over for takeout via text message. In the six days since I'd had my hand on his cock, his breathy moans had looped around my head like a Taylor Swift earworm, and I had an urgent need to hear the rest of the album.

At my door buzzer, the caterpillars crawling in my belly metamorphosed into full-grown butterflies. I made myself count to ten before opening up. He was wrapped in his fur hooded parka jacket and woollen beanie, as cute as a bug's ear and twice as charming.

"Hi." He lingered shyly on the threshold, with his messenger bag swung across his small frame and a couple of cans of beer poking out. Through all his damned hair, two damned aqua eyes peeked up at me.

"Hey." I took the bag, lightening his load. Boy, we'd travelled a long way. I helped him off with the heavy parka, too. "I know I invited you to slum it in the sub-penthouse, but us folks on the lesser levels do have heating installed, you know."

Shuffling forwards, he gave me a sheepish grin. "I... er... I told Frankie I was going out with work friends. So I had to look the part."

"What, instead of admitting you had a hot date with public enemy number one?"

He shook his head with amusement. "What, we're dating now, are we? That wasn't mentioned in the text."

"Sure, honey, we're dating," I drawled in my best Californian surfer accent. "Treat me good and I'll be your guy for prom night, too."

Cheekily, and ignoring his squeal of protest, I tugged the beanie off his head and jammed it down onto my own, leaving his hair all kinds of mussed. With his hands occupied by his sticks, someone had to smooth it down for him. I accompanied the gesture with a quick peck on the cheek, which had him blushing even more and me dancing around him even more clumsily than usual.

"Get off me, you big quarterbacker or linebacker or whatever overgrown sporting position you Americans have invented. I'm going to end up on my arse." His eyes darted around my living room. "Surprisingly tidy. In my mind I had you wading through piles of laundry and dirty dishes."

"It's a good thing you weren't here twenty minutes earlier. I always thought clothes picked themselves up. Turns out it was my mom all along! Who'd have thought?"

I fussed around him as he settled onto the sofa, parking his sticks within easy reach, and hanging up his jacket. "But seriously. The subterfuge with Frankie. Why didn't you tell him?"

Tristan shrugged. "Maybe because I like to have things in my life him and Maddie don't know about? Just because I live with him and he likes to overshare doesn't mean I do. Did you tell Lysander about... er... you know, the other night?"

"No," I answered honestly. "Because I'd get a lecture. I don't think he trusts me enough yet not to fuck up around you. He's seen we've mended our bridges, and that's enough for him. I suspect Frankie feels the same?"

That bought me another eyeroll. "What Frankie feels is beside the point. His opinion on you and me is irrelevant. Although he'd offer it, all the same. Then Maddie would give her ha'penny worth too. I don't need the aggro."

"Nice that they care, though."

"Yes, I suppose. But they like to interfere too. Being a triplet is like having two people walking around with the nuclear codes for making me mad." He let out a long sigh. "And anyhow. You're here for a few weeks longer and then going back. Not much to talk about anyway, is there? We're hardly planning a long-term future and setting up home together. Or even dating, to be honest."

So this had suddenly taking a depressing path I hadn't planned on strolling down. He was right, of course, and I'd drawn the same conclusion myself. We had no future, unless brothers-in-law on separate continents counted, at least while I finished my studies. I had another couple of years left if I wanted to follow my degree with a business masters.

All the same, thinking about it sucked.

"Right," I said brightly, plonking myself next to him. "I'll pretend I didn't hear all that. Let's make the most of what we have. I thought for our *second date*, we'd have Thai takeout, Netflix, and kissing."

"In that order?" A cute little pout crept across his face.

"I freaking hope not."

So we didn't get our money's worth out of my Netflix subscription. I mean, some shit was playing in the background, but at knifepoint I wouldn't have been able to recollect what. Because I was cuddled up to Tristan on the sofa, and we were fully dressed and necking like teenagers, as if our parents were out at work. And surprisingly, it was… enough.

"You have the softest, squishiest skin."

For some reason—me goofing around—our necking had extended to me shoving my head up his T-shirt and blowing raspberries on his belly. So classy.

"As compliments go, Dominic, that… um… isn't one?" He was amused, nonetheless.

"Aah, that's where you're wrong, babe." My voice muffled, I rubbed my nose in the dip under his ribcage. He smelled divine, like a slice of my mom's homecooked apple pie. "You're like the most satiny, velvety bedsheets money can buy. Fresh out the wrapper. Not like me, who's spent too many years already under the SoCal sun. They'll be able to make a leather sofa out of me when I'm dead."

"My mum used to hate it when I was younger."

Reluctantly, I stopped sniffing and pulled his T-shirt back down.

"My soft skin, I mean." His lips curved in a gentle smile. "I've never told anyone that before."

I waited for him to carry on, my head still resting on his soft belly.

"After I broke my ankle a few years ago, I spent some time recuperating with my parents. My mum got all the old family photos out, as parents are wont, and we went through a few million albums."

"She sounds as if she'd get on well with my mom. She's even kept a picture of my first dry diaper."

His tummy rippled underneath me as he chuckled. "I was a late developer, for obvious reasons. I learned to walk much later than Frankie and Maddie, and to talk too. Which meant that when we were around three or four, they would be zipping all over the place, getting into everything, and I would be sitting in my highchair, or a special beanbag thing we had, watching them."

I pressed my lips to the back of his hand. His skin was like melting butter there too. "And my mum hated it. Because those two would end the days covered in scratches and bruises and scabs. Their clothes would be filthy, but I'd still be as pristine as when she'd dressed me that morning. Like a doll. And she hated it, because she wished I could have the life they were living."

"Does she still?"

He shook his head. "No, not now. Not for a long time. When we were teens, Maddie was the most annoying monosyllabic creature on the planet, and Frankie thought he was God's gift to everyone. She used to say she'd exchange them both any day for two more like me. She still does occasionally."

He leaned down and kissed my mouth. "I'm happy most of the time. Don't feel sorry for me. I've always been this way, and I don't know any different."

I kissed his hand again. "I wouldn't want you any other way." So that was awkward. And a little heavy too. "Sorry, just me and my size twelves making you uncomfortable. I bet there are twenty different ways you'd prefer me."

Tristan peeked down at me, his upper lip curling into the hint of a smile. "No, this version is good."

Changing the subject, he asked me how the week with Pauline had gone. And that moved onto more talk about my internship and my presentation. Our food arrived. Suddenly realising we were both ravenous, we tucked in, not bothering with setting the table, but spreading it out on the floor at our feet. Everything was much simpler if we shared a plate and I fed Tristan. Which in itself was more straightforward if he sat in my lap. And he was still sitting there after we'd hoovered up all the food because what was the point of moving?

"I've never done this before," I observed.

We'd talked half the night away, which meant I'd have hell to pay with Pauline tomorrow, but it had been worth it. The heavier our eyelids, the more the words tumbled out, the more stories we exchanged, and the more hopes and dreams we shared. Tristan stayed drowsily sprawled across my lap, his face perfectly positioned for me to regularly drop my lips down onto his. I never wanted the evening to end.

"What? Pigged out on the sofa? Because you're very good at it for a beginner."

That comment earned him a tickle. "No, but you're right. I'm an expert at that. I meant this." I waved my hand over us both. "Just talking and kissing. It's… it's good."

I hesitated, wondering if I was bold enough to ask. "Do you want to stay the night? I don't expect anything else," I added hastily. "And I've got to be up in five hours, so we should probably get some sleep."

Said no horny twenty-one-year-old ever. Where the hell did that come from?

Tristan stretched a little in my lap, as loose-limbed as his flexed joints allowed. We'd spent some time rearranging cushions to find the most comfortable position—so comfortable, in fact, he was nearly asleep. Reaching up to my mouth, he traced a line with his thumb across my bottom lip, half-lidded gaze catching me right in the balls. "Thank you. I'd like that."

Some bed partners managed to hop in and out or slide around under the sheets with scarcely a ripple of the mattress. My Tristan wasn't quite so agile. He'd put in his hearing aids quietly enough, but silently shuffling his misbehaving body around to face me in order to conduct an exploratory journey with his tongue down my chest, not so much.

Not that I was gonna grumble. While his teeth tugged on my nipple piercing like the whole point of their freaking existence was to turn me on, his hand learned the contours of my belly. I sighed, long and happy. I didn't give a flying fuck about banking five hours of solid sleep if Tris was going to wake me up in this manner after only four.

"Keep going, babe."

His knuckles brushed against my shaft, then scurried away, like it was accidental. So damned cute. The second time, I dropped a subtle hint by pushing down first the duvet and then my boxer briefs, freeing my cock with a happy bounce. All hot and shiny and ready to play, it pointed straight up my belly, demanding attention. Staring at it like he'd never seen one before, Tristan's hands and mouth stilled. His warm exhale ghosted over the sensitive head, and I flexed, making it twitch.

"You're looking like you want to find out what it tastes like."

Tristan's pools of blue flicked up at me through a cloud of hair. A sweet shade of pink blossomed across his cheeks. "Yes." And flushed some more. All throaty with sleep, he sounded like a freaking porn star. "Can I?"

One of his hands disappeared inside the waistband of his boxers like he was squeezing himself, and my cock twitched again, without me putting in any effort. A pearl of precum glistened at the end, and Tris eyed it like the last one in a box of his favourite chocolates. I huffed out a sound caught between a laugh and a groan of freaking delight and gave it a long, lascivious pull, then clasped my hands behind my head, giving him a free rein.

"Babe, you never need to ask."

With a hand holding me still, he bent over my cock and licked that drop off like I was made of glass. And the one that took its place and the one after that. And then he followed that tiny torture up with a gazillion soft kisses all around my slit, making a sound in his throat as though it tasted even better than his favourite chocolate. Like he was worshipping the thing.

I nearly shot my load right then, all over my belly. And to make it even freaking wilder, from the rustling down below, he was bringing himself off too. The image of that baggy foreskin getting tighter and tighter as he shuttled it up and down, along with him dipping his tongue into my slit and swirling it around as if scooping up the last melted ice cream from the bottom of a cone, had me arching off the bed like the frigging Golden Gate Bridge.

"Jesus!"

His mouth popped off the end in alarm. "Is that okay? Did I hurt you?"

"No, babe, no, you... no. Christ, no."

Lips all wet and glistening, his greedy mouth smacked down on my cock again, swallowing a bit more this time. Such a hot, wet, thirsty heat, such a slow, teasing glide. Who the fuck taught him to suck cock this good? One lucky son of a bitch, that's who.

Around my root, his fist began a steady jerk in time to the action of his mouth. Urgently, I brought my hands down, rapidly winding my fingers through the waves of his long hair. Not to push him deeper, but to knock him off so I didn't come right that second. As I tugged, he made a little moan. "Pull it harder," he said around my knob, hardly breaking rhythm. "Feels nice."

Oh Jesus. About two more jerks, one more hollowing of his cheeks, one more of those freaking low moaning sounds, and a pathetic collapsing arch off the bed, and I exploded like a Fourth of July firework. Jizz all over the place. No warning. No buildup in my balls. Just freaking spewing everywhere. Like shooting stars, clinging to his hair, spraying over his face, across my belly. Some of it down his throat. Then, as he clumsily knelt up, grabbing my shoulder for support, some more splattered over my chest. Shooting out of him, not me.

Jesus, I was doomed.

CHAPTER 17

TRISTAN

Things I liked about living in the penthouse: part 9. My amazing brother, who put up with me cramping his style at school, at uni, and even now. But don't tell him I said so.

Frankie loitered in my bedroom doorway, cashmere overcoat in hand. Him and Lysander were off to a charity gig in Oxford and staying the night. He looked good—he had an eye for colour and the sort of skinny, angular frame made for a well-fitted suit. Not that I was going to offer that compliment, of course. "Lysander asked Dom to pop up later, just to check you have everything you need. He can drop by in the morning, too, if you like."

Guilt pulsed through me, until I reminded myself that telling him about Dominic and me would be akin to posting an advert in a national newspaper. He'd question whether I'd lost my mind and be late for his event. Instead, I threw him the kind of look invented exclusively for siblings.

"No need for that!" he chided. "Trust me, this is Lysander's doing. I couldn't give a shit if you fell arse over tit, bashed your head on the edge of the dining table, and spent the night on the floor in an unconscious stupor."

I kept my eyes glued to the TV, trying not to smile.

"But, bizarrely, Lysander does. And anyhow, it's good for you to spend some time getting to know Dom. He was fun last weekend, going over the wedding stuff, wasn't he? And I chatted to him at work the other day. He might not be as twattish as we both thought."

No shit.

"Anyway, we're going to bump into him periodically for the rest of our lives, so I'm giving him the benefit of the doubt."

Me too, buddy, me too.

"There's plenty of curry leftovers in the fridge if he hasn't eaten. You could offer him some. It just needs reheating on medium in the bottom oven for half an hour. Cover it in foil first, so it doesn't dry out."

"Thanks, Mum."

They left, but only after Lysander hauled Frankie back into their bedroom to suck his face off. How anyone could be so infatuated with a man who used to collect his toenail clippings in a used envelope and sprinkle them across my pillow was anyone's guess.

After they'd gone, I removed my hearing aids. I preferred subtitles anyhow. Flicking through the channels, I tried to relax. Challenging when Dominic might drop in at any moment. I hadn't seen him for twelve whole hours, not since my amateur attempt at a blowjob followed by my shuffle of shame from his warm bed and into my cold one in the early hours of the morning, before Frankie and Lysander woke.

The neighbours-with-benefits arrangement had already hurtled off track. My heart had divorced itself from my brain, taking its own foolish route. Last night's kissing and falling asleep in his arms, for instance. And him bloody carrying me to bed—or, rather, waltzing me to bed. Halfway there, he'd done a silly little twirl, and then another, and another one after that.

That wasn't normal for a casual fling, was it? Nor was the careful, almost reverent undressing which followed, nor the positioning of a pillow between my knees and the heat of his body melting my skin as he spooned me from behind. I'd been plucking up the courage to do something about the effect it had on my dick, but the next thing I knew, it was morning, and neither of us had moved. So I made up for it, as best I could. He came, pretty swiftly too, so it couldn't have been too terrible.

Who'd have imagined an evening spent with a testosterone-fuelled, sexually experienced neighbour would end up like that?

But it was too late now. As Milo suggested, we'd deal with my heart's fallout when Dominic was safely back in the US. Him or Frankie or anyone else never need to know.

Saying goodbye to this thing between us would hurt, but so did being a horny, deaf, and disabled virgin in a world of able-bodied people enjoying great sex. I trusted Dominic enough to expose my fears and unattractive body parts, and that would be enough.

And when he'd gone, and I'd finished licking my wounds, I'd feel better equipped to step out into the world and find a guy who would lick them for me.

The soft kiss landing on the top of my head, accompanying a slow sweep of Dominic's warm palm on the back of my neck, made all that a hell of a lot harder. "Hey, Tris," he mouthed, smiling down at me. "Missed you." Tingles shimmied up my spine. Tonight, in the dim glow from the side lights, his eyes shone a creamed coffee brown. Freshly showered, his thick hair was slicked back.

With an acknowledging raise of my hand, I reached for my hearing aids. Fantasising about him licking my bare arse was one thing; putting him through the horror of my deaf voice was a step too far.

"Was that okay? Did I startle you? Should I have buzzed first? Lys suggested I come up and say hello. So, hello, babe."

He kissed my forehead again, and then once more, just because he could, doing that eager-puppy thing, wanting to play. Endeavouring to ignore the dreamy suggestiveness in his inflection, I played it cool. "Yeah, it's fine. I half expected you—Frankie mentioned it. He thought spending some time together would be a good idea. We could get to know each other a little."

I accompanied the last part with a wry smile. Frankie had no fucking idea how excellent his suggestion sounded.

Dominic stepped further into the room and plopped down onto the sofa next to me, spreading his legs wide, making himself at home. Soft, grey, easy-access drawstring sweatpants. Ugh. I tried not to read anything into that. With a grin, he snaked his arm possessively around my shoulders. "He'll approve of this, then."

Kissing was as good as I'd remembered. Better in some ways, as his mouth was now so familiar. A casual observer might not have realised one of us was disabled. Just two guys *making out*, as my American toy boy would phrase it. Dominic smelled and tasted clean, of coconut shower gel and minty toothpaste.

"Frankie suggested I feed you, too," I said as we pulled apart. His eyes glinted wickedly, and I flushed.

"Uh-huh. I could get on board with that." He waggled his eyebrows. "Do you need me to give you a hand in the kitchen? My culinary expertise extends to grilled cheese, but I can follow a set of instructions."

Five minutes in, I reckoned even throwing two slices of bread sprinkled with cheddar under the grill might be beyond him. At home, I furniture-walked if I could, giving my shoulders a rest from supporting my weight through two canes. To that end, Lysander had strategically placed tables, sideboards, and other sturdy pieces so I could lurch from one to another.

Nonetheless, carrying heavy casseroles was a little tricky. Frankie was more than happy to let me struggle, so having Dominic awaiting my instruction was a rare treat.

"How does this freaking stove even switch on?"

"Um… the big silver knob on the front?" I'd been leaning against the giant stainless-steel fridge, admiring the view, but since our ridiculously intuitive oven seemed to be getting the better of him, I shuffled over to join in, steadying myself on the countertop.

"Nah, babe. I've got this." Looping an arm around my shoulders, he planted a kiss at my temple. "You can watch, but no interfering." Scanning the kitchen, he added, "And just to make sure, I'm gonna park your pretty ass right here."

A small step for mankind, a giant leap for Tristan Carter. With his usual brash confidence, Dominic secured his hands under each of my armpits and hoicked me up onto the work surface. Then, almost absently, brushed his lips against my forehead before turning back to the oven.

Unexpected tears pricked behind my eyelids. Sitting on a kitchen counter, chatting to someone as they moved between the triangle of the cooker, the fridge, and the sink was such a normal, mundane thing to do, but in all my twenty-six years, I never had. I'd never dangled my legs from a kitchen worktop, because... reasons.

Not appreciating the enormity of the moment, he'd already moved on. "The aluminum foil goes shiny side down?"

"Yeah. And it's *aluminium*, not aluminum."

"Cool beans. Where do you keep the plates? Or are we adding a pointless 'i' into every word now? Platies? And knivies and forkies?"

We had half an hour to kill, and Dominic had plenty of ideas to use that time, most of them centred around my mouth. As much as I enjoyed the alternate perspective of the kitchen from high on the counter, Dominic attempting to scoot between my open legs pushed the boundaries a little.

"My thighs don't spread apart." I was determined not to shrink from whatever we were getting in to. Didn't stop me finding it embarrassing, though. But we couldn't coyly skirt stuff, not with my disabilities. Years ago, I'd learned being up-front about what I could and couldn't do saved a whole pile of grief further down the line. Even if it killed the moment. "Not much, anyhow."

"I know, babe. And I don't care. I can reach you sitting up there just fine by leaning across like this." As he demonstrated,

Dominic's eyes travelled in a slow arc across my face, and his strong fingers interlaced with mine. I didn't need to clarify with Milo that fuck-buddy, friends-with-benefits etiquette didn't involve this degree of tenderness.

Yep, I was gonna be royally fucked when he went back to the US, and we had scarcely started.

"Listen, Tristan. You should have realised by now that I don't give a rat's ass about any of that. You know, your cerebral palsy shit. But you've got to talk to me. You tell me what you want and how you want it. And I'll oblige because right now, I want you, more than I've wanted anyone else, but I'm scared I'll fuck up."

A ball of emotion clogged my throat. His openness cut a swathe through my boundaries, as if he didn't see them, as if he wielded a pair of those giant scissors celebrities used to slice through ribbons to start races or open new supermarkets. And I was supposed to kid myself I was only in this for a quick fuck? God help me.

"I want you too," I answered, my voice almost a whisper. "I want to… to do a lot more than we did last week. Everything, in fact."

Comprehension and desire opened his eyes impossibly wide, more darkened pupil now than autumnal gold. He let out an incredulous laugh. "Wow, we got to that pretty quick. Seems you and me share the same wavelength."

My breathing eased. Thank God I wasn't going to have to spell it out. From that reaction, message received loud and clear. Sucking on his bottom lip, he contemplated me thoughtfully. If he was willing, I was ready for this. Not a relationship, and not dating, no matter how Dominic teased and no matter how much I loved it when he did. No dinners and candles or trips to the cinema, holding hands in the back row. Just sex. A straightforward friend—*neighbours* with benefits situation.

"So, I guess I know how I like it, Tristan, but I understand that might not be comfortable. Or possible, even." While he spoke, his hand roamed up and down my thigh, the other cradling the back of my neck. "You're gonna have to tell me what works for you, babe, so we can do this right."

We kissed again, long, and deep. As we pulled apart, he pressed his thumb to my chin, tipping it up to give me a look, aiming for stern.

"I'm waiting, Tris. I need to know how you normally do stuff."

I reminded myself I'd decided I could trust this bloke. "I don't... um... I don't normally do *anything*."

He took a second to process. "Shit. Are you... is... this is going to be your first time?"

"Yeah. It is." As if we couldn't make it any more complicated.

Dominic's jaw hung open. "What, and you're trusting *me* with that?"

"More than I trust you to safely deliver me from one side of the London to the other, yes. Or reheat a curry."

"Oh, shit. Have you met me?" He rubbed his face with both hands and blinked a few times, as if he wasn't sure he'd understood. "No one trusts me with anything, Tristan. I'm like... I'm like... whoa... and... like... yeah."

He was all that and more.

"It's no big deal." I shrugged. "Something I should have got out of the way years ago. Never got around to it, I suppose."

No big deal? No big deal? A bigger fucking deal did not exist.

Once he'd got over the shock, Dominic's confidence blew me away, sweeping me along with it. He plucked me off the kitchen counter with the same amount of irreverence with which he'd hoisted me up onto it. No one ever manhandled me in that carefree,

indelicate manner; a concept that simply didn't occur to him. I switched off the oven as we passed.

He undressed me, again without seeking permission first, haphazardly discarding my clothing around the room, before shimmying out of his own gear. Those drawstring sweatpants practically took themselves off. If my body appalled him, he didn't show it. He dived under the duvet, dragging me on top.

"Let's start working out what's good for you, babe."

My knees had kind of fallen between his spread thighs, a comfy, natural home for them. Lying on my belly was usually okay too, if I bunched a few strategic pillows underneath, and a Dominic-shaped version worked just fine. Even better, the nipple barbell, which had occupied way too many of my brain cells over the last few weeks, was within my grasp. I skimmed it with my fingers, the cool silver a sharp contrast to the heat of the flesh underneath. Boldly, I gave it a tweak, and Dominic hissed with shock. I followed with a lick, and he arched his back.

"Fuck, Tristan. I think you and me are gonna like exactly the same things."

Normally, Dominic ran full tilt at everything. He lived like he swam, like he drove. I expected his lovemaking to be the same, a quick count down then blast off. Not this. Not this unhurried build up, both of us feeling our way. Licking, biting, sucking. Slow kissing, passionate kissing. Neck kissing. Grinding. Pauses while we caught our breath, grinning at each other. Top-half stuff, teenage stuff.

Teenage stuff I'd missed out on.

Separated by our underwear, our dicks rubbed, desperately hard. A damp trail seeped through the fabric of his flimsy briefs and onto my belly. I think we both realised how far gone we were at around the same time. Dominic swept a warm palm down to my arse and squeezed.

"You gonna let me get my hands on that beautiful uncut diamond you're hiding down there, Tristan?"

My answer would have been a resounding yes—if my left leg hadn't chosen that precise second to spasm in protest at the unfamiliar posture. The unforgiving flat surface of my kneecap connected sharply with Dominic's balls.

"Ahh, fuck!"

Clutching his manhood, he threw me off. A grimace of piercing, unexpected agony contorted his handsome features, and he drew his knees up to his chest, wincing. "Ahh, fuck!"

"Shit, Dom, I'm so sorry. It just happened. My hip... my... fuck... I just..."

"Oh man, oh man, that freaking hurts."

We lay panting next to each other, Dominic cursing and massaging his bruised undercarriage and me digging my knuckles into my fucking stupid hip and trying not to make more of a scene. Hot tears stung my eyes; I clamped them shut, frantically plotting ways to creep out unseen, my mind flashing back to the night of the *thing*.

Fucking CP.

Like a colicky newborn baby, it never gave me a fucking second off. And the really stupid thing? My hip hadn't finished messing with me; involuntarily, I kicked out again, stifling a crippling wave of cramp.

But more than the pain, more than the utter, utter mortification, was the fucking *humiliation*. The fucking ludicrous idea that this had been within my grasp, That I'd kidded myself sex was possible. Lying there, gasping like a beached fish and half expecting a torrent of abuse, my humiliation at having tried for something beyond my reach and so ignominiously failed hurt more than the searing agony in my hip. Now would have been an excellent moment for an intruder to burst into the bedroom and kill me.

Strong fingers reached for mine across the gap between us, wrapping my hand up in their grasp. "Are you okay, babe? Can I do anything to help? Do you need me to rub it for you?"

"What?" The guy whose testicles I'd just walloped was asking *me* if *I* was okay? What sort of fuckery was this? Most blokes would be calling me every name under the sun.

"I said are you okay? Can I help? With the spasm thing?" Wincing, he turned on his side, and his hand left mine to start gently kneading at my hip. Under his warm palm, the tense rope of muscle eased a fraction. "It's okay, babe, it's okay. Is that starting to feel better?"

Vision watery, I nodded and gulped down a lump in my throat. How did this kid, sent to London in disgrace from a city I could barely identify on a map, manage to lull all my insecurities to sleep in a way no one else ever came close? Friends with benefits didn't soothe knots of coiled sinew, nor murmur sweet nothings and brush warm lips against necks and shoulders. Especially when they were the injured party.

"Are you sure you don't want to find a guy without CP to spend the night with?" My voice trembled. "There are plenty of them out there, you know. Uncircumcised, too. Guys that won't jeopardise your ability to produce kids when you're least expecting it."

"I know." His knuckles found the exact key to unlocking all the tightness in my hip. "But I don't want them. As I've already made clear. I want you."

The raw honesty of his words breached a corner of my heart I never knew existed. "But why?" I whispered. "Why, when someone else would be so much easier?"

Dominic just smiled and kept kneading. Deciding my boxers were an obstruction to the full hip massage treatment, he teased them lower, slipping them down beyond my knees. I kicked them all the way off. "Babe, if I answered that question truthfully and word got out, then everyone else would want a piece of you too."

Seemed the masseur's state of dress made massages easier because Dominic's underwear also disappeared. From the feel of his shaft, solid and hot against my thigh, he'd recovered from his ill-timed assault.

"I'm going to need to check a few of your other muscles aren't planning on ganging up on me." His palm tracked down my wasted thigh, skating over ridged scars from multiple operations, caressing the atrophied tissues dormant underneath my skin.

Whimpers I couldn't subdue escaped my throat, and I flung my arm over my face to keep them in check. My legs were hideous and useless. And this guy was stroking them as if they were as perfect as his own. Sensing my emotions threatening to overspill, Dominic rolled me onto my side, away from him, blanketing my bare back in his heat. I flailed around for a pillow to wedge between my knees.

"Are you comfier now?"

As he spooned me close, I nodded again. His dick, damp and leaking, slotted against my bottom. "Your massage technique is a little different to the osteopath I visit in Richmond. More thorough."

Chuckling, he rubbed his dick between my cheeks. "When I give a massage properly, I find it relieves the tension in my own cock, too." His fingers curled around my shaft, and he thrust up against my cleft again. "Seems to increase the tension in yours, though."

I hadn't realised sex could be funny. Or maybe I had, but not sex *with me*, or at least, not for any of the right reasons. I giggled as Dominic declared his undying love for my foreskin, teasing it back with his fingers, dipping his thumb into the slit and promising to donate his entire trust fund to it. Simultaneously, his dick wore a path down the crease of my arse, and our laughter dimmed, making way for soft moans and sighs. His rocking against my hole developed into a steady rhythm, in time with the curl of his palm lathing along my shaft and my own needy pushes back against him. At some point, I registered the snap of latex, and a cold lubed finger replaced his tip. Arching my back, I cried out with the unfamiliar sensation.

Instantly, he withdrew. "Shit, tell me if I'm hurting you." Dominic's honeyed voice was a low growl and full of concern.

I shook my head. "No, it's... you're... yes, fuck, yes."

One finger joined another, his steady coaxing open eased by the soothing words dripping from his velvet mouth as he sucked and nibbled and kissed the sensitive skin at the back of my neck. For my first time, he used plenty of lube; it trickled between my cheeks, coated my balls, painted my hole. His shaft rubbed needily along my crack, his ragged breaths scorched my ear, hitching with every inhale. The bedsheet twisted in my fist as I clamoured for purchase and ground back against him; my dick pulsed with every exquisite drag of his fingers against my prostate.

"Ready?"

"Yeah," I breathed. Already, a thicker, blunter push replaced his fingers, and I reflexively tensed, resisting the intrusion. A panicky sensation turned my guts watery, my useless legs scrabbled pointlessly, and I flung my arm back, grabbing on to his hip.

"Sshh, babe," he crooned. "I've got you. Push against me… there you go, nice and slow, nice and slow, nice and…"

His words were lost in his deep guttural groan and my sharp indrawn hiss as my passage stretched painfully around him. Soft kisses landed on my shoulders, his nose nuzzled into my neck, his lax mouth moved against my skin as he cursed and promised he'd never experienced a feeling so unreal. For a long second, I swore he'd split me in half; I took in a gulp of air, stifling a scream.

And then, with a thrust stealing the breath from my body, he was seated, and stilled, and a heavy arm wrapped itself around me, crushing my back against his chest. Hot lips sought mine as I craned my neck, sealed together, every inch of us touching.

"I can't hold it like this for very long, Tristan," he warned. "It's too good. You feel too good."

As I'd flailed around, my dick wilted, and the indescribable burn and fullness nearly had me begging him to pull out, but now it rose again, tall and strong, and I gave myself some firm strokes. My channel relaxed, accommodating him. The tension left my shoulders. Sensing it, Dominic batted my hand away, took over, and started up that delicious rocking again.

"Is this how you thought it would be, Tris?" he whispered.

"No," I gasped, "it's better." *Because he made me feel safe.* Not like protection from muggers or disease. Nor like mapping out a secure future, a career, finances, welfare. But the best kind of safe. The hidden, secret inner safety we all craved. The one allowing us to expose our fears, vulnerabilities, desires, my horrid legs, and, yes, even my arsehole. And the security of knowing that, for the next few hours, at least, someone held me close.

Cautious rocking wound up into more urgent drives. Dominic's weight and size and raw need pushed me more onto my belly, and I scrabbled with my arms. "That's it. Come up onto your elbows—ah, yeah, like that. Jeez, Tris, so fucking like that."

Up on his knees behind me, the changed position drove him deeper, a new angle. His balls slapped in a punishing rhythm against my arse. Each snap of his hips brushed my sensitive, hungry dick against the sheet just as each thrust milked the nub his clever fingers had sought. A greedy heat zipped up my spine, like he was hurtling me around the sharp corners of a rollercoaster. I felt out of control, my stiff limbs and tense muscles wrenched apart.

With one hand around my hip and the other at my neck, Dominic slammed into me like a punishment. His urgency felt filthy, crude, primeval and so fucking marvellous, all at the same time. Dominic, this untamed youth, wanted to fuck a man, and the man he'd chosen was me. He was taking what he needed, bending me to his need, no compromises, no thought for anything in this moment but his own want.

Sticking two fat fingers up to my disabilities.

I cried out as a rush of heat swept from my toes to the tips of my hair. A tightness in my throat, a whoosh of blood through my ears. Sensing my own release, he raised himself even higher, gripping and drawing my hips back as far as my spastic muscles would allow as he banged and banged and banged into me, chasing his own.

"I'm coming," he panted, pumping on and on. "Fuck, Tris, sorry, I'm—I can't stop, I'm coming."

A sudden heat flooded me; in swooping waves, my channel spasmed around him. A sound he'd never made before left his throat, tipping me over the edge. My balls clenched, my own cum drenched the sheet underneath. "That's right, Tris, oh fuck, Tris, oh fuck."

A numbness blanketed my legs and hips as I fought for oxygen. My head spun. I'd never come so hard or so intensely. I'd gone deaf in one ear. Utterly spent, Dominic stopped thrusting and collapsed heavily onto his side, still semi hard and filling me. He hauled me back with him, crushing me against his chest, bundled up in the circle of his arms. Chest still heaving, he fumbled under the pillow for a missing hearing aid and handed it to me. Limply, my head fell back, coming to rest on his shoulder.

"Fuck, Tris," he panted. "I got a little carried away at the end there. Please tell me I didn't hurt you."

I shook my head. His dick, now soft, slithered out, and he briefly let go to fiddle with the condom. Damp and sticky, smelling of sex and sweat and us, he curled against me once more as a well of silent, hysterical laughter bubbled up from my diaphragm, and tears threatened to spring from my eyes. One or two of the tears escaped, but I blinked rapidly; he'd never know.

I'd experienced being handled with kid gloves. On countless occasions. Colleagues, friends, even family sometimes went out of their way to pretend, but never quite succeed, they were free of inhibitions, for fear of hurting me. Which was ironic, because people like me experienced pain and discomfort to some degree every single day of our lives.

So, if Dominic wanted to fuck me hard? As long as we could find a good position, there would be no complaints from this quarter. Physically, I was the least fragile person I knew. Mentally, by the time Dominic had finished with me, I would be shattered into a thousand tiny shards.

I stretched within the confines of his delicious embrace. Not a casual, friend-with-benefits embrace, just like that had not been a casual, friend-with-benefits fuck. I'd deal with that later. I'd read that sex eased muscle spasms—something to do with endorphins. Floating in a sleepy haze, I concurred with the textbooks. I wasn't about to run any marathons; my thighs were pretty much super-glued together, and already, a creeping ache was making itself known in my arse. But yeah, I felt good.

"Babe, can I say something?" He nuzzled into the back of my neck. "I need to tell you, Tris, I think I'm falling for you."

"I think I'm falling for you, too." No thinking required. I knew already, with all of my soul. We were both quiet. Dominic squeezed me even tighter.

"We're fucked, aren't we? What with me not, like, living here?"

"Yeah." I couldn't have put it better myself.

CHAPTER 18
DOMINIC

Things I hated about London: I couldn't spend every second of my time in this city hanging out with the hot guy upstairs.

I couldn't lie—sex with Tristan was always going to be a little different. A swift kick in the balls was a novel form of foreplay I wasn't eager to repeat. A permanent reminder to never leave him for too long stretched out on my belly.

As much as I'd have liked to ignore his disabilities, we couldn't. He was never going to straddle me and ride me like a cowboy, for instance. And neither would I be slinging his legs over my shoulders, not without some pretty serious forethought. When I buried myself inside him next, I wanted to be face to face. I had a couple of ideas, but they required creativity that would only grow alongside deepening intimacy and goddamn old-fashioned practice. I planned on reaching that distant point.

In the meantime, I hadn't seen his face when he came, but the little appreciative sounds as I grazed his sweet spot, the high-pitched gasps and the low sighs, the fire crackling beneath his skin and the shuddery groan as that fucking gorgeous cock erupted—well, it more than made up for it.

Ensuring his pleasure slowed me down and heightened my own. Hell, I was twenty-one and horny, and I'd fucked plenty, but until last night with Tristan, I'd never made slow, sweet love. Or attempted to, anyhow. At the end, my little head had taken over proceedings and sped things up.

At any rate, both of us shared the newness of a gentler pace, although I kept those thoughts to myself. Tristan had been antsy enough, without me confiding that up until him, my mantra had been quantity over quality. Christ—he'd entrusted his virginity to me. Me! Of all people.

In the clear light of late morning, I watched him sleep, the magnetic pools of blue shuttered behind thickly fringed lids. He'd warned me sleep was his superpower, and, boy, he wasn't joking. I'd spooned him for nine hours straight, and he'd not stirred once, furled like a comma and tucked in close, his breathing light and steady. Those theories about other senses becoming hyperacute when one didn't work properly? Absolute horseshit. Nothing more than romantic myth. I'd wriggled around, gotten up and taken a piss, checked my phone (which held a message from Lys) and... nada.

Now curled towards each other, I snuggled a hand under the duvet and rubbed a thumb across his nipple. He'd enjoyed it last night; he'd enjoyed my mouth on it even more. I did it again, this time giving it a gentle tug.

Making an adorably sweet snuffling noise, Tristan's eyelids fluttered open. Finally, I'd found the on switch. As I tweaked a third time, the dawning of a smile played on his lips before he cheekily bobbed his tongue out at me, then closed his eyes again.

A ribbon of desire vibrated through my core at the carefree silliness of it. This was a glimpse of the real Tristan, the private Tristan, the Tristan he only revealed to a few. Watching him wake up next to me, I reckoned I'd penetrated a layer deeper than anyone.

Next time he teased his eyelids apart, I bobbed my tongue back at him and crossed my eyes. With a sound somewhere between a giggle and a groan of despair, he shifted, snuggling deeper into the mattress and hunching the duvet around his shoulders. Spun gold strands settled across his cheek. The guy was as cute as a freaking kitten.

"You going to stare at me all day?"

His deaf voice did freak me out a little. This morning, it came out as a loud bark. The monotone almost sounded computer generated. Moreover, it reminded me of our disastrous first meeting in the pool. But I liked it more than Tristan did, because his silliness of seconds ago evaporated. Instead, he regarded me self-consciously, as if suddenly hit by an awareness he'd woken to someone sharing his bed and peeking into his private deaf world.

Reaching across to the bedside table, I boldly plucked his hearing aids out of their little velvet nests and held them up in a questioning gesture. Two wary denim eyes blinked in assent.

I'd watched him do this a few times now. Thankfully, snapping them onto the hidden magnets buried beneath the skin behind his ears was as straightforward as he'd made it appear. I hadn't been prepared for the tender familiarity of it, though. And from his startled expression as my fingertips brushed through his hair, neither had Tristan.

"Did I misstep?" I asked urgently, the heel of my hand still resting on his cheek. "It has been known."

Smiling sweetly up at me, he circled my wrist, holding my hand against him. "You're strange, Dominic. You know that?" His voice slipped back into normal. "Most people are scared to even give me a quick hug because they think they're going to somehow damage me. A few hours ago, you banged me face down into the mattress. And *now* you're asking if you've done something wrong?"

"But did I?" I persisted. "Deciding it was time you needed to put your hearing aids in? Surely that's your decision?"

Chuckling, he shook his head before making a slight readjustment to his left hearing aid. "Yes, you did, but you seem to have a knack of getting away with it. And I don't know why."

I nearly told him he was falling for me, little by little, like raindrops coalescing into a puddle, just like I'd fallen for him. But the enormity scared me, so I responded with my most endearing boyish grin.

"How are you this morning? Are you okay? I know that it can... you know... hurt a little... after the first time."

A flush of colour crept up his neck, and I kissed it away. A bit late in the day for shyness. He might not know it, but his wanton neediness in bed held no room for bashfulness last night. He'd arched his back and pushed his arse onto my cock like he'd been doing it every night for the past month. The way his body begged for me? I couldn't recall the last time anyone had made me feel so much like goddamned British royalty.

"I'm okay," he mumbled. "Nothing a hot shower won't fix."

While he slept, I'd studied his roomy shower cubicle. It held a hell of a lot of potential. I leapt off the bed. "That can be arranged, babe. Join me in five."

My gorgeous man accepted my offer. "Um... that was installed for me to use?" He eyed me from the doorway, fingers grasped around one of the handholds for balance.

I sprawled in his plastic shower chair, dripping wet and idly playing with myself. He'd snuggled himself up in a big blue towelling robe and had no idea how adorable he looked, all sleep-mussed and rumpled.

"Don't you worry about a thing, babe. I'm saving a comfy seat for you right here." Patting my thighs, I spread them as wide as the confines of the chair would allow and fondled my cock with more purpose.

He tried to give me a disapproving look and failed dreadfully; his breathing sped up. "I have to take my hearing aids out for the shower." He reached for them. "So anything you want to say, say it now."

How could I refuse? "Just a warning that little E.T. down there, wrapped in his baggy hoodie and hidden under that robe, is going to get a very thorough soaping."

Tristan snorted with laughter. "Dominic? Did you just liken my dick to E.T.? He was a wrinkly grey alien!"

"A very cute wrinkly grey alien," I protested. "And the film made billions of dollars! It's a compliment!"

Did Tristan have a great body? Of course not. But I also thanked my lucky stars he'd chosen me to reveal it to, because the man I watched shedding his robe and making good use of all the handholds to creep towards me was one stunningly beautiful lover. With a beautiful uncut cock, obviously. My eyes were glued to it. Seemed I'd gotten myself a kink.

The shower chair was a bit of a squash for two, and it had arm supports, so Tris had to back up onto me, bent legs snuggled between mine. Which also meant the natural resting place for my hard cock was cosied up between his scrawny ass cheeks. My arms automatically slid around him, pulling him close and letting my hands fall where they fell. No prizes for guessing where that might be.

Tristan let his head tip back onto my shoulder, and we exchanged a sloppy, open-mouthed kiss. And then I pulled a ridiculous face at him, because this deaf, silent world gave me an insane immature urge to fill the void. Tristan giggled and tutted in a very non-deaf disapproving way. In retaliation, I tweaked his knob, and his ass wriggled wonderfully in my lap. And then wriggled again, a little more provocatively. My lover was fooling around. The next roll of his crack against the length of my cock was definitely deliberate.

"This will be a good position for us!" he barked, delighted he'd found a way to torture me. "No today, though. Too sore."

That he had relaxed sufficiently to use his deaf voice *and* refer to his tender parts warmed the cockles of my heart. Given that he was only on a transmit setting instead of receive, I kept that deliciousness to myself and played with my new favourite toy instead.

With my chin resting on his shoulder, I peeled back his foreskin, exposing the shiny swollen tip. Tristan watched too, flushing, and giving a little moan of pretend disgruntlement as I rolled it back and forth in a game of hide and seek. Kissing his cheek, I ran my tongue along the edge of his jaw and felt his breathing change, the restless shift of his ass in my lap. His bony fingers gripped his even bonier thighs.

As I enfolded my hand around his cock and began a slow, slick glide, a high whimper left his throat. My other hand dipped down to his balls, squeezing and cupping them, running them around my fingers. His lips parted as mine landed on the side of his neck; I sucked and nibbled at the soft skin, murmuring how freaking gorgeous he was even though he couldn't hear. His ass pressed against my cock, teasing me with the memory of last night.

Next time we took a shower together, I vowed to have that tight channel jammed down on my cock. I'd soap us both, he'd grip the handle bars either side of the seat, and I'd push up. He'd ride me so damned hard we'd gallop into next week.

As I jacked him, one of Tristan's small hands clamped around mine. His other stroked his own inner thigh like he didn't realise he was doing it, and wasn't that the fucking hottest thing ever? Hot water rained down on us. His writhing on my lap did evil things to my cock, rubbing it up against his crack, massaging my shaft like I massaged his. It throbbed, leaking precum as the slide of his tight foreskin in and out of the tunnel of our fists mesmerised the both of us. It felt intense. The silence, the inability to communicate, both of us watching him on the cusp of coming but saying nothing, added to the intensity.

Tristan's breathing quickened, he tensed, he made the fucking hottest noise on the planet, and jets of glorious spunk erupted from that beautiful narrow slit. So fucking awesome.

After, I soaped us both up thoroughly, kissed the hell out of my beautiful lover a whole lot more, then jacked myself extravagantly while Tris sat in his shower chair, like a Roman emperor watching the entertainment. From the way he bit his lip and fondled his own exhausted cock, he freaking adored it. And when I released all over his face, catching some on his lips, I reckon he adored it even more.

Now we'd moved to the kitchen. Once more, Tristan snuggled up in his bath robe and bossed me about, happy as a clam as I made a hash out of frying bacon and eggs. Picking him up, I deposited him on the worktop, partly because I knew he loved me throwing him around a little, but mostly to stop him from shuffling out of arm's reach.

"I had a text from Lysander while you were sleeping the morning away. We have a wedding practice dinner on Tuesday."

"Why do I need to practice how to eat dinner?" Tristan grumbled.

"So that Frankie can make sure we're doing it properly. He wants us to try all the menu choices and visualise how they look side by side."

Tris harrumphed. "Sounds like my brother."

"Are we gonna tell them about us?"

We regarded each other thoughtfully. "Do you think we should?"

On the one hand, sharing a relationship status with everyone else was nice. Equally, keeping it a secret felt attractive. And once people got wind of things, then they started asking questions. Like: *what the hell are you playing at when you haven't got much time left in England*? And then later, years later: *it must be awkward as hell having your brother-in-law and ex at every christening, wedding, funeral (delete as appropriate), and family gathering.*

I reached around his legs to gather him in my arms. Light, insubstantial almost, his body melded into mine. When the time came, I wanted to pack him into a suitcase and take him back to the US with me. Park him on my mom's kitchen table instead of this one, and let her make him some of her famous blueberry pancakes. And then whisk him back to bed.

"I think we should keep it just to ourselves for a while, don't you?"

CHAPTER 19

TRISTAN

Things I loved about living in the penthouse: part 10: yep, still the hot guy downstairs.

The lovebirds returned from their dirty—sorry—*work-related* weekend away and threw themselves into wedding preparation. Or rather, Frankie did; Lysander just tossed his abashed, dimpled grin at Frankie, then trailed after my brother with adoring puppy dog eyes. The guy must have had a screw loose.

Tuesday night found us piled into the restaurant of the fancy hotel booked for the wedding, the scene of Lysander's first declaration of sexy feelings towards Frankie. When our brother pointed out that nauseatingly romantic twist, Maddie and I ripped our brother to shreds.

Dominic clung to me like a limpet, determined we'd sit next to each other. Machinations not unmissed by Milo, who had taken up the seat to my left.

"We're going to be family, after all," I explained, quite casually considering Dominic's left hand danced a tango along my right inner thigh and his socked foot was crawling up my calf. Escape was at least another three hours away. "Brothers-in-law. It's only normal that we should sit together, isn't it? For a wedding rehearsal?"

I didn't know the rules of footsie in the US, but someone needed to tell Dominic it wasn't considered a competitive sport in the UK. I mean, the guy played to win. And by win, combined with his hand action, he was aiming for me to ejaculate into my trousers before we'd even got to the main course.

"The feng shui's not quite right," announced Frankie from the top of the table. "There's something wrong down the left side." Pursing his lips in consternation, his gaze travelled from person to person. "The seats aren't properly spaced. Tris, I know Milo's a bit whiffy sometimes, but shuffle back that way a little, can you? Mungo, petal, can you somehow make your shoulders look... narrower? Hunch them in, darling."

Following Bridezilla's orders was a relief in many ways. "See?" Milo hissed as I reluctantly manoeuvred my chair back towards him. "It's absolutely not normal to be practically sitting in your future brother-in-law's lap! Tell him to back off or else get yourselves a room upstairs."

Once we were all a regulation twenty centimetres apart, I tackled my warm goat's cheese crème brulée. Mungo, sat opposite, did the same, but in half the time. He licked his fork suggestively.

"Mmm. A pretty sexy starter. What's for main, Milo? Pigs in blankets? Pulled pork?"

He gave his best friend a direct look, and Milo waved him off.

"Spoilsport," Mungo grumbled.

I raised my eyebrows. "I'm not sure Frankie will allow smut at the wedding. Get it out of your system now."

Next to me, Dominic made the most of his devilled scotch egg accompanied with a soft-boiled quail's egg. As well he might. Frankie struck it from the final menu before he'd even got his lips around it. The crispy golden hue of the scotch egg clashed with the aesthetic of the table decorations.

Maddie had advised our brother to keep his full-throttle insanity under wraps until the ring was on his finger, but clearly, he hadn't listened. Tonight, dressed in one of his favourite sparkly halter neck tops, Frankie positively glittered with excitement. And I adored him for it.

"Darren, my love. Could you practise lifting your glass with your right hand, not your left? Much more favourable symmetry from the top end of the table." Fortunately, whatever my brother slipped into his fiancé's cocoa every night did the trick. Otherwise, a man as rational and pleasant and fabulously gorgeous as Lysander would easily see my brother was an absolute, monumental—

I sucked the last of the deliciously runny goat's cheese from my finger, taking my time over it, relishing the sharp flavour. Checking Frankie's beady eyes weren't looking in my direction, I swept my finger across my empty plate, searching for a few drops more, before sucking on it again. I moaned with contentment. God, it tasted good.

"Go to the men's room." Dominic's low voice growled next to my ear, so only I could hear. "Now."

"Now? What? Why?" So much for snaffling the last piece of smoked ciabatta toast slathered in watermelon and pomegranate terrine before Mungo got his thieving mitts on it. Although another opportunity would present itself at the actual wedding breakfast. Its dusky pink blush contrasted beautifully with the silk ceiling drapes, hence passing the Bridezilla test with flying colours.

Dominic's tone held urgency, and I swiped my fingers across my mouth. Did I have goat's cheese stuck to my chin? Loose snot in my nose?

"Go on," he urged. "Stop licking your freaking fingers like that and go to the bathroom."

"But I don't... what..."

His chin jerked towards the gents with a stern glare.

"Okay, whatever." Clearly, doing what he asked was the only way to find out what was bothering him. As I heaved myself out of my seat, reaching for my canes, the chair scraped noisily, no doubt damaging the aesthetic even more. Everyone looked up.

"Hey, Tris, let me help you," Dominic insisted, as if he hadn't ordered me to excuse myself. Bolting upright, he pushed his own chair back.

"Um... the toilets are just there?" I pointed to the gents, and the unobstructed route leading to them. "Like, twenty paces away?"

"I know." He grabbed my arm. "But you can't be too careful. And anyhow, a team trip to the john is always more fun than going alone."

He was being even goofier than usual. "Is it? I mean, I kind of get when teenage girls go in pairs and..."

"Yes, it is!" he hissed. "Christ, Tristan! Just let me freaking come with you!"

We paraded to the toilets under Frankie's suspicious gaze. The feng shui would be all sorts of fucked up now. Maybe he'd put cardboard cut-outs or actors in our places until we came back, like at the Oscars to make the auditorium look full for the cameras. I would have suggested it for laughs, except Frankie might actually take it seriously.

"Secret wedding stuff," Dominic mouthed at him with an exaggerated wink. *Liar*. But from Frankie's idiotic beam of delight, he'd earned another gold star against his name, so I couldn't knock it.

The gents were empty, and as soon as the door closed on us, Dominic shoved me into the disabled cubicle.

"Very thoughtful," I murmured, "but I'm...um...quite happy standing at the urinals?" A firm hand gripped my jaw as his hungry mouth plastered itself against mine.

"But I can't do this with you at the urinals. And Christ, Tristan, I really, really need to."

The meaning of 'this' became abundantly clear as Dominic worked his own belt open, then tackled mine. Grabbing my hand, he brought it onto his rock-solid dick, closing my fist around him. At the sound he made, my own dick rapidly swelled.

"Are you okay propped up against the wall like that? Keep hold of your canes for balance."

I huffed out a laugh. Sandwiched between him and the flimsy side of the cubicle, I could hardly go anywhere.

"All freaking night I've had to watch you," he whispered around his kiss. "Putting stuff into your mouth."

All night was somewhat over-egging it; we'd only sat down three-quarters of an hour earlier. Not that I was complaining.

He pulled my dick out of my trousers to join his, then spat on his palm, looping it around us both. "Stuff that wasn't me. No way can I sit through dinner, pudding, coffee and more beers without getting off."

Hitching his leg up onto the closed lid of the toilet, he ground against me. My head fell back hard against the side wall at the same time a door banged. With a sigh of relief, someone pissed a loud stream into the urinal. I patted behind Dominic for the flush, yanking it down hard to drown out the sound of him, and more importantly *us*. One of my canes clattered to the floor, rolling away from me. On legs like string, I clutched at him, slipping down the wall.

"I've got you, babe, I've got you." His hand never leaving its grip on my hips, Dominic sank to his knees. His hot mouth circled the head of my knob. As his wet finger probed at my hole, I nearly joined him.

Forget Frankie slipping love potions into Lysander's drinks; someone must have sprinkled fairy dust into mine, because I'd been transported to a parallel universe where a hot guy sucked my dick and finger-fucked me in the disabled toilet cubicle of a Michelin-starred restaurant. Things like that did not happen to Tristan Carter halfway through his dinner.

And yet... here I was. *Me*. Not Frankie, reliably the most sought-after guy in the room. And not Milo either—I'd lost count of the times I'd witnessed him bat his eyes at a waiter before discreetly following him into the staff changing area. Oh no, out of the three of us, only little old me would be enjoying an orgasm between the starter and the main course tonight.

"Oh, fuck, Dominic," I gasped. "Oh fuck, I'm gonna…"

Another door banged, and someone with a brisk, trotting walk entered the gents. Stifling a panicked scream, I clapped my hand over my mouth. I was so close, so close, thrusting desperately into Dominic's throat, chasing my orgasm, twisting his hair in my hands. Then, with one last delicious drag of his finger, I came in a gush, clamping onto my palm to stifle my moans, knowing I hadn't managed it, and aware of an echoing moan from my lover as he released into his hand.

Blindly, I fumbled around. I flushed the toilet again, then collapsed sideways onto it, Dominic steadying my fall. As the noise of the cistern faded, the movement outside of the cubicle went quiet too—thank God.

Standing over me, panting heavily, Dominic wiped the back of his hand across his mouth, then tore off some sheets of loo roll, looking hella satisfied.

"Feeling better now?" I asked. "Jesus, Dominic, I nearly had a heart attack when that second bloke walked in."

He buttoned his fly, for all the world like a man who'd just strolled in for a piss. "Much better." He kissed the top of my head. "And ready for my seared sea bass fillet served with a saffron and crab potato cake."

I, on the other hand, was going to need a few moments to pull myself together. "You go first. I'll follow in a couple of minutes so it's not weird."

He wiped me clean, tucked me back in, and zipped me up a hell of a lot quicker than I'd have managed. With another kiss to my forehead, he swept my hair back and patted it down tidily. "Sure?"

I nodded. "Everyone expects me to take ages in the bogs."

He unlocked the door. "Missing you already, babe."

I passed the two minutes sitting on the closed lid, waiting for my legs to stop trembling and processing the whirlwind that had just blown through the gents. What the fuck I was going to do when Dominic returned to the United States? Aside from weep, which went without saying.

Most of my hours at work today had been spent pondering the same question. Unexpectedly crashing into my life, he'd bullied me, humiliated me, reduced me to tears, and then undone his mistakes so, so brilliantly. Hard to believe the sweet Dominic who gathered me in his arms and twirled me into bed and the immature wanker who tossed my clothes onto the floor were one and the same.

Judging enough time had passed, I shuffled out of the cubicle. Milo stepped out of the adjacent one. Why was I not surprised? I raised an eyebrow at him. "Bloody hell, Frankie's feng shui is totally ruined now."

Wordlessly, he handed me my cane. "Really, Tristan? In a toilet cubicle? Flower, when I suggested you should live and love each other in the here and now, I didn't mean fuck in public like a pair of alley cats!"

I cast a look back at the toilet, cool as you like. A hot masc guy had just emptied my balls, exactly as Milo prescribed; I was on top of the world. "What's your problem? I've been for a piss in the disabled bog. And I'm... um... disabled?"

"Oh for goodness sake! As if! You've got to get up very early to con me, sunshine." His eyes danced. "Come on, spill the beans! How did the weekend go? Successfully, I'm judging, from this evening's shenanigans. Did he break your back like a glow stick?" His eyes flicked down to my feet and back up. "I've been trying to decide whether you've been hobbling more than usual."

Friends, eh? Who needed them? Nonetheless, finally having something to tell was rather delicious. And knowing I intended to deprive him of every single juicy detail was even better.

"You know, I kind of came in here to do something? Can you move out of the way, so I can *hobble* over to the urinal, please?"

"Yes, yes. Piss and talk, flower. And be quick, otherwise your toy boy will accuse me of chancing my arm too."

I shook my head at him. "You wouldn't get very far. I'm a little... tender."

That shut him up, enabling me to empty my bladder in peace. Sometimes, you had to play these extrovert types at their own game.

"He's all over you like flies on flypaper tonight, flower. I'm not sure he's even noticed anyone else is here. I'm staggered they can't see it. Frankie's usually like a bloodhound. Maybe his impending nuptials are distracting him."

I thought otherwise. "They're not looking for it. Frankie and Lysander are behaving as if they personally invented marriage, Mungo only has eyes for you, and you damn well know it," Milo rolled his own eyes at this, "and Maddie and Darren are so thrilled to have a night off baby duties, the confit duck leg on a bed of wild mushroom rice could have a topping of dried maggots and neither of them would notice."

He waggled a knowing finger at me. "Seeing as you've brought up the subject of topping, are you going to tell them you and Baby Brother are at it like sex-starved cavemen? They're going to be staggered when they find out."

I shook my head firmly. God, confiding in Milo was like having my own conscience talking back at me. Once Dominic returned to the US, this relationship with me would rapidly become nothing more than a footnote in his frat boy life. I'd get over it myself too, one day, although I had a feeling it would take a lot longer.

"No, they won't, because they aren't going to find out. There's no point. He'll be heading back to San Diego soon, and it will only make things awkward further down the line. You know, at family gatherings and things."

"When is he returning? Do you have a date?"

"No."

I couldn't decide if not knowing how much time Dominic and I had left together was better or worse. On the one hand, no torturing myself counting down the days. I couldn't tick off a mental checklist of 'this will be the last time he burns the scrambled eggs', or 'this will be the last time he calls me babe' in that dreamy suggestive drawl.

Instead, I kicked the can further down the road, floating on a cloud—a heavenly St. Cloud—pretending my current bliss might go on forever. Except when I was alone. Then dark voices inside my head reminded me the only path leading from the top of the world was down.

And I harboured a strong suspicion Dominic felt the same way.

"Well, I hope your acting is better than your cleaning." Bringing me back to the present, Milo's eyes expertly assessed my dishevelled appearance. "For getting spunk out of denim, I recommend a rub with hand soap followed by copious amounts of hot water—and immediately, before it dries. Then hang your nether regions over the Dyson dryer."

CHAPTER 20

DOMINIC

Things I hated about London: time travelled too fast, flying west over our heads, back to sunnier climes.

The phone call came when I least expected it—in the gym with Lysander, spotting for each other. Afterwards, I planned to grab Tristan and maul him in the hot tub.

"I thought you'd be pleased, honey?" Our mom's puzzled tone caught Lysander's attention, and he stopped, mid-rep, to listen. "I spoke to your tutor—she says you can re-enrol again after the spring break with two credits to make up. We can all travel back the day after the wedding together."

"That's only a week away." The phone call didn't only piss on my dreams of a happy end to my day—it drowned me in a whole set of emotions I wouldn't have imagined lurked within three months ago. A profound and sickening sense of unfairness came first, followed by anger, a childish gut reaction. Why me? Why us? Why now?

A steel band tightened around my rib cage, as if the 185-pound weight I'd been bench pressing now squatted on my chest. Only seven days left of Tristan. Seven mornings of waking, tangled in a pile of limbs and pillows, holding the only thing I've ever wanted. Seven nights of rediscovering all the secret places that made him gasp with delight, that briefly loosened the cords of muscle binding him so tightly. Seven days to prepare to walk away from him.

"Which gives you time to wrap things up with the St. Clouds. Your dad's lawyer did a great job, didn't he?"

My voice faltered. "I guess."

"Honey, we've shifted hell and high water to get you out of this mess. A little more appreciation would be nice."

Lysander replaced his weights. Sitting up, he wiped his face with a towel, never taking his eyes off me. I wandered away a couple of paces, turning my back slightly. Sweat cooled on my body, prickling and itchy. My mom gabbled on a while longer, some logistical stuff I didn't hear and didn't care about.

"Good news," he said warily as I wound up the call.

"Great news," I answered.

"Is everything okay, Dom? You sounded a little off with Mom."

Lysander's kind eyes looked up into mine. Gripped by an overwhelming urge to burst into tears, I stepped around him, heading for the shower. Dropping my shorts, I banged the shower knob with my elbow.

"Nah." I raised my voice over the noise. "It's a shock, I guess. Came a little sooner than I expected. I was getting into things at work."

Lysander joined me. Screwing my eyes up tight, I tilted my head, letting the hot water cascade across my face. I was too old to be the kid brother with his very own Olympic hero to dry his tears.

"Then come back in two years, when you've finished your college degree. Jump straight back in where you left off."

"What if I don't finish it? I mean, do I need to? I've got a job for life here anyhow."

His hand had already lifted for the shower knob. "You're seriously thinking about doing that? Dom, is there some other thing bothering you that you haven't told Mom about?"

Oh God. Was there ever. Tristan, picking his way to the hot tub without me ready to catch his fall, flashed before my eyes. Dreadlocked Neil, with his cool style and dogged persistence hanging around the record shop.

Did I tell Lys? Or would it complicate things? It would stress Frankie out, and the guy was already on a knife edge building up to the wedding. I opened my mouth to speak, but Lysander hadn't finished.

"Because she's so stoked one of her boys is going to graduate from college. I don't want to be the one to tell her it ain't going to happen."

I barked with laughter. "Lys, her other son is literally a world-record-breaking Olympian!"

"But he hasn't got a college degree. And neither has she. You're the first on her side of the family, so you'd better believe it when I say she's proud. As am I."

Stepping into the space next to me, he began soaping up. "Listen, Dom. You and me, we're the future of this family business whether we like it or not. Daphne's visions need us to see them through. And in that future, I need you beside me, with the smarts I never got. Never mind your confidence. So go back to the US next week, finish your studies, do our mom proud—do *me* proud. Then come back and we'll smash it together."

Eggs broke. Not hearts. Breaking wasn't a brutal enough word. Shattered or demolished were much more accurate descriptors. And hearts plural. Tristan's was going to splinter into a million pieces too. After a restless night alone, I collected him from the record shop in place of Maureen.

"What are you doing here?" I heard the tapping of his canes on the floor before he came through the door. His voice was laced with pleasure he made no effort to hide as he gave me that damned shy look through his gossamer gold curtain.

Yesterday evening, his siblings had commandeered him. A

cheery text, signed off with a row of purple hearts, told me not to wait up. He'd spend the night over at Maddie's, blowing out candles for baby Rosie's first birthday. One of the precious nights left to us already lost.

I took his messenger bag, and he tweaked my tie. "I thought I'd surprise you." I jerked my chin in the direction of outside. "Your useless British sun must be drunk on love or something because it's still in the sky, so I sneaked out of the office early. I thought we could find a park and enjoy the last of the daylight."

He worked it out then, I think. We'd fooled around, but outside the apartment, we hadn't done the dating thing, not really. Arranging to meet up, to go out for dinner, to the theatre or for a walk, felt too permanent. Laughable, really, because instead we'd stoked the fires at home, falling much deeper and harder than sharing popcorn at the movies or sipping beer together in a pub would've facilitated.

I drove us to a nearby small park. London was crammed full of them, and I'd hardly explored any. Tristan had a natty disabled parking permit, so we made use of a space right by the entrance. Plenty of folk had had the same idea, groups of two and three were dotted over the grass, stretching as far down to the lake. Above our heads, the sun weirdly continued to shine. The usual grey clouds must have been hanging low over another town. Don't get me wrong—it wasn't California, but it was the first time in a while some real heat had scorched my bones.

Tristan pottered along beside me, giving me oodles of time to smell the flowers, as my mom always said, something I'd neglected until I'd met him. I nearly asked if he had a hat hidden in that damned leather satchel he carried everywhere, to protect his delicate skin, but it would earn me a withering look, so I stayed quiet.

"You're going back soon, aren't you?"

He said the words in a soft voice, head down, planting his sticks on even patches of ground. I spied an empty bench ahead and steered him towards it.

"The day after the wedding." I blew out a breath, rubbing my palm across my stubbly jaw. "My mom's flying over tomorrow—she's going to stay in my apartment with me. And she's got tickets to travel back together. College starts three days later."

Settling himself, he balanced his sticks next to him. "At least everything is sorted now. With the fire engine thing."

"Yeah. The lawyer and my dad have made sure it's quietly disappeared. I'm going to visit her, though – the firefighter's wife. And they can't stop me. I'm going to do exactly what you said. Knock on her door, look her in the eye, and say I'm sorry."

"Good for you. You're good at apologies."

"I've had some practice."

Down near the lake, some lads kicked a ball around, showing off as a group of girls nearby sat up to watch them. A couple of the boys held cans of beer, a raucous bunch, the sort I might have been amongst not so long ago.

"It doesn't have to be the end, Tristan," I blurted. "Me going back. It's only two years. It will be over in a blink. And then I'll come back here and work for the firm. I've already told Pauline my plans. I'm going to start at the bottom and make my way up. I've got other ideas too, about how the management could stay in touch with the workers. I'm presenting them this week. So you and I could still…"

"Shhh," Tristan interrupted. "Let's not make promises we might not be able to keep."

"I'm not! I could fly back and visit you in the holidays. At spring break. Or even better—you could come and visit me."

Even as the words tumbled from my lips, that sounded unlikely. I had a single dorm on the third floor, with no elevator and no handholds in sight. Never mind a loving supporting cast of friends and siblings. Tristan couldn't imagine our bold future, but he also couldn't imagine leaping on or off aeroplanes, towing suitcases, nipping across town, springing up the stairs to my dorm, or any of the other inconsequential steps to visit me in San Diego. How could he, when he relied on brothers, sisters, friends, drivers, hot tubs, and goddamn walking sticks every single fucking day of his life?

I ploughed on anyhow. "We could still make it work."

"Two years is a long time when you're twenty-one, Dominic. People change a lot. You'll change a lot."

"How I feel about you won't. We'll FaceTime every day. And we could travel back and forth."

With a low laugh, Tristan shook his head. "Dominic, do I look like a frequent flyer to you?"

No, he didn't. He looked like the most beautiful creature on God's green earth, and I had no idea how I'd get through the days ahead without him. But telling him that was no use. Instead, I plucked his hand out of his lap and held it in my own.

He glanced down at our intertwined fingers. "People are going to think you're my carer if you do that."

"People are assholes."

CHAPTER 21
TRISTAN

If you love someone, set them free. Wasn't that the quote? And if they came back, they were yours. And if they didn't, then they never were anyhow.

Dominic wouldn't return. Not for a few years at any rate. One day, of course, he'd build a home here in London, as the CEO of Cloud Construction, as sure as eggs were eggs. It was written in his genetic code. He'd steer the ship, and Lysander would keep it steady.

But between now and then, he had a hell of a lot of living to do in California. He could kid himself all he wanted, but give him a few weeks, and he'd slip straight back into his college life as if he'd never left. A more mature version of himself, definitely; kinder, and more considerate. Someone with an eye on his future too, because one day, my Californian beach boy would grow into a force to be reckoned with.

Dead weight like me had no place in that life, amongst the rich handsome jocks and the pretty spoiled girls.

With that in mind, I made the most of the precious time we had left. Every minute slipped through our fingers too fast, like grains of salt. The arrival of Dominic's mother rightly occupied him. Impossibly glamorous and charming, and very, very present in the flat downstairs. And Frankie and Lysander's last remaining wedding preparations didn't miraculously prepare themselves. Neither did the record shop close just because one of its employees felt too bloody sad to haul himself out of bed in the mornings.

After a late burst of effort over the last few days, spring decided enough was enough for one year and taken itself off to bed. I'd have liked to join it. Fighting a losing battle, the windscreen wipers threw themselves hopelessly at the sheets of rain beating down on the glass, perfectly reflecting my mood.

"I had a fella once," stated Maureen as she steered the Lexus (ever so smoothly) through the morning traffic.

"You've got four daughters, Maureen, so I think you had him more than once."

"He was a cut above the rest," she continued, ignoring me. "He had a car for starters, an Austin Allegro. It looked like a giant chocolate lime sweet on wheels coming down the road. Bright green on the outside and with brown velour seats."

I pulled a face. If you wanted your mouth to taste like a freshly cleaned urinal all day, then suck on a chocolate lime.

"I was nineteen and had a job in a hairdresser's. I paid my ma rent, but she still wouldn't let him stay over on a Saturday night. Worried what the neighbours would think with that bloody car stuck outside the house all night."

Our own car idled at a junction as Maureen wittered on. Last night, Dominic and his mother had joined us for dinner in the penthouse. My lover and I sat chastely side by side while excited wedding chatter swirled around us, hardly joining in, only existing for each other. I couldn't recall what we ate.

"He booked us a camping trip, two nights in Wales—Pembrokeshire. So we could have a bit of time alone. Borrowed a tent off his mate; we bought a sleeping bag each and those roll-up sponge mats. Teabags and a little camping stove."

Despite myself, I listened, letting another one of her tales carry me out of the unfinished narrative inside my head.

"Anyhow, we drove a couple of hours to this campsite on the Friday after work. It had been drizzling a bit in Birmingham, but by the time we reached the Welsh border, the sky was chucking it down. Like it is now. And it was pitch dark. The lad was all for turning back and giving it another go next weekend, but I'd had my nails done and had bought two new pairs of knickers. I wasn't going to let that expense go to waste, for the sake of a few drops of water."

Even in my current mood, Maureen could put a smile on my face. I pictured her—a younger version obviously—all dolled up and erecting a tent in the driving rain, determined to get a shag out of this bloke, whatever the weather.

Stalled behind a taxi rank, she paused. We weren't far from the record shop. "Anyhow, by the time we eventually found the bloody campsite—no satnav in those days, just a big road atlas spread across my lap—we'd criss-crossed most of Wales and were both getting what you youngsters would call hangry. We didn't have a name for it in those days, but if he asked me one more time whether I wanted to bleeding turn back home, I'd have socked him."

"What happened?"

We pulled into our usual spot outside the record shop, and Maureen switched off the engine. As much as I enjoyed my job, on a day like today, I'd have much rather sat in the car all day, letting Maureen and her stories wash over me. My customer service skills would be seriously below par today; I planned on skulking in the back room as much as possible.

She chortled happily. "Jesus, what *didn't* happen? Ten o'clock at night and there we were: up to our knees in a bleeding swamp, with the rain pissing down and giving each other the evils. Then the daft bugger opens the boot of the car. And he's only gone and forgotten the bloody tent poles, hasn't he? They're still sitting in the middle of his dad's bloody drive, aren't they?"

I snorted. If young Maureen had been anywhere near as feisty as old Maureen, that lad would have wished he'd never been born.

"Anyhow," she continued, "I'm back in the car, bawling my eyes out, mascara ruined. I'm insisting he drive me straight back home again or I'm phoning my dad to come and get me, when the lad picks that moment of all bloody moments to ask me to marry him! No bleeding chance!"

She helped me out onto the pavement and fussed with the hood of my parka. And then, even though she was getting soaked and it wasn't a special morning, like my birthday or anything, she pulled me into a hug too. "There you go, my darling. Snug as a bug."

"I'm only walking five feet across the pavement."

Maureen handed me my bag. "Can't have you with wet hair all day. You'll catch your death."

"Did you ever wonder what happened to him?"

She laughed, her throaty, smoker's laugh. "Oh, love, I know what bloody happened to him. Three years later, he turns up on my ma's doorstep. At eight o'clock one morning to carpet the lounge and hallway. Never been so shocked to see someone in my life! All bright-eyed and bushy tailed, he was. And I looked a right bloody mess—I still had my hair in curlers. Looked me straight in the eye and said my sleeping bag was still at his house if I wanted to go round and collect it some time. The daft bugger."

"Did you?" I asked curiously.

"Of course I bloody did! Cost me fourteen quid in Woolworths. And right in front of my ma, he said he'd never stopped loving me. That I was the one for him. I've been married to him forty-two years this October." She fiddled with my parka hood, again. "Not been on any camping holidays together, mind."

My awesome, infuriating, glorious older brother (by three minutes) married the stunningly handsome, kind, and wonderful love of his life at four-fifteen on a wet and windy Friday in March. Thank God the only role expected of me was to turn up.

Maddie performed best man duties, partly as Frankie's way of sticking two fingers up to patriarchal heteronormative traditions but mostly because she did that shit so much more fluently than I ever could and had enough words for all three of us. After that, my newly minted brother-in-law stood up and said a few off-the-cuff sentences about dear Lysander, with such fatal sincerity I regretted wearing my hearing aids and had to look away and squeeze my eyes shut.

In truth, a fat lump clogged my throat from start to finish. It had nothing to do with the extravagance; the Carter-St. Cloud union was always going to be a swanky affair. Steeped in glitz and glamour, combining Frankie's over-the-top gay flair with Lysander's gazillions and his understated elegance. Yet however they did it, even in a garden shed, their special day was always going to strike the right note. True love tended to do that.

Mobility issues and deafness weren't without their advantages. Nobody (and by nobody I meant older well-meaning relatives) ever felt the urge to look at my newly married brother and my partnered-up sister and come out with a hackneyed, 'It will be you next!' Secretly, they didn't share that expectation. Neither did I, to be honest, so even when my own heart was crumbling, I could embrace Frankie's happiness to the full. As an added bonus, people's expectations of me on Frankie's nuptials were also set reassuringly low. Parked on a comfy seat with a glass of bubbly in my hand, next to the great-aunts and doddery grandparents, I was left to my own devices, free to watch Dominic politely work the room.

"He gives Lysander a run for his money dressed in that suit," remarked Milo, sliding in alongside me. "Shame he's taken, really."

"Not for much longer. He's heading back to the US tomorrow."

He gave me a sidelong appraisal. "You kept that quiet."

"Didn't want to spoil Frankie's big day."

"How do you feel about it?" He frowned. "Say... on a scale with yellow Liquorice Allsorts at the bottom, the ones that look and taste like eyeballs, to blackcurrant Jellybabies at the top?"

Like I was on a fairground ride hurtling out of control? Clinging on for dear life as every blurred second whizzing past brought me closer to the hideous moment Dominic St. Cloud would collect his belongings and stroll out of not only his apartment, but London, England, Europe, and my whole fucking universe forever?

"Sick as a dog. But for God's sake, don't start being nice to me. Not here, not now. Please, Milo, I won't be able to take it."

"Does he feel the same?"

Unable to speak, I nodded, my eyes blurring.

"So why the fuck is he going?"

"He has to. He needs..." God, pushing the words out was hard. "He needs to finish his college degree. And he should. He's still very young and... and silly sometimes. He doesn't believe it yet, but he'll soon get over me."

And knowing he wouldn't be there to catch me when I fell was a most exquisite pain, a level of self-destruction I hadn't thought possible.

"Why don't you ask him to take you with him? Or follow after him in a few weeks? There's no reason why you can't go."

Believe me, I'd thought about it; the request had been on the tip of my tongue more than once this week. "Milo. He's a student, for fuck's sake! He doesn't need to be saddled with someone like me. How would I cope in student digs? What would I do? I'd be home again by the summer, and we'd have to spend the rest of our lives trying to pretend none of that embarrassing interlude happened."

"So what will you do instead? Are you going see if you can make it work long distance?"

"Maybe?" I shrugged. "Is that really possible? It's what he wants. And maybe if he was older, then we'd have a chance, but I've got to let him live his life between now and then. So yes, we'll give it a go, but I won't ask him to make me any promises."

His gaze moved away from Dominic, seeking out Mungo. We both spied him at the same time, an arm slung around one of Dominic's grumpy-looking relatives named Pauline. Mungo was the only person today who had coaxed a laugh from her. No surprise; the man could charm birds from the skies.

"For what it's worth, Tris, I think you're very brave. Much braver than me. You've had the nerve to taste heaven, flower. Dominic sounds like he's been worth it."

"Your slice of heaven is right over there. Ready for the taking. He's just waiting for you to realise."

Milo gave a soft chuckle. "Oh, flower. I've realised. I can't trust myself not to fuck it up, though, and lose him. Mungo's way too precious for that."

Pauline tipped her head back, laughing uproariously at whatever Mungo was telling her. Earlier, one of Lysander's work colleagues had been flirting with him. "He won't wait forever, you know."

Not long after, Milo left, eye caught by a chunky darkhaired waiter bearing a passing similarity to Mungo. Seemed I wasn't the only one faking smiles today.

And so the evening wound merrily onwards, with the groom and groom floating on Cloud Ten, exactly as they should. Happiness was toasted, cakes were cut, old acquaintances remade, and new friendships formed. Like every other wedding I'd ever attended, except with added rainbow glitter. From the looks of things on the dancefloor, even the posh white middle-aged straights had found their inner groove.

"Hey, babe. It's our song."

Dominic's voice in my ear, his hand on my shoulder. Lost in my own thoughts, I hadn't noticed him join me. Nor heard the Spice Girls warbling in harmony. "Viva Forever." If only. I dredged up a smile.

"It's a naff song."

"I know, Mr Super Cool. But now it's my favourite ever. And I sneaked it onto Frankie's playlist, so he may have me killed later. Before he does, will you dance with me? Please?"

The floor was packed with bodies. Drunken, mostly, of all shapes and sizes and in all combinations. Over at the far end, my mum and dad were jigging enthusiastically, strutting their stuff next to the dowdy CEO of Cloud Ten and her even dowdier husband. Maureen was getting down and dirty with Mungo, while Milo was making absolutely no headway with the bear of a guy balancing a tray of drinks. Most weirdly, Doorman Dave was wooing Dominic's uber-glamorous mother in the middle of the dancefloor, and from the shaking of her booty, she was loving every second of it.

Shuffling our feet in our dark corner, we were safe. No one noticed our lack of rhythm, nor heard the cracks in my heart widening, smooshed up against the fine wool of my fabulous brother-in-law's suit jacket. A steady stream of hot tears dripping onto his silk paisley tie went unremarked too. And, over the sound of five young women reminding me *I'll be waiting, everlasting, like the sun*, as if I didn't fucking already know, my brother-in-law didn't hear me whispering along to the sugary-sweet truth.

CHAPTER 22
DOMINIC

Things I hated about living in London: very little, actually.

Apart from that uniquely hellish wedding. Sure, I played my part; I was happy for Lysander, even if I would always likely be a little fearful of his sassy new husband. My brother looked like he'd licked all the fondant off a rack of homemade cupcakes and got clean away with it.

As soon as Tristan was decent, I dragged him out of there, not the first to leave but not making it through to the last round of tipsy toasts either. Tristan's CP carried the can for all sorts of inconvenient truths. No one batted an eyelid when he pleaded tiredness, and Frankie radiated sunshine once I insisted I would happily escort him safely to his door.

I saw him a lot farther along than that. Through the door, through the living room and into his bedroom. Between urgent kisses, I made light work of his smart suit and then my own. Scooping him up, I tossed him into the middle of the bed, because he loved a little rough manhandling, and then threw myself on top of him. We only had a few hours left, but I planned on making the most of them.

"Need any more pillows?" I checked. "Are you comfortable?"

I'd landed with my elbows either side of his head, perfect for covering every inch of his face with my mouth. I couldn't fully lie over him, because his legs didn't spread or straighten out at the knees, but as long as I rested most of my weight through my arms and spread my own knees wide, with him tucked in the middle, we were peachy. And the cute guy Tristan kept down below, wrapped in his little hoodie, got to rub up against my belly.

"More than." Breathing out a long blissful sigh, he pushed up against my groin. His fingers circled one of his own nipples, then pinched it between finger and thumb, our contented moans the only sounds in the hush of the night. He snaked a hand down between us, eyes shot wide and focused on mine, and his swollen lips parted as he gave himself a long, slow pull.

So fucking beautiful; I wanted to parcel that image up and take it back to the States. Carry it around with me, take it out and examine it when I was alone, pray over it, hope it would still be waiting for me when I returned. He did it again, teasing me, biting down on his lip, putting on a show, loving his own body in a way I didn't think he ever believed he would.

His hand moved again, and he pushed up, fingers searching for my cock to circle them together. A bit of lube and a wet palm, two cocks gliding together as one. His hand moved again, he pushed up again, and…

And… and… nothing. Tristan's fingers tapped around between us; his blissful expression slid into an almost cross-eyed puzzlement. Which would have been freaking hilarious if it wasn't my cock he was struggling to locate. On our last freaking night together. Humiliating didn't begin to cover it.

"This has… um…" An ugly sound escaped my throat, somewhere between a laugh and a sob. "This has never happened to me before. I'm so sorry."

Rolling off him, I lay on my back, an arm flung across my face. "For fuck's sake," I muttered, "I wanted tonight to be perfect."

Tristan's fingers looped into mine as he turned on his side to face me. "Hey, shush. It is perfect. Your brain is too full, that's all. Mine too."

"I don't want it to be." Perilously close to tears, I lifted my head and slammed it down again on the pillow. "I want you to have something to remember me by." I was almost shouting. Even to my ears, I sounded like a spoiled brat having a hissy fit. "I don't want to go."

Tristan flopped onto his back, loosening my hand. A tense silence hummed between us, loud, obnoxious, and unwelcome. I don't know how long it lasted. Long enough for me to come up with a hundred panicked reasons why my cock wasn't working, all of them involving a devastating terminal illness. Which was crazy. Tristan had already summarised the cause perfectly.

"I can hear you staring at the ceiling," he observed. "Even with my shite auditory skills." Once more, his fingers found mine and gave them a squeeze.

"I don't have to go, Tris. I could stay here. We could carry on as we are."

"Yeah, you do. We've been through this. Go back to San Diego and finish college. Make everyone proud. Including yourself. Including me."

"Really?"

"Yeah, really." He huffed a laugh. "You'll regret it if you don't. And I don't want to be the cause. You'd always resent me."

"I wouldn't ever do that."

"I'm just saying. It could happen. Finish being a student and enjoy it—trust me, the rest of life is long. The thrill of getting up and going to work every day soon wears off. And you need to go and find that woman, the one whose husband died, and say sorry to her."

Out of all of this, that one thing made sense.

"I'll come back to you, Tris. I mean it. I'll visit you and call every day and…"

A kiss swallowed my words. "Shhh," he whispered into my mouth. "If it's meant to be, it's meant to be. No promises, okay? Promise?" He grinned. Fuck knew how he managed; I didn't think I'd ever grin again. "Except that one."

Another brush of his lips against mine. Softer this time, the tenderness saying more than my clumsy words ever could. A cool palm skimmed up my belly, well away from my flaccid freaking cock. "Come on, Dominic. Instead of talking, soothe my aches away. My shoulders and arms are killing me after standing around and supporting my weight all day."

And so I did, letting my eyes drift closed, losing myself in him, mapping out his body with my fingertips, storing every imperfect inch of it away. The sweeping undulations of his biceps and their unexpected strength. The dip of his elbows, the slender circle of his wrists. Then up again to the satiny softness of his narrow chest, the barely there valley dividing it, each rung on the ladder of his ribs and the hollows between them. His soft belly.

At some point, my mouth followed the path of my fingers, tasting salt as he restlessly arched into my touch. I stored his breathy sighs in my memory, the tiny noises as my tongue laved at the modest bump of one nipple, then the other. Tilting him onto his side, I rediscovered the planes of his back, a slow sweep of my fingers up each peak of his spine, running my tongue down the shallow coves of his shoulder blades, ignoring the push of his velvety butt against my groin.

I stopped overthinking; biological instinct kicked in. I was hard now, and needy, my cock leaking a trail. I slipped a hand between his thighs, nestling into the warmth, and a low groan escaped him when I cupped his heavy balls.

"Soothed some aches, and created a couple more," I murmured into his neck. "Are you ready for me, Tristan?"

He answered on a long exhale, his voice breaking. "Always."

CHAPTER 23

TRISTAN

Things I loved about the penthouse: part 10: very little, actually.

There were fifty ways to leave your lover. Fifty fucked-up sets of emotion to go along with it, too. Some folks, I'm sure, ran the gamut of grief, relief, joy, nostalgia, a sense of rightness, and a sense of new beginnings. Dominic, I suspected, simply carried a bittersweet sadness.

But when you were the guy left behind? Only one way to feel. Absolutely fucking wrecked.

As he vowed he would, Dominic slipped out of my room early while I slept. His flight wasn't until the evening, but he had his bags to pack, a presentation to deliver, and then a heap of family to say goodbye to, before finally re-joining his mother. I blissfully slept though his departure, another advantage of deafness, thus avoiding a dreadful, undignified scene during which I couldn't have trusted myself not to desperately cling to him and beg him to stay.

When I woke, nothing remained except a cold sheet outlining the shape of the body that had made love to me so sweetly a few hours before.

Leaving a text message with the Cloud Ten carpool, I called in sick to work. Maureen, Irene, and Emily would guess why. They wouldn't push; they knew I'd talk about it when I was ready. Maureen wanted to come over, but I gave her some batshit excuse about Maddie bringing the baby and our plans to spend the day together.

An unstoppable stream of tears seeped from my eyes. Already, Dominic's absence draped itself everywhere. A chair empty of his discarded clothing; a tube of toothpaste next to the sink, squeezed in the middle; a damp towel carelessly abandoned on the bathroom floor. My satiated, well-used body and the loose liquid ache within. A part of Dominic within. No condom last night. I hadn't wanted one, and he hadn't argued.

Masochistically imagining what Dominic was doing every minute of the day had already started. The world didn't stop just because our love had been ripped apart. At ten o'clock, he'd stand before the board, minus Lysander, delivering his presentation. I visualised him in my mind's eye, tall and straight in his navy suit, wearing it for the last time before exchanging it for jeans, a baseball cap, and sun cream.

Midday: farewell drinks with the family. Shaking hands, promising to keep in close touch, having serious discussions about developing the property empire across the pond. Four o'clock: picking his mother up from the apartment, a text from one of the drivers, maybe even Maureen. Then lifting his case into the back of the car, a last check of his passport in his jacket inside pocket before heading out to Heathrow in the relentless London traffic.

And still, the tears endlessly flowed as I huddled under a duvet drenched with his scent. Like a shrivelled, desiccated husk, my body curled in on itself. My eyes ached, the skin on my face crusted with salt.

Mid-afternoon, I headed out. Frankie and Lysander had booked the honeymoon suite at the hotel for the night of the wedding, so they would be home in a couple of hours. I did not need them to see me like this. Not ready to face Maureen either, I called an Uber, directing the driver to Kensington Gardens, a park not far from Maddie's place. Younger than me, the guy navigated the city like a seasoned pro, with none of the unpredictable jerks, swearing, and sudden slamming-on of brakes I'd grown accustomed to with Dominic. None of the chatter of Maureen either. Another bout of tears threatened the smooth silence of the car.

For two hours I sat in that damned park, bony arse parked on a cold hard bench, staring at nothing. Most passers-by ignored me, but within minutes of the school day ending, I remembered society didn't appreciate single men loitering around public spaces, especially near a primary school and with swingsets for the use of small children. And even more so an unusual-looking single man like me.

After some conflab with her friend, an anxious mother wandered over and asked me if I needed any help, if there was anyone she could contact. Polite at first, she addressed me in a slow and wary voice, as if I wasn't quite the full ticket and shouldn't be out without a carer. As if I'd escaped them.

Her friend walked over to join her, both looming over me and suggesting they could phone social services on my behalf. I'd like to report that at least it distracted me from wondering if Dominic had forgotten about us already, but honestly? Like a drag sideshow, it hardly registered. But when they walked a short distance away to whisper behind their hands, and the word *police* floated across the grass, I decided it was time to move on.

I phoned Maddie from the bottom of their torturous wrought-iron staircase. Two seconds later, Darren flew out the door and down towards me, three steps at a time, as if his arse was on fire.

"Thank fuck. She was on the edge of phoning the police!"

I didn't bother telling him a stranger had almost done it for her. I didn't bother saying anything at all. Somewhere in amongst all the fucking misery, their concern fuelled a flare of irritation. Couldn't a man go off grid for a few hours in peace, without sparking a manhunt?

With my disabilities, it would seem not.

Silent and patient, Darren hovered behind me as I dragged

myself up the steps, stumbling on one of them. My vision had become a watery film, my body so fucking damn tired after dragging myself across South Ken to theirs. He caught me easily, strong arms only serving to remind me they were the wrong strong arms, and set me back upright.

Maddie, hands on hips and toe-tapping furiously, waited at the top.

"Where the hell have you been? I had Emily from work on the phone worried about you, saying you were upset, but she wouldn't tell me why. Your nice woman from the driving pool hasn't seen hide nor hair of you either. You told her you had a hangover, apparently, and were spending the day with me!"

"And look. Here I am."

Knowing she'd follow, I shuffled past her, eyes fixed on the floor.

"Frankie got home and assumed you'd gone to work as normal, so of course, he's having fucking kittens now, racing around London trying to find you, which is not how he planned his first day of married life at all. And Mum and Dad are in a complete tailspin imagining you lying dead in a ditch somewhere, because he texted Mum wondering if you'd sprung them a surprise visit. For fuck's sake, Tris!" Already, her thumbs flew across her phone screen in a blur, no doubt calling off the search.

"Hello to you, too." I shrugged, tricky when every cell of my being wanted to curl up in a ball on the floor and wail. "Ah, well. As you can see, I'm still in one piece."

"Is that it? You start a bloody citywide manhunt and then turn up here, cool as you like, as if you'd just popped out for a bloody pint of milk?"

"I never pop out for a bloody pint of milk."

I never fucking *popped* anywhere. I slithered and crawled and ached and hauled, always with a fucking audience of drivers and co-workers and siblings and friends. Or do-gooders like the strangers in the park, assuming they knew what was best for me, because somehow having visible disabilities made me public property.

"I didn't ask anyone to go looking for me."

"We shan't bother next time, if this is how you show your gratitude!"

Deafness had its upsides. Sinking gratefully into Maddie's sofa, I rested my head back and reached for my hearing aids to remove them. Trouble was Maddie was familiar with my tricks.

"Oh no you don't," she ordered. "You don't just bloody turn up and do that."

Would the childish delight in thwarting my bossy, capable siblings ever disappear? Taunting her, I flipped off them both and dropped them onto the coffee table. "Watch me."

I closed my eyes after that, retreating into my deaf world. Past experiences taught me tears were easier to contain. By now, Dominic would be at the airport, settled into departures. Check-in times were so early these days. Or maybe he was at the bar in the business lounge, passing the tedious hours of waiting with a beer and texting his mates, setting up a welcome-home party.

A gentle nudge: Darren, proffering a mug of tea. Maddie was nowhere to be seen, so I slipped my hearing aids back on and took it from him.

"She's putting Rosie to bed," he offered.

The curtains had been closed and the lights switched on. I must have slept; it was later than I thought. Not much longer until Dominic's flight was called.

"She's only worried about you."

"I know." I took a sip. "I'll apologise. I just fancied a few hours on my own, without everyone knowing where I was."

"I told her that." He hesitated. "Anything I can do to help?"

Fucking tears threatened again, and I forcibly pushed them back down. When had I become such a self-pitying watering can? My heart could cry all it wanted, but never my eyes. I shook my head dumbly. There was nothing anyone could do. My wounds would scab over one day, although God knew how I'd survive until then.

An insistent buzzing sounded at the door, and I groaned. Like a swarm of angry bees, it buzzed again. It had to be Frankie; no-one else was that immediate. Fucking marvellous. And the whole gang—well, Milo and Mungo—barrelled in after him. Lysander entered at a more measured pace.

Maddie must have warned our brother I wasn't my usual outgoing cheery self, as he approached me cautiously. "All right, Tris?" With his hands thrust in his jean pockets, he threw the question out as if I could regularly be found lying on my sister's sofa with a blotchy, tearstained face, having gone AWOL for the greater part of the day. I loved my brother dearly (not that I'd tell him), but not insisting I fill him in immediately on what the hell had led me to this pathetic juncture must have killed him.

"No, he's not okay." Barging past him, Milo sank to his knees, grasping my hands in his. "It's the fuckening," he announced dramatically. "It's happened." He kissed me on my forehead, exactly like Dominic used to. "My poor flower."

"Yeah." My throat closed.

"What the hell are you talking about?" Frankie and Maddie demanded in unison.

We ignored them. Milo stroked my hair back from my face. This soft side of him was a revelation to all of us. "I bet you were so brave," he murmured. "I'm so proud of you."

This almost generated a smile from me. "I tried. I tried to make it easier at the end for him."

Confident outgoing siblings didn't like being excluded from conversations.

"Will. Someone. Please. Tell. Me. What. The. Fuck is going on?" Frankie screeched, voice bordering on panic. He flailed around for Lysander. Suddenly, I realised this wasn't an angry, left-out sibling at all. This was raw fear, mirrored in Maddie's face too. Hurt one of us and we all bled.

"Shit, Tris, we've been worried sick about you." Frankie slid to his knees on the floor next to Milo. Maddie slid in next to him, and they held onto each other. "And you've been acting so weird recently. We've hardly seen you. Please tell us what the hell's happening. I can't bear it."

The burden of grief, already settled in at home in my chest, eased by the minutest fraction. Every journey I undertook was hard, long or short. Countless times over the years, I'd needed Frankie and Maddie's help, sometimes even with the simplest ones, like walking to the bathroom and back. And their support, too, either in the form of an arm around my shoulder or a quiet presence when I didn't feel like talking. Why the hell had I thought this journey, the most arduous of all, would be something I could tackle alone?

"I'm sorry," I whispered, "You were so busy with the wedding. I didn't want to worry you." I looked up at Maddie. "Nor you, busy with the baby."

"What? What didn't you tell us? Christ, Tris."

Oh God, they were utterly petrified. And for what? Only a stupid broken heart, after all. I let my eyes drift shut. A tear seeped out anyhow. "Tell them, Milo. Tell them everything."

CHAPTER 24

DOMINIC

I'd learned a lot from my recent monumental fuck-ups. Hell, I'd almost developed a fondness for them; they'd turned me into a much better person than before. Into the kind of guy, in fact, that I'd like to know.

Nevertheless, I wasn't so enamoured I was going to add to their number by committing the most stupid fuck-up of all.

You could say I owed my future to United Airlines. I came to my senses while working my way through their tedious online checking-in process, sitting next to my mom in the back of the Lexus as Doorman Dave drove us to the airport.

Everyone exploited an opportunity to flog extra stuff you didn't need these days, and airlines were no exception. Checking in should simply take a couple of clicks, right? Thumb in the flight reference number, confirm the seat allocation, and bingo. Job done.

But like the rest, United was determined to screw its customers for every cent, and so I ended up suffering through a few more screens. Did I want to book a hire car on arrival? No. A driver? No. Did I want a hotel for the night? No. Extra baggage? Extra leg room? Holiday insurance? The vegetarian option on the plane? No, no, and no.

Surely after wading through all that jazz, I deserved the goddamn *'your check-in is complete'* page, but United hadn't finished with me. Another page opened up, listing even more possible ways to part me from my dollars: duty-free goods, a massage in the executive lounge, priority boarding, and so on.

But the reams and reams of advertising shit on this penultimate page didn't make me slam my arm down onto the seat divider, so ferociously my mom jumped. Hell, no. It was the simply worded question printed *above* the advertising shit: *Anything else you might have forgotten?*

I stared and stared at those six words until Dave pulled the car to the kerb, twisted around, winked at my mother, and politely wished us a safe trip. We'd reached the airport drop-off zone. My blushing mom got out, still bitching about how she always preferred the first-class seating in American over United, and I'd not processed a single sentence.

Dave pulled our cases from the trunk, my mom handed him a hefty tip, and my eyes drifted to the blanket of lead hanging low over our heads. A plane climbed away from the airport, immediately gobbled up by the clouds, taking a few hundred people out of this rainy city to God knew where. Millions were left behind. London teemed with folk, everywhere you looked, of every size, colour, and nationality. One of those people was dearer to me than all the rest put together, and yet here I was, on the cusp of leaving him behind. And a piece of me behind with him.

Anything else you might have forgotten?
Anything else you might have forgotten?
Yes. The love of my whole freaking life.
"Mom? I'm not coming. Not now, anyhow."
"Honey, we're cutting it fine as it is." She tapped her foot.
"Sorry, I didn't make myself clear. I'm not coming on this flight with you. There's something I need to do first."

Lysander had inherited my mom's eyes. Big dopey brown things. I'd always been secretly envious. Lys had learned to use them to good effect, especially around Frankie, but not so well as my mom. Her eyes narrowed to two glittery slits, like polished cherrywood. Not dopey all the time; my dad had never stood a chance. "Dominic St. Cloud, you explain yourself right now. You have thirty seconds."

"Mom. Listen. You remember, ages ago, I told you there was a guy. The not guy-guy."

"Sure, honey. I remember." She tapped her foot again.

"Well, he's turned into a guy-guy. But not any guy-guy. He's *the* guy-guy, and you've already met him, and he thought you were nice, and you thought he was nice too. And I'm not coming home unless I can persuade him to come and join us. I need him to join us. Even if that means jacking everything in."

She pretended to look over my shoulder. Dave was on the phone in the driver's seat, about to leave. "Unless you've started crushing on men older than your own dad, I don't see anyone joining us. And I can tell you one thing for sure, honey. Dave's straight."

The information in that answer I had neither the time nor the inclination to unpick. "I have to go back and get him. He might not be able to come straight away, but that's fine, because it gives us time to get everything ready. I'll follow with him in a day or two, but you need to go now and start looking for a place for us both. Somewhere with easy disabled access. Situated between home and college. A condo might be best. It will need handrails in the bathroom and a shower seat. I want a Lexus like this one too—the same model, in fact. And the condo needs a garden big enough for a hot tub. Hire one, or buy one, I don't care. It's not like we don't have the money. Oh, and for Christ's sake, hide my Michael Bublé albums."

Bewildered, my mom tried to work out how the fuck someone had managed to dispose of her feckless youngest son and replace him with a facsimile without her noticing. "You… you mean… Frankie's brother, Tristan?"

"Yes, I mean Tristan. He's the love of my goddamned life, Mom. I'm going to persuade him to come back with me. I might start college a few days late, but I'll make it up. I promise. And I want to change my minor, from general studies to international finance. I'm a St. Cloud. Me and Lysander are the future of Cloud Ten Construction. I need to start taking that shit more seriously."

As a San Diego native, I'd bummed around water all my life. The beach, the lake, aquatic centres, the plunge pool in our back yard. Even in London it called to me, as Tristan found to his dismay all those weeks ago. Being an Olympic champion's younger brother accounted for some of it. As a kid, I was dragged kicking and screaming to all his swim meets.

Lysander used the water for swimming all his worries away, but not being a worrier myself, I tended to just jump in to lose myself in the swirling blue depths. That first dive down was my favourite part: breaking the seal on the thin meniscus separating air from liquid, all sound vanishing, aside from the pulsing of my own blood in my ears. That first feeling of joyous weightless freedom. I guessed it was a close as I would come to understanding Tristan's mindset sinking his battered body into the hot tub.

This late at night, I knew exactly where to find him. He'd been better at pretending our love affair wasn't the real thing, especially at the end, but even if his words didn't give him away, those fucking phenomenal aqua eyes sure did. The shy glances, peeking out beyond that glorious swish of golden waves. As did the breathy moans when we made love, the way he opened up for me, so desperate and needy. The relaxed sprawl of his limbs afterwards, fingers entangled in mine, the delight he failed to mask behind an eyeroll when I blew raspberries on his soft belly. The sadness he failed to shield from me during our last night together.

Tristan would be hurting too, and when Tristan hurt, he headed for the hot tub.

A subdued golden glow enveloped the pool room, still and silent except for the steady melodic trickling of water through the pool filters. Not that Tristan would be aware of it. I carefully placed the neat case containing his hearing aids out of the way of my exuberant front crawl and wandered over to the edge of the water.

Only then did I dare look up.

Dense shadows played across the hot tub corner, so I couldn't see Tristan very well. He'd be able to see me, though. An unaccustomed tremble ran through me as I poked a toe into the glassy sheet of water. I didn't need to see him. I sensed his presence right down to my bones. He belonged to me as I belonged to him, and it was as simple as that.

We might not look like pieces of the same jigsaw, but his hand fit into mine like they were designed that way. My long body curved around his shorter one like skin on an unripe banana, and when our mouths slotted together, the world and my place in it slid into view so clearly.

All that remained was for me to jump right in.

Staring straight at where I knew Tristan lay, I dropped the towel. Baring myself. I wasn't above working my assets to get what I needed. A naked offering. A healthy, fit young body, attached to a soul, his for the taking for as long as he wanted me. Which I prayed would be for a very long time. And with everything I had to offer exposed to him, I hit the water in what I hoped was a graceful swallow dive. With my current nerves, it was probably closer to a belly flop. Hell, the guy had seen Lysander in action plenty of times—I'd always look ordinary in comparison.

I powered through twenty or so lengths, feeling as streamlined and swift as a dolphin at the helm of a pod, but probably as lumpen and uncoordinated as a walrus waddling on dry land. Swimming—the only sport where the coach would shout at you for freaking *breathing*, and boy, did my swim team coach used to shout. My mom joked it was water off a duck's back. Literally. She knew I was never going to be another Lysander, not when I could dive-bomb my mates and ogle the girl's synchro team instead.

When my lungs burned and I couldn't stand another second without touching Tristan, I heaved myself out of the pool. The towel stayed on the floor. Anxiety pricked at my scalp as I slicked my hair back with my hands, picked up the case containing his hearing aids, and strolled as calmly as my pounding heart allowed towards the tub.

Chest heaving, I opened the case and, the heel of my palm brushing his cheeks, secured each little device behind his ears. And then we stared at each other—him in the water, me outside of it, hands on hips and dripping onto the cold tiles. A similar pose to one not so long ago, when I was an immature, thoughtless dick. That guy had fucked off for good.

"You came back."

"I never left. I couldn't."

"You're shivering."

Even bedroom eyes couldn't detract from the dark hollows below them, which spoke of Tristan's pain more eloquently than the words both of us had bottled inside. And my body was trembling, not shivering, choked up on the words I should have said and deeds I should have done. While Dave drove me back from the airport, I rehearsed my speech, then went over it again while I swam up and down. But here, it fled my mind. Fancy words were for boardrooms and wedding ceremonies. What I had to say was plain and simple.

"When I got to the airport today, I realised I'd left behind someone very important to me. Someone I couldn't live without. So I came back to beg him to make a home with me in San Diego until I finish my college degree. I can't wait two years, Tristan."

A ghost of a smile crossed his lips, and damn if it didn't make my belly flop upside down.

"I've got my mom organising everything. A place for us to live together. She's going to get modifications for you." I took a step closer to the hot tub. "And we're going to install a tub, like this one, except you'll hardly need it, because the sun will warm your bones and ease the ache in them nearly every freaking day anyhow. And while I'm in class, you can occupy yourself doing nothing or anything. There's a really cool district close to college; you could find work in a record store—you'd fit right in. Or sit on your pretty ass all day in the sunshine. I don't freaking mind. I just want *you*, Tristan. I want to care for you, and I need you to care for me. And if…"

My voice faltered, "And if you might want that too, then you have to tell me, because it's a big step. You already know I'm a doofus, and I'll probably fuck things up a million times, but if we don't give ourselves this chance, then…"

He interrupted me with a throaty chuckle, and my stomach performed another loop. "Yes."

"What?"

"Yes. I'll come. I'm scared shitless, but I'll come. Now, get in, *doofus*. You'll catch your death standing there. And what sort of word is *doofus*?"

In two strides, I hopped in next to him. "An American one. And you'll hear plenty more like it if you come with me. Though I need to warn you, you're going to discover gravy isn't what you think it is, and the green stuff you like to decorate your salad with isn't called rocket. And I'd also just like to say that none of this was in the speech I prepared on the way over. Can I put my arm around you?"

"Do you normally ask?" The tiny smile had transformed into a bigger one. I mean, he was trying to hide it, but when a dripping-wet, naked man with all his floppy bits dangling bombards you with weird bits of food-based information and says he's buying you a hot tub to use five thousand miles away, I guessed it would seem quite amusing.

I did more than put my arm around him. I smothered him in kisses, then dragged him onto my lap. And suddenly, my bare cock wasn't quite as floppy anymore.

"Are you really going to come? I just need to check again. And you don't need to be scared. You'll have me. I'll be there to look after you."

He twisted around, and we kissed again. "That's the part that scares me the most."

With a chuckle, I fiddled with the waistband of his shorts. "Did E.T. miss me?"

A peal of laughter rang out across the empty pool. "Dominic, you were gone for one day!"

"So? I'm obsessed with it! And have you heard of docking? Because we're doing that. too."

He kissed me again. And again after that, then once more for luck. Tristan wriggled in my lap, making himself comfortable and me more uncomfortable. Jeez, it had only been a day!

"Your worried family is waiting in the penthouse, Tris," I informed him. My hot date with his dick was going to have to wait a while. "And Milo and Mungo are there too. I phoned Lys from the airport when I knew I had to come back."

"Our family," he corrected with an upwards curve of his lips. "Brother-in-law. That's going to take some getting used to."

"I think we're going to manage just fine, once we get through tonight. As you can imagine, Frankie has… more questions. Listed on a clipboard."

He cuddled into me. "He'll have to wait."

"I used to make my own lists when I first arrived here," I began. "In my mind. Of every single thing I hated about London. It was quite long. Things like the fact it rains every freaking day, and that Brits moan about it constantly, but none of you carry a goddamned umbrella. That potato chips are called crisps and come in roast chicken or *bolognese* flavours. The way y'all drinks pints of brown shit in pubs and seem to like it."

Funnily enough, none of this was in my original speech either. Tristan raised an amused eyebrow.

"I had no idea you felt so strongly about… um… crisp flavours."

"You never asked. But it doesn't matter. Because then I met you, and the list petered out. None of those things mattered any more. In its place in my mind, I created another list, entitled 'things I love about London'."

He threw me his shy smile, the one I absolutely freaking adored. "I hope that was just as long."

I shook my head. "Nah. I only ever wrote two words on it. Tristan Carter."

THE END

To: maureen@cloudten.com
From: tristan@trisanddom.com

> *Omg. The driving? I've found out it had nothing to do with being on the left. The guy is a menace.*
> *Wish you were here. No, seriously, I do. And then you wouldn't send me so many pictures of Chewbacca. I had no idea zip files could be so freaking big. Freaking! Omg, I'm turning into a Cali boy!*

To: emilyandirene@vinyltap.com
From: tristan@trisanddom.com

> *I finally found his record stash in the bottom of his wardrobe, sorry,* closet. *Michael Bolton. Michael Bublé. Shania Twain. NSYNC. Coldplay. I might be dying. Send help.*

To: frankiecarterstcloud@cloudten.com
From: tristan@trisanddom.com

> *FFS! No more saccharine honeymoon photos! I don't need diabetes on top of everything else. And BTW, before I forget, Lys's mother says 'hi' to Doorman Dave.*
> *Okay, here goes: please read once, show to Maddie, then delete what I am about to write. Henceforth, I shall deny any knowledge or will lay the blame on too much sun and being indoctrinated by emotionally incontinent Californians. But I just wanted to thank you both. Thank you for putting up with my moodiness (and sorry for being an even more miserable git at the wedding—I had*

reasons). Thank you for standing up for me, advocating for me, pretending not to notice my tears, for rearranging my belongings, for all the lovingly curated toenail clippings. For saying yes when I'm thinking no. For ensuring I live my best life.
You are both amazing, in all your crazy diamond glory. Lys and Darren are lucky men. As am I.

To: lysander@thesceneisgreen.com
From: tristan@trisanddom.com

> *I'll never know all the reasons why you left sunny California for dreary London, but I'm so glad you did. Not only for making my brother happy but for accepting all the parts of him that can be hard to understand. Not least of all for accepting me as part of the Frankie package. Oh, and for not sending your own brother back to the US with a flea in his ear. Because you were right. He is good people. The best, in fact.*

To: mungo@bearswithbeards.com
From: tristan@trisanddom.com

> *You would literally drown in twinks over here.*
> *Don't give up on Milo. He needs you.*

To: milo@hungryflower.com
From: rumpleforeskin@trisanddom.com

> *Milo. So, docking. I thought Dom was joking, but apparently, it's*

a thing. The man is obsessed with my foreskin. Any tips? I mean, obvs it is all about tips, but...yeah.
Anyhow...life is good. I still pinch myself that it's mine.
PS Mungo won't wait around forever. Just saying.

ABOUT THE AUTHOR

Fearne Hill resides deep in the British countryside, in the county of Dorset, surrounded by animals. She likes it that way.

Her popular Rossingley series was nominated in nine separate categories of the 2021 Goodreads M/M Romance awards and received an Honourable Mention in the 2021 Rainbow Awards.

She can be found on social media:
- Facebook group: Fearne Hill's House
- On Instagram: instagram.com/fearnehill_author
- On Twitter: twitter.com/FearneHill
- On Bookbub: bookbub.com/authors/fearne-hill

ALSO BY FEARNE HILL

Nailed It! series
Cloud Ten
Cloud Nine
Cloud White *(Releasing Autumn 2023)*

Surfing the Waves series
Brushed with Love
Dipped in Sunshine

Rossingley Series
To Hold A Hidden Pearl
To Catch A Fallen Leaf
To Take A Quiet Breath
To Melt A Frozen Heart
To Mend a Broken Wing

Standalone Romance
The Last of the Moussakas
Two Tribes

Printed in Great Britain
by Amazon